Here for the Fir—————————————
Are Two Brilliant Books by the Author
of America's Number One Bestseller

IN COLD BLOOD

THE GRASS HARP is a story about people in
search of love. They defy the narrow conventions
of a small town in order to find their own brand of
freedom, enjoy momentary heady release, and then
make their individual compromises with reality.

"A charming human warmth pervades these
pages, a feeling for the positive quality of life,
despite life's abiding sadness. . . ."
—*New York Herald Tribune*

In A TREE OF NIGHT and other stories Truman
Capote explores the misery, horror and loneliness
of modern life. Two of these tales, "Miriam" and
"Shut A Final Door," have won O. Henry awards.

"Truman Capote stands out as a master of fear
and the borderland between sanity and the neu-
rotic wastes of the mind . . . the writing is un-
obtrusively beautiful . . . a superlative book."
—*The Washington Post*

Great Novels from SIGNET

(0451)

- [ ] **BREAKFAST AT TIFFANY'S** by Truman Capote.
  (099591—$2.25)*
- [ ] **THE GRASS HARP and TREE OF NIGHT** by Truman Capote.
  (099605—$2.25)
- [ ] **IN COLD BLOOD** by Truman Capote. (099583—$2.95)*
- [ ] **MUSIC FOR CHAMELEONS** by Truman Capote.
  (099346—$3.50)*
- [ ] **OTHER VOICES, OTHER ROOMS** by Truman Capote.
  (099613—$2.25)
- [ ] **THE ARMIES OF THE NIGHT** by Norman Mailer.
  (113209—$2.95)
- [ ] **THE NAKED AND THE DEAD** by Norman Mailer.
  (097025—$3.50)
- [ ] **THE CHAPMAN REPORT** by Irving Wallace. (094565—$2.95)
- [ ] **THE PRIZE** by Irving Wallace. (094557—$2.95)
- [ ] **THE FABULOUS SHOWMAN** by Irving Wallace.
  (113853—$1.50)
- [ ] **THE THREE SIRENS** by Irving Wallace. (113594—$3.50)
- [ ] **TWENTY-SEVENTH WIFE** by Irving Wallace. (092333—$2.50)
- [ ] **THE SECOND LADY** by Irving Wallace. (110641—$3.95)
- [ ] **GOD'S LITTLE ACRE** by Erskine Caldwell. (511670—$1.75)
- [ ] **TOBACCO ROAD** by Erskine Caldwell. (515099—$1.95)

*Price slightly lighter in Canada

Buy them at your local bookstore or use this convenient coupon for ordering.

THE NEW AMERICAN LIBRARY, INC.,
P.O. Box 999, Bergenfield, New Jersey 07621

Please send me the books I have checked above. I am enclosing $_____
(please add $1.00 to this order to cover postage and handling). Send check
or money order—no cash or C.O.D.'s. Prices and numbers are subject to change
without notice.

Name_____

Address_____

City _____ State _____ Zip Code _____
Allow 4-6 weeks for delivery.
This offer is subject to withdrawal without notice.

The Grass Harp

and

A Tree of Night

AND OTHER STORIES

Truman Capote

A SIGNET BOOK

NEW AMERICAN LIBRARY

SIGNET TRADEMARK REG. U.S. PAT. OFF. AND FOREIGN COUNTRIES
REGISTERED TRADEMARK—MARCA REGISTRADA
HECHO EN CHICAGO, U.S.A.

SIGNET, SIGNET CLASSIC, MENTOR, PLUME, MERIDIAN AND NAL
BOOKS *are published by New American Library,
1633 Broadway, New York, New York 10019*

16   17   18   19   20   21   22   23   24

PRINTED IN THE UNITED STATES OF AMERICA

CONTENTS

THE GRASS HARP

One

WHEN was it that first I heard of the grass harp? Long before the autumn we lived in the China tree; an earlier autumn, then; and of course it was Dolly who told me, no one else would have known to call it that, a grass harp.

If on leaving town you take the church road you soon will pass a glaring hill of bonewhite slabs and brown burnt flowers: this is the Baptist cemetery. Our people, Talbos, Fenwicks, are buried there; my mother lies next to my father, and the graves of kinfolk, twenty or more, are around them like the prone roots of a stony tree. Below the hill grows a field of high Indian grass that changes color with the seasons: go to see it in the fall, late September, when it has gone red as sunset, when scarlet shadows like firelight breeze over it and the autumn winds strum on its dry leaves sighing human music, a harp of voices.

Beyond the field begins the darkness of River Woods. It must have been on one of those September days when we were there in the woods gathering roots that Dolly said: Do you hear? that is the grass harp, always telling a story—it knows the stories of all the people on the hill, of all the people who ever lived, and when we are dead it will tell ours, too.

After my mother died, my father, a traveling man, sent me to live with his cousins, Verena and Dolly Talbo, two unmarried ladies who were sisters. Before that, I'd not ever been allowed into their house. For reasons no one ever got quite clear, Verena and my father did not speak. Probably Papa asked Verena to lend him some money, and she refused; or perhaps she did make the loan, and he never returned it. You can be sure that the trouble was over money, because nothing else would have mattered to them so much, especially Verena, who was the richest person in town. The drugstore, the drygoods store, a filling station, a grocery, an office building, all this was hers, and the earning of it had not made her an easy woman.

Anyway, Papa said he would never set foot inside her house. He told such terrible things about the Talbo ladies. One of the stories he spread, that Verena was a morphodyte, has never stopped going around, and the ridicule he heaped on Miss Dolly Talbo was too much even for my mother: she told him he ought to be ashamed, mocking anyone so gentle and harmless.

I think they were very much in love, my mother and father. She used to cry every time he went away to sell his frigidaires. He married her when she was sixteen; she did not live to be thirty. The afternoon she died Papa, calling her name, tore off all his clothes and ran out naked into the yard.

It was the day after the funeral that Verena came to the house. I remember the terror of watching her move up the walk, a whip-thin, handsome woman with shingled peppersalt hair, black, rather virile eyebrows and a dainty cheekmole. She opened the front door and walked right into the house. Since the funeral, Papa had been breaking things, not with fury, but quietly, thoroughly: he would amble into the parlor, pick up a china figure, muse over it a moment, then throw it against the wall. The floor and stairs were littered with cracked glass, scattered silverware; a ripped nightgown, one of my mother's, hung over the banister.

Verena's eyes flicked over the debris. "Eugene, I want a word with you," she said in that hearty, coldly exalted voice, and Papa answered: "Yes, sit down, Verena. I thought you would come."

That afternoon Dolly's friend Catherine Creek came over and packed my clothes, and Papa drove me to the impressive, shadowy house on Talbo Lane. As I was getting out of the car he tried to hug me, but I was scared of him and wriggled out of his arms. I'm sorry now that we did not hug each other. Because a few days later, on his way up to Mobile, his car skidded and fell fifty feet into the Gulf. When I saw him again there were silver dollars weighting down his eyes.

Except to remark that I was small for my age, a runt, no one had ever paid any attention to me; but now people pointed me out, and said wasn't it sad? that poor little Collin Fenwick! I tried to look pitiful because I knew it pleased people: every man in town must have treated me to a Dixie Cup or a box of Crackerjack, and at school I got good grades for the first time. So it was a long while before I calmed down enough to notice Dolly Talbo.

And when I did I fell in love.

Imagine what it must have been for her when first I came to the house, a loud and prying boy of eleven. She skittered at the sound of my footsteps or, if there was no avoiding me, folded like the petals of shy-lady fern. She was one of those people who can disguise themselves as an object in the room, a shadow in the corner, whose presence is a delicate happening. She wore the quietest shoes, plain virginal dresses with hems that touched her ankles. Though older than her sister, she seemed someone who, like myself, Verena had adopted. Pulled and guided by the gravity of Verena's planet, we rotated separately in the outer spaces of the house.

In the attic, a slipshod museum spookily peopled with old display dummies from Verena's drygoods store, there were many loose boards, and by inching these I could look down into almost any room. Dolly's room, unlike the rest of the house, which bulged with fat dour furniture, contained only a bed, a bureau, a chair: a nun might have lived there, except for one fact: the walls, everything was painted an outlandish pink, even the floor was this color. Whenever I spied on Dolly, she usually was to be seen doing one of two things: she was standing in front of a mirror snipping with a pair of garden shears her yellow and white, already brief hair; either that, or she was writing in pencil on a pad of coarse Kress paper. She kept wetting the pencil on the tip of her tongue, and sometimes she spoke aloud a sentence as she put it down: *Do not touch sweet foods like candy and salt will kill you for certain.* Now I'll tell you, she was writing letters. But at first this correspondence was a puzzle to me. After all, her only friend was Catherine Creek, she saw no one else and she never left the house, except once a week when she and Catherine went to River Woods where they gathered the ingredients of a dropsy remedy Dolly brewed and bottled. Later I discovered she had customers for this medicine throughout the state, and it was to them that her many letters were addressed.

Verena's room, connecting with Dolly's by a passage, was rigged up like an office. There was a rolltop desk, a library of ledgers, filing cabinets. After supper, wearing a green eyeshade, she would sit at her desk totaling figures and turning the pages of her ledgers until even the street-lamps had gone out. Though on diplomatic, political terms with many people, Verena had no close friends at all. Men were afraid of her, and she herself seemed to be afraid of women. Some years before she had been greatly attached to a blonde jolly girl called Maudie Laura Murphy, who worked for a bit in the post office here and who finally married a liquor salesman from St. Louis. Verena had been very bitter over this and said publicly that the man was no account. It was therefore a surprise when, as a wedding present, she gave the couple a honeymoon trip to the Grand Canyon. Maudie and her husband never came back; they opened a filling station nearby Grand Canyon, and from time to time sent Verena Kodak snapshots of themselves. These pictures were a pleasure and a grief. There were nights when she never opened her ledgers, but sat with her forehead leaning in her hands, and the pictures spread on the desk. After she had put them away, she would pace around the room with the lights turned off, and presently there would come a hurt rusty crying sound as though she'd tripped and fallen in the dark.

That part of the attic from which I could have looked down into the kitchen was fortified against me, for it was stacked with trunks like bales of cotton. At that time it was the kitchen I most wanted to spy upon; this was the real living room of the house, and Dolly spent most of the day there chatting with her friend Catherine Creek. As a child, an orphan, Catherine Creek had been hired out to Mr. Uriah Talbo, and they had all grown up together, she and the Talbo sisters, there on the old farm that has since become a railroad depot. Dolly she called Dollyheart, but Verena she called That One. She lived in the back yard in a tin-roofed silvery little house set among sunflowers and trellises of butterbean vine. She claimed to be an Indian, which made most people wink, for she was dark as the angels of Africa. But for all I know it may have been true: certainly she dressed like an Indian. That is, she had a string of turquoise beads, and wore enough rouge to put out your eyes; it shone on her cheeks like votive taillights. Most of her teeth were gone; she kept her jaws jacked up with cotton wadding, and Verena would say Dammit Catherine, since you can't make a sensible sound why in creation won't you go down to Doc Crocker and let him put some teeth in your head? It was true that she was hard to understand: Dolly was the only one who could fluently translate her friend's muffled, mumbling noises. It was enough for Catherine that Dolly understood her: they were always together and everything they had to say they said to each other: bending my ear to an attic beam I could hear the tantalizing tremor of their voices flowing like sapsyrup through the old wood.

To reach the attic, you climbed a ladder in the linen closet, the ceiling of which was a trapdoor. One day, as I started up, I saw that the trapdoor was swung open and, listening, heard above me an idle sweet humming, like the pretty sounds small girls make when they are playing alone. I would have turned back, but the humming stopped, and a voice said: "Catherine?"

"Collin," I answered, showing myself.

The snowflake of Dolly's face held its shape; for once she did not dissolve. "This is where you come—we wondered," she said, her voice frail and crinkling as tissue paper. She had the eyes of a gifted person, kindled, transparent eyes, luminously green as mint jelly: gazing at me through the attic twilight they admitted, timidly, that I meant her no harm. "You play games up here—in the attic? I told Verena you would be lonesome." Stooping, she rooted around in the depths of a barrel. "Here now," she said, "you can help me by looking in that other barrel. I'm hunting for a coral castle; and a sack of pearl pebbles, all colors. I think Catherine will like that, a bowl of goldfish, don't you? For her birthday. We used to have a bowl of tropical fish—devils, they were: ate each other up. But I remember when we bought them; we went all the way to Brewton, sixty miles. I never went sixty miles before, and I don't know that I ever will again. Ah see, here it is, the castle." Soon afterwards I found the pebbles; they were like kernels of corn or candy, and: "Have a piece of candy," I said, offering the sack. "Oh thank you," she said, "I love a piece of candy, even when it tastes like a pebble."

We were friends, Dolly and Catherine and me. I was eleven, then I was sixteen. Though no honors came my way, those were the lovely years.

I never brought anyone home with me, and I never wanted to. Once I took a girl to the picture show, and on the way home she asked couldn't she come in for a drink of water. If

I'd thought she was really thirsty I would've said all right; but I knew she was faking just so she could see inside the house the way people were always wanting to, and so I told her she better wait until she got home. She said: "All the world knows Dolly Talbo's gone, and you're gone too." I liked that girl well enough, but I gave her a shove anyway, and she said her brother would fix my wagon, which he did: right here at the corner of my mouth I've still got a scar where he hit me with a Coca-Cola bottle.

I know: Dolly, they said, was Verena's cross, and said, too, that more went on in the house on Talbo Lane than a body cared to think about. Maybe so. But those were the lovely years.

On winter afternoons, as soon as I came in from school, Catherine hustled open a jar of preserves, while Dolly put a foot-high pot of coffee on the stove and pushed a pan of biscuits into the oven; and the oven, opening, would let out a hot vanilla fragrance, for Dolly, who lived off sweet foods, was always baking a pound cake, raisin bread, some kind of cookie or fudge: never would touch a vegetable, and the only meat she liked was the chicken brain, a pea-sized thing gone before you've tasted it. What with a woodstove and an open fireplace, the kitchen was warm as a cow's tongue. The nearest winter came was to frost the windows with its zero blue breath. If some wizard would like to make me a present, let him give me a bottle filled with the voices of that kitchen, the ha ha ha and fire whispering, a bottle brimming with its buttery sugary bakery smells—though Catherine smelled like a sow in the spring. It looked more like a cozy parlor than a kitchen; there was a hook rug on the floor, rocking chairs; ranged along the walls were pictures of kittens, an enthusiasm of Dolly's; there was a geranium plant that bloomed, then bloomed again all year round, and Catherine's goldfish, in a bowl on the oilcloth-covered table, fanned their tails through the portals of the coral castle. Sometimes we worked jigsaw puzzles, dividing the pieces among us, and Catherine would hide pieces if she thought you were going to finish your part of the puzzle before she finished hers. Or they would help with my homework; that was a mess. About all natural things Dolly was sophisticated; she had the subterranean intelligence of a bee that knows where to find the sweetest flower: she could tell you of a storm a day in advance, predict the fruit of the fig tree, lead you to mushrooms and wild honey, a hidden nest of guinea hen eggs. She looked around her, and felt what she saw. But about homework Dolly was as ignorant as Catherine. "America must have been called America before Columbus came. It stands to reason. Otherwise, how would he have known it was America?" And Catherine said: "That's correct. America is an old Indian word." Of the two, Catherine was the worst: she insisted on her infallibility, and if you did not write down exactly what she said, she got jumpy and spilled the coffee or something. But I never listened to her again after what she said about Lincoln: that he was part Negro and part Indian and only a speck white. Even I knew this was not true. But I am under special obligation to Catherine; if it had not been for her who knows whether I would have grown to ordinary human size? At fourteen I was not much bigger than Biddy Skinner, and people told how he'd had offers from a circus. Catherine said don't worry yourself honey, all you need is a little stretching. She pulled at my arms, legs, tugged at my head as though it were an apple latched to an unyielding bough. But it's the truth that within two years she'd stretched me from four feet nine to five feet seven, and I can prove it by the breadknife knotches on the pantry door, for even now when so much has gone, when there is only wind in the stove and winter in the kitchen, those growing-up scars are still there, a testimony.

Despite the generally beneficial effect Dolly's medicine appeared to have on those who sent for it, letters once in a while came saying Dear Miss Talbo we won't be needing any more dropsy cure on account of poor Cousin Belle (or whoever) passed away last week bless her soul. Then the kitchen was a mournful place; with folded hands and nodding heads my two friends bleakly recalled the circumstances of the case, and Well, Catherine would say, we did the best we could Dollyheart, but the good Lord had other notions. Verena, too, could make the kitchen sad, as she was always introducing a new rule or enforcing an old one: do, don't, stop, start: it was as though we were clocks she kept an eye on to see that our time jibed with her own, and woe if we were ten minutes fast, an hour slow: Verena went off like a cuckoo. That One! said Catherine, and Dolly would go hush now! hush now! as though to quiet not Catherine but a mutinous inner whispering. Verena in her heart wanted, I think, to come into the kitchen and be a part of it; but she was too like a lone man in a house full of women and children, and the only way she could make contact with us was through assertive outbursts: Dolly, get rid of that kitten, you want to aggravate my asthma? who left the water running in the bathroom? which one of you broke my umbrella? Her

ugly moods sifted through the house like a sour yellow mist.
That One. Hush now, hush.

Once a week, Saturdays mostly, we went to River Woods.
For these trips, which lasted the whole day, Catherine fried a
chicken and deviled a dozen eggs, and Dolly took along a chocolate layer cake and a supply of divinity fudge. Thus armed,
and carrying three empty grain sacks, we walked out the church
road past the cemetery and through the field of Indian grass.
Just entering the woods there was a double-trunked China
tree, really two trees, but their branches were so embraced
that you could step from one into the other; in fact, they were
bridged by a tree-house: spacious, sturdy, a model of a tree-
house, it was like a raft floating in the sea of leaves. The boys
who built it, provided they are still alive, must by now be very
old men; certainly the tree-house was fifteen or twenty years
old when Dolly first found it and that was a quarter of a cen-
tury before she showed it to me. To reach it was easy as climbing stairs; there were footholds of gnarled bark and tough vines
to grip; even Catherine, who was heavy around the hips and
complained of rheumatism, had no trouble. But Catherine felt
no love for the tree-house; she did not know, as Dolly knew
and made me know, that it was a ship, that to sit up there was
to sail along the cloudy coastline of every dream. Mark my
word, said Catherine, them boards are too old, them nails are
slippery as worms, gonna crack in two, gonna fall and bust our
heads don't I know it.

Storing our provisions in the tree-house, we separated into
the woods, each carrying a grain sack to be filled with herbs,
leaves, strange roots. No one, not even Catherine, knew altogether what went into the medicine, for it was a secret Dolly
kept to herself, and we were never allowed to look at the
gatherings in her own sack: she held tight to it, as though
inside she had captive a blue-haired child, a bewitched prince.
This was her story: "Once, back yonder when we were children (Verena still with her babyteeth and Catherine no higher
than a fence post) there were gipsies thick as birds in a blackberry patch—not like now, when maybe you see a few strag-
gling through each year. They came with spring: sudden, like
the dogwood pink, there they were—up and down the road and
in the woods around. But our men hated the sight of them, and
daddy, that was your great-uncle Uriah, said he would shoot
any he caught on our place. And so I never told when I saw
the gipsies taking water from the creek or stealing old winter
pecans off the ground. Then one evening, it was April and

falling rain, I went out to the cowshed where Fairybell had a new little. calf; and there in the cowshed were three gipsy women, two of them old and one of them young, and the young one was lying naked and twisting on the cornshucks. When they saw that I was not afraid, that I was not going to run and tell, one of the old women asked would I bring a light. So I went to the house for a candle, and when I came back the woman who had sent me was holding a red hollering baby upside down by its feet, and the other woman was milking Fairybell. I helped them wash the baby in the warm milk and wrap it in a scarf. Then one of the old women took my hand and said: Now I am going to give you a gift by teaching you a rhyme. It was a rhyme about evergreen bark, dragon-fly fern—and all the other things we come here in the woods to find: *Boil till dark and pure if you want a dropsy cure.* In the morning they were gone; I looked for them in the fields and on the road; there was nothing left of them but the rhyme in my head."

Calling to each other, hooting like owls loose in the daytime, we worked all morning in opposite parts of the woods. Towards afternoon, our sacks fat with skinned bark, tender, torn roots, we climbed back into the green web of the China tree and spread the food. There was good creek water in a mason jar, or if the weather was cold a thermos of hot coffee, and we wadded leaves to wipe our chicken-stained, fudge-sticky fingers. Afterwards, telling fortunes with flowers, speaking of sleepy things, it was as though we floated through the afternoon on the raft in the tree; we belonged there, as the sun-silvered leaves belonged, the dwelling whippoorwills.

About once a year I go over to the house on Talbo Lane, and walk around in the yard. I was there the other day, and came across an old iron tub lying overturned in the weeds like a black fallen meteor: Dolly—Dolly, hovering over the tub dropping our grain-sack gatherings into boiling water and stirring, stirring with a sawed-off broomstick the brown as tobacco spit brew. She did the mixing of the medicine alone while Catherine and I stood watching like apprentices to a witch. We all helped later with the bottling of it and, because it produced a fume that exploded ordinary corks, my particular job was to roll stoppers of toilet paper. Sales averaged around six bottles a week, at two dollars a bottle. The money, Dolly said, belonged to the three of us, and we spent it fast as it came in. We were always sending away for stuff advertised in magazines: Take

Up Woodcarving, Parcheesi: the game for young and old, Anyone Can Play A Bazooka. Once we sent away for a book of
French lessons: it was my idea that if we got to talk French
we would have a secret language that Verena or nobody would
understand. Dolly was willing to try, but "Passez-moi a spoon"
was the best she ever did, and after learning "Je suis fatigué,"
Catherine never opened the book again: she said that was all
she needed to know.

Verena often remarked that there would be trouble if anyone ever got poisoned, but otherwise she did not show much
interest in the dropsy cure. Then one year we totaled up and
found we'd earned enough to have to pay an income tax.
Whereupon Verena began asking questions: money was like a
wildcat whose trail she stalked with a trained hunter's muffled
step and an eye for every broken twig. What, she wanted to
know, went into the medicine? and Dolly, flattered, almost
giggling, nonetheless waved her hands and said Well this and
that, nothing special.

Verena seemed to let the matter die; yet very often, sitting
at the supper table, her eyes paused ponderingly on Dolly, and
once, when we were gathered in the yard around the boiling
tub, I looked up and saw Verena in a window watching us
with uninterrupted fixity: by then, I suppose, her plan had
taken shape, but she did not make her first move until summer.

Twice a year, in January and again in August, Verena went
on buying trips to St. Louis or Chicago. That summer, the
summer I reached sixteen, she went to Chicago and after two
weeks returned accompanied by a man called Dr. Morris Ritz.
Naturally everyone wondered who was Dr. Morris Ritz? He
wore bow ties and sharp jazzy suits; his lips were blue and he
had gaudy small swerving eyes; altogether, he looked like a
mean mouse. We heard that he lived in the best room at the
Lola Hotel and ate steak dinners at Phil's Café. On the streets
he strutted along bobbing his shiny head at every passerby; he
made no friends, however, and was not seen in the company of
anyone except Verena, who never brought him to the house
and never mentioned his name until one day Catherine had the
gall to say, "Miss Verena, just who is this funny looking little
Dr. Morris Ritz?" and Verena, getting white around the
mouth, replied: "Well now, he's not half so funny looking as
some I could name."

Scandalous, people said, the way Verena was carrying on
with that little Jew from Chicago: and him twenty years
younger. The story that got around was that they were up to

something out in the old canning factory the other side of town. As it developed, they were; but not what the gang at the pool-hall thought. Most any afternoon you could see Verena and Dr. Morris Ritz walking out toward the canning factory, an abandoned blasted brick ruin with jagged windows and sagging doors. For a generation no one had been near it except school-kids who went there to smoke cigarettes and get naked to-gether. Then early in September, by way of a notice in the *Courier*, we learned for the first time that Verena had bought the old canning factory; but there was no mention as to what use she was planning to make of it. Shortly after this, Verena told Catherine to kill two chickens as Dr. Morris Ritz was coming to Sunday dinner.

During the years that I lived there, Dr. Morris Ritz was the only person ever invited to dine at the house on Talbo Lane. So for many reasons it was an occasion. Catherine and Dolly did a spring cleaning: they beat rugs, brought china from the attic, had every room smelling of floorwax and lemon polish. There was to be fried chicken and ham, English peas, sweet potatoes, rolls, banana pudding, two kinds of cake and tutti-frutti ice cream from the drugstore. Sunday noon Verena came in to look at the table: with its sprawling centerpiece of peach-colored roses and dense fancy stretches of silverware, it seemed set for a party of twenty; actually, there were only two places. Verena went ahead and set two more, and Dolly, seeing this, said weakly Well, it was all right if Collin wanted to eat at the table, but that she was going to stay in the kitchen with Cath-erine. Verena put her foot down: "Don't fool with me, Dolly. This is important. Morris is coming here expressly to meet you. And what-is more, I'd appreciate it if you'd hold up your head: it makes me dizzy, hanging like that."

Dolly was scared to death: she hid in her room, and long after our guest had arrived I had to be sent to fetch her. She was lying in the pink bed with a wet washrag on her forehead, and Catherine was sitting beside her. Catherine was all sleeked up, rouge on her cheeks like lollipops and her jaws jammed with more cotton than ever; she said, "Honey, you ought to get up from there—you're going to ruin that pretty dress." It was a calico dress Verena had brought from Chicago; Dolly sat up and smoothed it, then immediately lay down again: "If Verona knew how sorry I am," she said helplessly, and so I went and told Verena that Dolly was sick. Verena said she'd see about that, and marched off leaving me alone in the hall with Dr. Morris Ritz.

Oh he was a hateful thing. "So you're sixteen," he said, winking first one, then the other of his sassy eyes. "And throwing it around, huh? Make the old lady take you next time she goes to Chicago. Plenty of good stuff there to throw it at." He snapped his fingers and jiggled his razzle-dazzle, dagger-sharp shoes as though keeping time to some vaudeville tune: he might have been a tapdancer or a soda-jerk, except that he was carrying a brief case, which suggested a more serious occupation. I wondered what kind of doctor he was supposed to be; indeed, was on the point of asking when Verena returned steering Dolly by the elbow.

The shadows of the hall, the tapestried furniture failed to absorb her; without raising her eyes she lifted her hand, and Dr. Ritz gripped it so ruggedly, pumped it so hard she went nearly off balance. "Gee, Miss Talbo; am I honored to meet you!" he said, and cranked his bow tie.

We sat down to dinner, and Catherine came around with the chicken. She served Verena, then Dolly, and when the doctor's turn came he said, "Tell you the truth, the only piece of chicken I care about is the brain: don't suppose you'd have that back in the kitchen, mammy?"

Catherine looked so far down her nose she got almost cross-eyed; and with her tongue all mixed up in the cotton wadding she told him that, "Dolly's took those brains on her plate."

"These southern accents, Jesus," he said, genuinely dismayed.

"She says I have the brains on my plate," said Dolly, her cheeks red as Catherine's rouge. "But please let me pass them to you."

"If you're sure you don't mind . . ."

"She doesn't mind a bit," said Verena. "She only eats sweet things anyway. Here, Dolly: have some banana pudding."

Presently Dr. Ritz commenced a fit of sneezing. "The flowers, those roses, old allergy . . ."

"Oh dear," said Dolly who, seeing an opportunity to escape into the kitchen, seized the bowl of roses: it slipped, crystal crashed, roses landed in gravy and gravy landed on us all. "You see," she said, speaking to herself and with tears teetering in her eyes, "you see, it's hopeless."

"Nothing is hopeless, Dolly; sit down and finish your pudding," Verena advised in a substantial, chin-up voice. "Besides, we have a nice little surprise for you. Morris, show Dolly those lovely labels."

Murmuring "No harm done," Dr. Ritz stopped rubbing

gravy splotches off his sleeve, and went into the hall, returning with his brief case. His fingers buzzed through a sheaf of papers, then lighted on a large envelope which he passed down to Dolly.

There were gum-stickers in the envelope, triangular labels with orange lettering: Gipsy Queen Dropsy Cure: and a fuzzy picture of a woman wearing a bandana and gold earloops. "First class, huh?" said Dr. Ritz. "Made in Chicago. A friend of mine drew the picture: real artist, that guy," Dolly shuffled the labels with a puzzled, apprehensive expression until Verena asked: "Aren't you pleased?"

The labels twitched in Dolly's hands. "I'm not sure I understand."

"Of course you do," said Verena, smiling thinly. "It's obvious enough. I told Morris that old story of yours and he thought of this wonderful name."

"Gipsy Queen Dropsy Cure: very catchy, that," said the doctor. "Look great in ads."

"*My* medicine?" said Dolly, her eyes still lowered. "But I don't need any labels, Verena. I write my own."

Dr. Ritz snapped his fingers. "Say, that's good! We can have labels printed like her own handwriting: personal, see?"

"We've spent enough money already," Verena told him briskly; and, turning to Dolly, said: "Morris and I are going up to Washington this week to get a copyright on these labels and register a patent for the medicine—naming you as the inventor, naturally. Now the point is, Dolly, you must sit down and write out a complete formula for us."

Dolly's face loosened; and the labels scattered on the floor, skimmed. Leaning her hands on the table she pushed herself upward; slowly her features came together again, she lifted her head and looked blinkingly at Dr. Ritz, at Verena. "It won't do," she said quietly. She moved to the door, put a hand on its handle. "It won't do: because you haven't any right, Verena. Nor you, sir."

I helped Catherine clear the table: the ruined roses, the uncut cakes, the vegetables no one had touched. Verena and her guest had left the house together; from the kitchen window we watched them as they went toward town nodding and shaking their heads. Then we sliced the devil's-food cake and took it into Dolly's room.

Hush now! hush now! she said when Catherine began lighting into That One. But it was as though the rebellious inner whispering had become a raucous voice, an opponent she must outshout: Hush now! hush now! until Catherine had to put her arms around Dolly and say hush, too.

We got out a deck of Rook cards and spread them on the bed. Naturally Catherine had to go and remember it was Sunday; she said maybe we could risk another black mark in the Judgment Book, but there were too many beside her name already. After thinking it over, we told fortunes instead. Sometime around dusk Verena came home. We heard her footsteps in the hall; she opened the door without knocking, and Dolly, who was in the middle of my fortune, tightened her hold on my hand. Verena said: "Collin, Catherine, we will excuse you."

Catherine wanted to follow me up the ladder into the attic, except she had on her fine clothes. So I went alone. There was a good knothole that looked straight down into the pink room; but Verena was standing directly under it, and all I could see was her hat, for she was still wearing the hat she'd put on when she left the house. It was a straw skimmer decorated with a cluster of celluloid fruit. "Those are facts," she was saying, and the fruit shivered, shimmered in the blue dimness. "Two thousand for the old factory, Bill Tatum and four carpenters working out there at eighty cents an hour, seven thousand dollars worth of machinery already ordered, not to mention what a specialist like Morris Ritz is costing. And why? All for you!"

"All for me?" and Dolly sounded sad and failing as the dusk. I saw her shadow as she moved from one part of the room to another. "You are my own flesh, and I love you tenderly; in my heart I love you. I could prove it now by giving you the only thing that has ever been mine: then you would have it all. Please, Verena," she said, faltering, "let this one thing belong to me."

Verena switched on a light. "You speak of giving," and her voice was hard as the sudden bitter glare. "All these years that I've worked like a fieldhand: what haven't I given you? This house, that . . ."

"You've given everything to me," Dolly interrupted softly. "And to Catherine and to Collin. Except, we've earned our way a bit: we've kept a nice home for you, haven't we?"

"Oh a fine home," said Verena, whipping off her hat. Her face was full of blood. "You and that gurgling fool. Has it not struck you that I never ask anyone into this house? And for a very simple reason: I'm ashamed to. Look what happened today."

I could hear the breath go out of Dolly. "I'm sorry," she said faintly. "I am truly. I'd always thought there was a place for us here, that you needed us somehow. But it's going to be all right now, Verena. We'll go away."

Verena sighed. "Poor Dolly. Poor poor thing. Wherever would you go?"

The answer, a little while in coming, was fragile as the flight of a moth: "I know a place."

Later, I waited in bed for Dolly to come and kiss me good-night. My room, beyond the parlor in a faraway corner of the house, was the room where their father, Mr. Uriah Talbo, had lived. In his mad old age, Verena had brought him here from the farm, and here he'd died, not knowing where he was. Though dead ten, fifteen years, the pee and tobacco old-man smell of him still saturated the mattress, the closet, and on a shelf in the closet was the one possession he'd carried away with him from the farm, a small yellow drum: as a lad my own age he'd marched in a Dixie regiment rattling this little yellow drum, and singing. Dolly said that when she was a girl she'd liked to wake up winter mornings and hear her father singing as he went about the house building fires; after he was old, after he'd died, she sometimes heard his songs in the field of Indian grass. Wind, Catherine said; and Dolly told her: But the wind is us—it gathers and remembers all our voices, then sends them talking and telling through the leaves and the fields —I've heard Papa clear as day.

On such a night, now that it was September, the autumn winds would be curving through the taut red grass, releasing all the gone voices, and I wondered if he was singing among them, the old man in whose bed I lay falling asleep.

Then I thought Dolly at last had come to kiss me good-night, for I woke up sensing her near me in the room; but it was almost morning, beginning light was like a flowering foliage at the windows, and roosters ranted in distant yards. "Shhh, Collin," Dolly whispered, bending over me. She was wearing a woolen winter suit and a hat with a traveling veil that misted her face. "I only wanted you to know where we are going."

"To the tree-house?" I said, and thought I was talking in my sleep.

Dolly nodded. "Just for now. Until we know better what our plans will be." She could see that I was frightened, and put her hand on my forehead.

"You and Catherine: but not me?" and I was jerking with a chill. "You can't leave without me."

The town clock was tolling; she seemed to be waiting for it to finish before making up her mind. It struck five, and by the time the note had died away I had climbed out of bed and rushed into my clothes. There was nothing for Dolly to say except: "Don't forget your comb."

Catherine met us in the yard; she was crooked over with the weight of a brimming oilcloth satchel; her eyes were swollen, she had been crying, and Dolly, oddly calm and certain of what she was doing, said it doesn't matter, Catherine—we can send for your goldfish once we find a place. Verena's closed quiet windows loomed above us; we moved cautiously past them and silently out the gate. A fox terrier barked at us; but there was no one on the street, and no one saw us pass through the town except a sleepless prisoner gazing from the jail. We reached the field of Indian grass at the same moment as the sun. Dolly's veil flared in the morning breeze, and a pair of pheasants, nesting in our path, swept before us, their metal wings swiping the cockscomb-scarlet grass. The China tree was a September bowl of green and greenish gold: Gonna fall, gonna bust our heads, Catherine said, as all around us the leaves shook down their dew.

Two

IF IT hadn't been for Riley Henderson, I doubt anyone would have known, or at least known so soon, that we were in the tree.

Catherine had loaded her oilcloth satchel with the leftovers from Sunday dinner, and we were enjoying a breakfast of cake and chicken when gunfire slapped through the woods. We sat there with cake going dry in our mouths. Below, a sleek bird dog cantered into view, followed by Riley Henderson; he was shouldering a shotgun and around his neck there hung a garland of bleeding squirrels whose tails were tied together. Dolly lowered her veil, as though to camouflage herself among the leaves.

He paused not far away, and his wary, tanned young face tightened; propping his gun into position he took a roaming aim, as if waiting for a target to present itself. The suspense was too much for Catherine, who shouted: "Riley Henderson, don't you dare shoot us!"

His gun wavered, and he spun around, the squirrels swinging like a loose necklace. Then he saw us in the tree, and after a moment said, "Hello there, Catherine Creek; hello, Miss Talbo. What are you folks doing up there? Wildcat chase you?"

"Just sitting," said Dolly promptly, as though she were

afraid for either Catherine or I to answer. "That's a fine mess of squirrels you've got."

"Take a couple," he said, detaching two. "We had some for supper last night and they were real tender. Wait a minute, I'll bring them up to you."

"You don't have to do that; just leave them on the ground." But he said ants would get at them, and hauled himself into the tree. His blue shirt was spotted with squirrel blood, and flecks of blood glittered in his rough leather-colored hair; he smelled of gunpowder, and his homely well-made face was brown as cinnamon. "I'll be damned, it's a tree-house," he said, pounding his foot as though to test the strength of the boards. Catherine warned him that maybe it was a tree-house now, but it wouldn't be for long if he didn't stop that stamping. He said, "You build it, Collin?" and it was with a happy shock that I realized he'd called my name: I hadn't thought Riley Henderson knew me from dust. But I knew him, all right.

No one in our town ever had themselves so much talked about as Riley Henderson. Older people spoke of him with sighing voices, and those nearer his own age, like myself, were glad to call him mean and hard: that was because he would only let us envy him, would not let us love him, be his friend.

Anyone could have told you the facts.

He was born in China, where his father, a missionary, had been killed in an uprising. His mother was from this town, and her name was Rose; though I never saw her myself, people say she was a beautiful woman until she started wearing glasses; she was rich too, having received a large inheritance from her grandfather. When she came back from China she brought Riley, then five, and two younger children, both girls; they lived with her unmarried brother, Justice of the Peace Horace Holton, a meaty spinsterish man with skin yellow as quince. In the following years Rose Henderson grew strange in her ways: she threatened to sue Verena for selling her a dress that shrank in the wash; to punish Riley, she made him hop on one leg around the yard reciting the multiplication table; otherwise, she let him run wild, and when the Presbyterian minister spoke to her about it she told him she hated her children and wished they were dead. And she must have meant it, for one Christmas morning she locked the bathroom door and tried to drown her two little girls in the tub: it was said that Riley broke the door down with a hatchet, which seems a tall order for a boy of nine or ten, whatever he was. Afterwards, Rose was sent off to a place on the Gulf Coast, an institution, and she may still be living there, at least I've never heard that she died. Now Riley and his uncle Horace Holton couldn't get on. One night he stole Horace's Oldsmobile and drove out to the Dance-N-Dine with Mamie Curtiss: she was fast as lightning, and maybe five years older than Riley, who was not more than fifteen at the time. Well, Horace heard they were at the Dance-N-Dine and got the Sheriff to drive him out there: he said he was going to teach Riley a lesson and have him arrested. But Riley said Sheriff, you're after the wrong party. Right there in front of a crowd he accused his uncle of stealing money that belonged to Rose and that was meant for him and his sisters. He offered to fight it out on the spot; and when Horace held back, he just walked over and socked him in the eye. The Sheriff put Riley in jail. But Judge Cool, an old friend of Rose's, began to investigate, and sure enough it turned out Horace had been draining Rose's money into his own account. So Horace simply packed his things and took the train to New Orleans where, a few months, later, we heard that, billed as the Minister of Romance, he had a job marrying couples on an excursion steamer that made moon-light cruises up the Mississippi. From then on, Riley was his own boss. With money borrowed against the inheritance he was coming into, he bought a red racy car and went skidding round the countryside with every floozy in town; the only nice girls you ever saw in that car were his sisters—he took them for a drive Sunday afternoons, a slow respectable circling of the square. They were pretty girls, his sisters, but they didn't have much fun, for he kept a strict watch, and boys were afraid to come near them. A reliable colored woman did their housework, otherwise they lived alone. One of his sisters, Eliza-beth, was in my class at school, and she got the best grades, straight A's. Riley himself had quit school; but he was not one of the pool-hall loafs, nor did he mix with them; he fished in the daytime, or went hunting; around the old Holton house he made many improvements, as he was a good carpenter; and a good mechanic, too: for instance, he built a special car horn, it wailed like a train-whistle, and in the evening you could hear it howling as he roared down the road on his way to a dance in another town. How I longed for him to be my friend! and it seemed possible, he was just two years older. But I could remember the only time he ever spoke to me. Spruce in a pair of white flannels, he was off to a dance at the clubhouse, and he came into Verena's drugstore, where I sometimes helped out on Saturday nights. What he wanted was a package of Shadows, but I wasn't sure what Shadows were, so he had to come behind the counter and get them out of the drawer himself; and he laughed, not unkindly, though it was worse than if it had been: now he knew I was a fool, we would never be friends.

Dolly said, "Have a piece of cake, Riley," and he asked did we always have picnics this early in the day? then went on to say he considered it a fine idea: "Like swimming at night," he said. "I come down here while it's still dark, and go swimming in the river. Next time you have a picnic, call out so I'll know you're here."

"You are welcome any morning," said Dolly, raising her veil. "I daresay we will be here for some while."

Riley must have thought it a curious invitation, but he did not say so. He produced a package of cigarettes and passed it around; when Catherine took one, Dolly said: "Catherine Creek, you've never touched tobacco in your life." Catherine allowed as to how she may have been missing something: "It must be a comfort, so many folks speak in its favor; and Dolly-heart, when you get to be our age you've got to look for comforts." Dolly bit her lip; "Well, I don't suppose there's any harm," she said, and accepted a cigarette herself.

There are two things that will drive a boy crazy (according to Mr. Hand, who caught me smoking in the lavatory at school) and I'd given up one of them, cigarettes, two years before: not because I thought it would make me crazy, but because I thought it was imperiling my growth. Actually, now that I was a normal size, Riley was no taller than me, though he seemed to be, for he moved with the drawn-out cowboy awkwardness of a lanky man. So I took a cigarette, and Dolly, gushing un-inhaled smoke, said she thought we might as well all be sick together; but no one was sick, and Catherine said next time she would like to try a pipe, as they smelled so good. Whereupon Dolly volunteered the surprising fact that Verena smoked a pipe, something I'd never known: "I don't know whether she does any more, but she used to have a pipe and a can of Prince Albert with half an apple cut up in it. But you musn't tell that," she added, suddenly aware of Riley, who laughed aloud.

Usually, glimpsed on the street or seen passing in his car, Riley wore a tense, trigger-tempered expression; but there in the China tree he seemed relaxed: frequent smiles enriched his whole face, as though he wanted at least to be friendly, if not friends. Dolly, for her part, appeared to be at ease and en-joying his company. Certainly she was not afraid of him: perhaps it was because we were in the tree-house, and the tree-house was her own.

"Thank you for the squirrels, sir," she said, as he prepared to leave. "And don't forget to come again."

He swung himself to the ground. "Want a ride? My car's up by the cemetery."

Dolly told him: "That's kind of you; but really we haven't any place to go."

Grinning, he lifted his gun and aimed it at us; and Catherine yelled: You ought to be whipped, boy; but he laughed and waved and ran, his bird dog barking, booming ahead. Dolly said gaily, "Let's have a cigarette," for the package had been left behind.

By the time Riley reached town the news was roaring in the air like a flight of bees: how we'd run off in the middle of the night. Though neither Catherine nor I knew it, Dolly had left a note, which Verena found when she went for her morning coffee. As I understand it, this note simply said that we were going away and that Verena would not be bothered by us any more. She at once rang up her friend Morris Ritz at the Lola Hotel, and together they traipsed off to rouse the sheriff. It was Verena's backing that had put the sheriff into office; he was a fast-stepping, brassy young fellow with a brutal jaw and the bashful eyes of a cardsharp; his name was Junius Candle (can you believe it? the same Junius Candle who is a Senator today!). A searching party of deputies was gathered; telegrams were hurried off to sheriffs in other towns. Many years later, when the Talbo estate was being settled, I came across the handwritten original of this telegram—composed, I believe, by Dr. Ritz. *Be on lookout for following persons traveling together. Dolly Augusta Talbo, white, aged 60, yellow grayish hair, thin, height 5 feet 3, green eyes, probably insane but not likely to be dangerous, post description bakeries as she is cake eater. Catherine Creek, Negro, pretends to be Indian, age about 60, toothless, confused speech, short and heavy, strong, likely to be dangerous. Collin Talbo Fenwick, white, age 16, looks younger, height 5 feet 7, blond, gray eyes, thin, bad posture, scar at corner of mouth, surly natured. All three wanted as runaways.* They sure haven't run far, Riley said in the post office; and postmistress Mrs. Peters rushed to the telephone to say Riley Henderson had seen us in the woods below the cemetery.

While this was happening we were peaceably setting about

to make the tree-house cozy. From Catherine's satchel we took
a rose and gold scrapquilt, and there was a deck of Rook
cards, soap, rolls of toilet paper, oranges and lemons, candles,
a frying pan, a bottle of blackberry wine, and two shoeboxes
filled with food: Catherine bragged that she'd robbed the pantry of everything, leaving not even a biscuit for That One's
breakfast.

Later, we all went to the creek and bathed our feet and faces
in the cold water. There are as many creeks in River Woods
as there are veins in a leaf: clear, crackling, they crook their
way down into the little river that crawls through the woods
like a green alligator. Dolly looked a sight, standing in the
water with her winter suit-skirt hiked up and her veil pester-
ing her like a cloud of gnats. I asked her, Dolly, why are you
wearing that veil? and she said, "But isn't it proper for ladies
to wear veils when they go traveling?"

Returning to the tree, we made a delicious jar of orangeade
and talked of the future. Our assets were: forty-seven dollars
in cash, and several pieces of jewelry, notably a gold fraternity
ring Catherine had found in the intestines of a hog while
stuffing sausages. According to Catherine, forty-seven dollars
would buy us bus tickets anywhere: she knew somebody who
had gone all the way to Mexico for fifteen dollars. Both Dolly
and I were opposed to Mexico: for one thing, we didn't know
the language. Besides, Dolly said, we shouldn't venture outside the state, and wherever we went it ought to be near a
forest, otherwise how would we be able to make the dropsy
cure? "To tell you the truth, I think we should set up right
here in River Woods," she said, gazing about speculatively.

"In this old tree?" said Catherine. "Just put that notion out
of your head, Dollyheart." And then: "You recall how we saw
in the paper where a man bought a castle across the ocean
and brought it every bit home with him? You recall that?
Well, we maybe could put my little house on a wagon and haul
it down here." But, as Dolly pointed out, the house belonged
to Verena, and was therefore not ours to haul away. Catherine
answered: "You wrong, sugar. If you feed a man, and wash
his clothes, and born his children, you and that man are married, that man is yours. If you sweep a house, and tend its fires
and fill its stove, and there is love in you all the years you are
doing this, then you and that house are married, that house is
yours. The way I see it, both those houses up there belong
to us: in the eyes of God, we could put That One right out."

I had an idea: down on the river below us there was a forsaken houseboat, green with the rust of water, half-sunk; it had been the property of an old man who made his living catching catfish, and who had been run out of town after applying for a certificate to marry a fifteen-year-old colored girl. My idea was, why shouldn't we fix up the old houseboat and live there?

Catherine said that if possible she hoped to spend the rest of her life on land: "Where the Lord intended us," and she listed more of His intentions, one of these being that trees were meant for monkeys and birds. Presently she went silent and, nudging us, pointed in amazement down to where the woods opened upon the field of grass.

There, stalking toward us, solemnly, stiffly, came a distinguished party: Judge Cool, the Reverend and Mrs. Buster, Mrs. Macy Wheeler; and leading them, Sheriff Junius Candle, who wore high-laced boots and had a pistol flapping on his hip. Sunmotes lilted around them like yellow butterflies, brambles brushed their starched town clothes, and Mrs. Macy Wheeler, frightened by a vine that switched against her leg, jumped back, screeching: I laughed.

And, hearing me, they looked up at us, an expression of perplexed horror collecting on some of their faces: it was as though they were visitors at a zoo who had wandered accidentally into one of the cages. Sheriff Candle slouched forward, his hand cocked on his pistol. He stared at us with puckered eyes, as if he were gazing straight into the sun. "Now look here . . ." he began, and was cut short by Mrs. Buster, who said: "Sheriff, we agreed to leave this to the Reverend." It was a rule of hers that her husband, as God's representative, should have first say in everything. The Reverend Buster cleared his throat, and his hands, as he rubbed them together, were like the dry scraping feelers of an insect. "Dolly Talbo," he said, his voice very fine-sounding for so stringy, stunted a man, "I speak to you on behalf of your sister, that good gracious woman . . ."

"That she is," sang his wife, and Mrs. Macy Wheeler parroted her.

". . . who has this day received a grievous shock."

"That she has," echoed the ladies in their choir-trained voices.

Dolly looked at Catherine, touched my hand, as though asking us to explain what was meant by the group glowering below like dogs gathered around a tree of trapped possums. Inadvertently, and just, I think to have something in her hands, she picked up one of the cigarettes Riley had left.

"Shame on you," squalled Mrs. Buster, tossing her tiny baldish head: those who called her an old buzzard, and there were several, were not speaking of her character alone: in addition to a small vicious head, she had high hunched shoulders and a vast body. "I say shame on you. How can you have come so far from God as to sit up in a tree like a drunken Indian—sucking cigarettes like a common . . ."

"Floozy," supplied Mrs. Macy Wheeler.

". . . floozy, while your sister lies in misery flat on her back."

Maybe they were right in describing Catherine as dangerous, for she reared up and said: "Preacher lady, don't you go calling Dolly and us floozies; I'll come down there and slap you bowlegged." Fortunately, none of them could understand her; if they had, the sheriff might have shot her through the head: no exaggeration; and many of the white people in town would have said he did right.

Dolly seemed stunned, at the same time self-possessed. You see, she simply dusted her skirt and said: "Consider a moment, Mrs. Buster, and you will realize that we are nearer God than you—by several yards."

"Good for you, Miss Dolly. I call that a good answer." The man who had spoken was Judge Cool; he clapped his hands together and chuckled appreciatively. "Of course they are nearer God," he said, unfazed by the disapproving, sober faces around him. "They're in a tree, and we're on the ground."

Mrs. Buster whirled on him. "I'd thought you were a Christian, Charlie Cool. My ideas of a Christian do not include laughing at and encouraging a poor mad woman."

"Mind who you name as mad, Thelma," said the Judge. "That isn't especially Christian either."

The Reverend Buster opened fire. "Answer me this, Judge. Why did you come with us if it wasn't to do the Lord's will in a spirit of mercy?"

"The Lord's will?" said the Judge incredulously. "You don't know what that is any more than I do. Perhaps the Lord told these people to go live in a tree; you'll admit, at least, that He never told you to drag them out—unless, of course, Verena Talbo is the Lord, a theory several of you give credence to, eh Sheriff? No, sir, I did not come along to do anyone's will but my own: which merely means that I felt like taking a walk—

the woods are very handsome at this time of year." He picked some brown violets and put them in his buttonhole.

"To hell with all that," began the Sheriff, and was again interrupted by Mrs. Buster, who said that under no circumstances would she tolerate swearing: Will we, Reverend? and the Reverend, backing her up, said he'd be damned if they would. "I'm in charge here," the Sheriff informed them, thrusting his bully-boy jaw. "This is a matter for the law."

"Whose law, Junius?" inquired Judge Cool quietly. "Remember that I sat in the courthouse twenty-seven years, rather a longer time than you've lived. Take care. We have no legal right whatever to interfere with Miss Dolly."

Undaunted, the Sheriff hoisted himself a little into the tree. "Let's don't have any more trouble," he said coaxingly, and we could see his curved dog-teeth. "Come on down from there, the pack of you." As we continued to sit like three nesting birds he showed more of his teeth and, as though he were trying to shake us out, angrily swayed a branch.

"Miss Dolly, you've always been a peaceful person," said Mrs. Macy Wheeler. "Please come on home with us; you don't want to miss your dinner." Dolly replied matter-of-factly that we were not hungry: were they? "There's a drumstick for anybody that would like it."

Sheriff Candle said, "You make it hard on me, ma'am," and pulled himself nearer. A branch, cracking under his weight, sent through the tree a sad cruel thunder.

"If he lays a hand on any one of you, kick him in the head," advised Judge Cool. "Or I will," he said with sudden gallant pugnacity: like an inspired frog he hopped and caught hold to one of the Sheriff's dangling boots. The Sheriff, in turn, grabbed my ankles, and Catherine had to hold me around the middle. We were sliding, that we should all fall seemed inevitable, the strain was immense. Meanwhile, Dolly started pouring what was left of our orangeade down the Sheriff's neck, and abruptly, shouting an obscenity, he let go of me. They crashed to the ground, the Sheriff on top of the Judge and the Reverend Buster crushed beneath them both. Mrs. Macy Wheeler and Mrs. Buster, augmenting the disaster, fell upon them with crow-like cries of distress.

Appalled by what had happened, and the part she herself had played, Dolly became so confused that she dropped the empty orangeade jar: it hit Mrs. Buster on the head with a ripe thud. "Beg pardon," she apologized, though in the furor no one heard her.

When the tangle below unraveled, those concerned stood apart from each other embarrassedly, gingerly feeling of themselves. The Reverend looked rather flattened out, but no broken bones were discovered, and only Mrs. Buster, on whose skimpy-haired head a bump was pyramiding, could have justly complained of injury. She did so forthrightly. "You attacked me, Dolly Talbo, don't deny it, everyone here is a witness, everyone saw you aim that mason jar at my head. Junius, arrest her!"

The Sheriff, however, was involved in settling differences of his own. Hands on hips, swaggering, he bore down on the Judge, who was in the process of replacing the violets in his buttonhole. "If you weren't so old, I'd damn well knock you down."

"I'm not so old, Junius: just old enough to think men ought not to fight in front of ladies," said the Judge. He was a fair-sized man with strong shoulders and a straight body: though not far from seventy, he looked to be in his fifties. He clenched his fists and they were hard and hairy as coconuts. "On the other hand," he said grimly, "I'm ready if you are."

At the moment it looked like a fair enough match. Even the Sheriff seemed not so sure of himself; with diminishing bravado, he spit between his fingers, and said Well, nobody was going to accuse him of hitting an old man. "Or standing up to one," Judge Cool retorted. "Go on, Junius, tuck your shirt in your pants and trot along home."

The Sheriff appealed to us in the tree. "Save yourselves a lot of trouble: get out of there and come along with me now." We did not stir, except that Dolly dropped her veil, as though lowering a curtain on the subject once for all. Mrs. Buster, the lump on her head like a horn, said portentously, "Never mind, Sheriff. They've had their chance," and, eyeing Dolly, then the Judge, added: "You may imagine you are getting away with something. But let me tell you there will be a retribution —not in heaven, right here on earth."

"Right here on earth," harmonized Mrs. Macy Wheeler.

They left along the path, erect, haughty as a wedding procession, and passed into the sunlight where the red rolling grass swept up, swallowed them. Lingering under the tree, the Judge smiled at us and, with a small courteous bow, said: "Do I remember you offering a drumstick to anybody that would like it?"

He might have been put together from parts of the tree, for

his nose was like a wooden peg, his legs were strong as old roots, and his eyebrows were thick, tough as strips of bark. Among the topmost branches were beards of silvery moss the color of his center-parted hair, and the cowhide sycamore leaves, sifting down from a neighboring taller tree, were the color of his cheeks. Despite his canny, tomcat eyes, the general impression his face made was that of someone shy and countrified. Ordinarily he was not the one to make a show of himself, Judge Charlie Cool; there were many who had taken advantage of his modesty to set themselves above him. Yet none of them could have claimed, as he could, to be a graduate of Harvard University or to have twice traveled in Europe. Still, there were those who were resentful and felt that he put on airs: wasn't he supposed to read a page of Greek every morning before breakfast? and what kind of a man was it that would always have flowers in his buttonhole? If he wasn't stuck up, why, some people asked, had he gone all the way to Kentucky to find a wife instead of marrying one of our own women? I do not remember the Judge's wife; she died before I was old enough to be aware of her, therefore all that I repeat comes second-hand. So: the town never warmed up to Irene Cool, and apparently it was her own fault. Kentucky women are difficult to begin with, keyed-up, hellion-hearted, and Irene Cool, who was born a Todd in Bowling Green (Mary Todd, a second cousin once removed, had married Abraham Lincoln) let everyone around here know she thought them a backward, vulgar lot: she received none of the ladies of the town, but Miss Palmer, who did sewing for her, spread news of how she'd transformed the Judge's house into a place of taste and style with Oriental rugs and antique furnishings. She drove to and from Church in a Pierce-Arrow with all the windows rolled up, and in church itself she sat with a cologned handkerchief against her nose: *the smell of God ain't good enough for Irene Cool.* Moreover, she would not permit either of the local doctors to attend her family, this though she herself was a semi-invalid: a small backbone dislocation necessitated her sleeping on a bed of boards. There were crude jokes about the Judge getting full of splinters. Nevertheless, he fathered two sons, Todd and Charles Jr., both born in Kentucky where their mother had gone in order that they could claim to be natives of the bluegrass state. But those who tried to make out the Judge got the brunt of his wife's irritableness, that he was a miserable man, never had much of a case, and after she died even the hardest of their critics had to admit old Charlie must surely have loved his Irene. For during the last two years of her life, when she was very ill and fretful, he retired as circuit judge, then took her abroad to the places they had been on their honeymoon. She never came back; she is buried in Switzerland. Not so long ago Carrie Wells, a schoolteacher here in town, went on a group tour to Europe; the only thing connecting our town with that continent are graves, the graves of soldier boys and Irene Cool; and Carrie, armed with a camera for snapshots, set out to visit them all: though she stumbled about in a cloud-high cemetery one whole afternoon, she could not find the Judge's wife, and it is funny to think of Irene Cool, serenely there on a mountain-side still unwilling to receive. There was not much left for the Judge when he came back; politicians like Meiself Tallsap and his gang had come into power: those boys couldn't afford to have Charlie Cool sitting in the courthouse. It was sad to see the Judge, a fine-looking man dressed in narrowcut suits with a black silk band sewn around his sleeve and a Cherokee rose in his button-hole, sad to see him with nothing to do except go to the post office or stop in at the bank. His sons worked in the bank, prissy-mouthed, prudent men who might have been twins, for they both were marshmallow-white, slump-shouldered, watery-eyed. Charles Jr., he was the one who had lost his hair while still in college, was vice-president of the bank, and Todd, the younger son, was chief cashier. In no way did they resemble their father, except that they had married Kentucky women. These daughters-in-law had taken over the Judge's house and divided it into two apartments with separate entrances; there was an arrangement whereby the old man lived with first one son's family, then the other. No wonder he'd felt like taking a walk to the woods.

"Thank you, Miss Dolly," he said, wiping his mouth with the back of his hand. "That's the best drumstick I've had since I was a boy."

"It's the least we can do, a drumstick; you were very brave." There was in Dolly's voice an emotional, feminine tremor that struck me as unsuitable, not dignified; so, too, it must have seemed to Catherine: she gave Dolly a reprimanding glance. "Won't you have something more, a piece of cake?"

"No ma'm, thank you, I've had a sufficiency." He unloosened from his vest a gold watch and chain, then lassoed the chain to a strong twig above his head; it hung like a Christmas ornament, and its feathery faded ticking might have been the heart-beat of a delicate thing, a firefly, a frog. "If you can hear time passing it makes the day last longer. I've come to appreciate a long day." He brushed back the fur of the squirrels, which lay curled in a corner as though they were only asleep. "Right through the head: good shooting, son."

Of course I gave the credit to the proper party. "Riley Henderson, was it?" said the Judge, and went on to say it was Riley who had let our whereabouts be known. "Before that, they must have sent off a hundred dollars' worth of telegrams," he told us, tickled at the thought. "I guess it was the idea of all that money that made Verena take to her bed."

Scowling, Dolly said, "It doesn't make a particle of sense, all of them behaving ugly that way. They seemed mad enough to kill us, though I can't see why, or what it has to do with Verena: she knew we were going away to leave her in peace, I told her, I even left a note. But if she's sick—is she, Judge? I've never known her to be."

"Never a day," said Catherine.

"Oh, she's upset all right," the Judge said with a certain contentment. "But Verena's not the woman to come down with anything an aspirin couldn't fix. I remember when she wanted to rearrange the cemetery, put up some kind of mausoleum to house herself and all you Talbos. One of the ladies around here came to me and said Judge, don't you think Verena Talbo is the most morbid person in town, contemplating such a big tomb for herself? and I said No, the only thing morbid was that she was willing to spend the money when not for an instant did she believe she was ever going to die."

"I don't like to hear talk against my sister," said Dolly curtly. "She's worked hard, she deserves to have things as she wants them. It's our fault, someway we failed her, there was no place for us in her house."

Catherine's cotton-wadding squirmed in her jaw like chewing tobacco. "Are you my Dollyheart? or some hypocrite? He's a friend, you ought to tell him the truth, how That One and the little Jew was stealing our medicine. . . ."

The Judge applied for a translation, but Dolly said it was simply nonsense, nothing worth repeating and, diverting him, asked if he knew how to skin a squirrel. Nodding dreamily, he gazed away from us, above us, his acornlike eyes scanning the sky-fringed, breeze-fooled leaves. "It may be that there is no place for any of us. Except we know there is, somewhere; and if we found it, but lived there only a moment, we could count ourselves blessed. This could be your place," he said, shivering as though in the sky spreading wings had cast a cold shade. "And mine."

Subtly as the gold watch spun its sound of time, the afternoon curved toward twilight. Mist from the river, autumn haze, trailed moon-colors among the bronze, the blue trees, and a halo, an image of winter, ringed the paling sun. Still the Judge did not leave us: "Two women and a boy? at the mercy of night? and Junius Candle, those fools up to God knows what? I'm sticking with you." Surely, of the four of us, it was the Judge who had most found his place in the tree. It was a pleasure to watch him, all twinkly as a hare's nose, and feeling himself a man again, more than that, a protector. He skinned the squirrels with a jackknife, while in the dusk I gathered sticks and built under the tree a fire for the frying pan. Dolly opened the bottle of blackberry wine; she justified this by referring to a chill in the air. The squirrels turned out quite well, very tender, and the Judge said proudly that we should taste his fried catfish sometime. We sipped the wine in silence; a smell of leaves and smoke carrying from the cooling fire called up thoughts of other autumns, and we sighed, heard, like sea-roar, singings in the field of grass. A candle flickered in a mason jar, and gipsy moths, balanced, blowing about the flame, seemed to pilot its scarf of yellow among the black branches.

There was, just then, not a footfall, but a nebulous sense of intrusion: it might have been nothing more than the moon coming out. Except there was no moon; nor stars. It was dark as the blackberry wine. "I think there is someone—something down there," said Dolly, expressing what we all felt.

The Judge lifted the candle. Night-crawlers slithered away from its lurching light, a snowy owl flew between the trees. "Who goes there?" he challenged with the conviction of a soldier. "Answer up, who goes there?"

"Me, Riley Henderson." It was indeed. He separated from the shadows, and his upraised, grinning face looked warped, wicked in the candlelight. "Just thought I'd see how you were getting on. Hope you're not sore at me: I wouldn't have told where you were, not if I'd known what it was all about."

"Nobody blames you, son," said the Judge, and I remembered it was he who had championed Riley's cause against his uncle Horace Holton: there was an understanding between them. "We're enjoying a small taste of wine. I'm sure Miss Dolly would be pleased to have you join us."

Catherine complained there was no room; another ounce,

and those old boards would give way. Still, we scrunched together to make a place for Riley, who had no sooner squeezed into it than Catherine grabbed a fistful of his hair. "That's for today with you pointing your gun at us like I told you not to; and this," she said, yanking again and speaking distinctively enough to be understood, "pays you back for setting the Sheriff on us."

It seemed to me that Catherine was impertinent, but Riley grunted good-naturedly, and said she might have better cause to be pulling somebody's hair before the night was over. For there was, he told us, excited feelings in the town, crowds like Saturday night; the Reverend and Mrs. Buster especially were brewing trouble: Mrs. Buster was sitting on her front porch showing callers the bump on her head. Sheriff Candle, he said, had persuaded Verena to authorize a warrant for our arrest on the grounds that we had stolen property belonging to her.

"And Judge," said Riley, his manner grave, perplexed, "they've even got the idea they're going to arrest you. Disturbing the peace and obstructing justice, that's what I heard. Maybe I shouldn't tell you this—but outside the bank I ran into one of your boys, Todd. I asked him what he was going to do about it, about them arresting you, I mean; and he said Nothing, said they'd been expecting something of the kind, that you'd brought it on yourself."

Leaning, the Judge snuffed out the candle; it was as though an expression was occurring in his face which he did not want us to see. In the dark one of us was crying, after a moment we knew that it was Dolly, and the sound of her tears set off silent explosions of love that, running the full circle round, bound us each to the other. Softly, the Judge said: "When they come we must be ready for them. Now, everybody listen to me. . . ."

Three

We must know our position to defend it; that is a primary rule. Therefore: what has brought us together? Trouble. Miss Dolly and her friends, they are in trouble. You, Riley: we both are in trouble. We belong in this tree or we wouldn't be here." Dolly grew silent under the confident sound of the Judge's voice; he said: "Today, when I started out with the Sheriff's party, I was a man convinced that his life will have passed uncommunicated and without trace. I think now that I will not have been so unfortunate. Miss Dolly, how long? fifty, sixty years? it was that far ago that I remember you, a stiff and blushing child riding to town in your father's wagon—never getting down from the wagon because you didn't want us town-children to see you had no shoes."

"They had shoes, Dolly and That One," Catherine muttered. "It was me that didn't have no shoes."

"All the years that I've seen you, never known you, not ever recognized, as I did today, what you are: a spirit, a pagan . . ."

"A pagan?" said Dolly, alarmed but interested.

"At least, then, a spirit, someone not to be calculated by the eye alone. Spirits are accepters of life, they grant its differences—and consequently are always in trouble. Myself, I

40

should never have been a Judge; as such, I was too often on the wrong side: the law doesn't admit differences. Do you remember old Carper, the fisherman who had a houseboat on the river? He was chased out of town—wanted to marry that pretty little colored girl, I think she works for Mrs. Postum now; and you know she loved him, I used to see them when I went fishing, they were very happy together; she was to him what no one has been to me, the one person in the world—from whom nothing is held back. Still, if he had succeeded in marrying her, it would have been the Sheriff's duty to arrest and my duty to sentence him. I sometimes imagine all those whom I've called guilty have passed the real guilt on to me: it's partly that that makes me want once before I die to be right on the right side."

"You on the right side now. That One and the Jew . . ."

"Hush," said Dolly.

"The one person in the world." It was Riley repeating the Judge's phrase; his voice lingered inquiringly.

"I mean," the Judge explained, "a person to whom everything can be said. Am I an idiot to want such a thing? But ah, the energy we spend hiding from one another, afraid as we are of being identified. But here we are, identified: five fools in a tree. A great piece of luck provided we know how to use it: no longer any need to worry about the picture we present —free to find out who we truly are. If we know that no one can dislodge us; it's the uncertainty concerning themselves that makes our friends conspire to deny the differences. By scraps and bits I've in the past surrendered myself to strangers—men who disappeared down the gangplank, got off at the next station: put together, maybe they would've made the one person in the world—but there he is with a dozen different faces moving down a hundred separate streets. This is my chance to find that man—you are him, Miss Dolly, Riley, all of you."

Catherine said, "I'm no man with any dozen faces: the notion," which irritated Dolly, who told her if she couldn't speak respectably why not just go to sleep. "But Judge," said Dolly, "I'm not sure I know what it is you have in mind we should tell each other. Secrets?" she finished lamely.

"Secrets, no, no." The Judge scratched a match and re-lighted the candle; his face sprang upon us with an expression unexpectedly pathetic: we must help him, he was pleading. "Speak of the night, the fact there is no moon. What one says hardly matters, only the trust with which it is said, the sympathy with which it is received. Irene, my wife, a remarkable woman, we might have shared anything, and yet, yet nothing in us combined, we could not touch. She died in my arms, and at the last I said, Are you happy, Irene? have I made you happy? Happy happy happy, those were her last words: equivocal. I have never understood whether she was saying yes, or merely answering with an echo: I should know if I'd ever known her. My sons. I do not enjoy their esteem: I've wanted it, more as a man than as a father. Unfortunately, they feel they know something shameful about me. I'll tell you what it is." His virile eyes, faceted with candle-glow, examined us one by one, as though testing our attention, trust. "Five years ago, nearer six, I sat down in a train-seat where some child had left a child's magazine. I picked it up and was looking through it when I saw on the back cover addresses of children who wanted to correspond with other children. There was a little girl in Alaska, her name appealed to me, Heather Falls. I sent her a picture postcard; Lord, it seemed a harmless and pleasant thing to do. She answered at once, and the letter quite astonished me; it was a very intelligent account of life in Alaska—charming descriptions of her father's sheep ranch, of northern lights. She was thirteen and enclosed a photograph of herself—not pretty, but a wise and kind looking child. I hunted through some old albums, and found a Kodak made on a fishing trip when I was fifteen—out in the sun and with a trout in my hand: it looked new enough. I wrote her as though I were still that boy, told her of the gun I'd got for Christmas, how the dog had had pups and what we'd named them, described a tent-show that had come to town. To be growing up again and have a sweetheart in Alaska—well, it was fun for an old man sitting alone listening to the noise of a clock. Later on she wrote she'd fallen in love with a fellow she knew, and I felt a real pang of jealousy, the way a youngster would; but we have remained friends: two years ago, when I told her I was getting ready for law school, she sent me a gold nugget—it would bring me luck, she said." He took it from his pocket and held it out for us to see: it made her come so close, Heather Falls, as though the gently bright gift balanced in his palm was part of her heart.

"And that's what they think is shameful?" said Dolly, more piqued than indignant. "Because you've helped keep company a lonely little child in Alaska? It snows there so much."

Judge Cool closed his hand over the nugget. "Not that they've mentioned it to me. But I've heard them talking at night, my sons and their wives: wanting to know what to do about me. Of course they'd spied out the letters. I don't believe in locking drawers—seems strange a man can't live without keys in what was at least once his own house. They think it all a sign of . . ." He tapped his head.

"I had a letter once. Collin, sugar, pour me a taste," said Catherine, indicating the wine. "Sure enough, I had a letter once, still got it somewhere, kept it twenty years wondering who was wrote it. Said Hello Catherine, come on to Miami and marry with me, love Bill."

"Catherine. A man asked you to marry him—and you never told one word of it to me?"

Catherine lifted a shoulder. "Well, Dollyheart, what was the Judge saying? You don't tell anybody everything. Besides, I've known a peck of Bills—wouldn't study marrying any of them. What worries my mind is, which one of the Bills was it wrote that letter? I'd like to know, seeing as it's the only letter I ever got. It could be the Bill that put the roof on my house; course, by the time the roof was up—my goodness, I have got old, been a long day since I've given it two thoughts. There was Bill that came to plow the garden, spring of 1913 it was; that man sure could plow a straight row. And Bill that built the chicken-coop: went away on a Pullman job; might have been him wrote me that letter. Or Bill—uh uh, his name was Fred—Collin, sugar, this wine is mighty good."

"I may have a drop more myself," said Dolly. "I mean, Catherine has given me such a . . ."

"Hmn," said Catherine.

"If you spoke more slowly, or chewed less . . ." The Judge thought Catherine's cotton was tobacco.

Riley had withdrawn a little from us; slumped over, he stared stilly into the inhabited dark: I, I, I, a bird cried, "I—you're wrong, Judge," he said.

"How so, son?"

The caught-up uneasiness that I associated with Riley swamped his face. "I'm not in trouble: I'm nothing—or would you call that my trouble? I lie awake thinking what do I know how to do? hunt, drive a car, fool around; and I get scared when I think maybe that's all it will ever come to. Another thing, I've got no feelings—except for my sisters, which is different. Take for instance, I've been going with this girl from Rock City nearly a year, the longest time I've stayed with one girl. I guess it was a week ago she flared up and said where's your heart? said if I didn't love her she'd as soon die.

So I stopped the car on the railroad track; well, I said, let's just sit here, the Crescent's due in about twenty minutes. We didn't take our eyes off each other, and I thought isn't it mean that I'm looking at you and I don't feel anything except . . ."

"Except vanity?" said the Judge.

Riley did not deny it. "And if my sisters were old enough to take care of themselves, I'd have been willing to wait for the Crescent to come down on us."

It made my stomach hurt to hear him talk like that; I longed to tell him he was all I wanted to be.

"You said before about the one person in the world. Why couldn't I think of her like that? It's what I want, I'm no good by myself. Maybe, if I could care for somebody that way, I'd make plans and carry them out: buy that stretch of land past Parson's Place and build houses on it—I could do it if I got quiet."

Wind surprised, pealed the leaves, parted night clouds; showers of starlight were let loose: our candle, as though intimidated by the incandescence of the opening, star-stabbed sky, toppled, and we could see, unwrapped above us, a late wayaway wintery moon: it was like a slice of snow, near and far creatures called to it, hunched moon-eyed frogs, a claw-voiced wildcat. Catherine hauled out the rose scrapquilt, insisting Dolly wrap it around herself; then she tucked her arms around me and scratched my head until I let it relax on her bosom—You cold? she said, and I wiggled closer: she was good and warm as the old kitchen.

"Son, I'd say you were going at it the wrong end first," said the Judge, turning up his coat-collar. "How could you care about one girl? Have you ever cared about one leaf?"

Riley, listening to the wildcat with an itchy hunter's look, snatched at the leaves blowing about us like midnight butterflies; alive, fluttering as though to escape and fly, one stayed trapped between his fingers. The Judge, too: he caught a leaf; and it was worth more in his hand than in Riley's. Pressing it mildly against his cheek, he distantly said, "We are speaking of love. A leaf, a handful of seed—begin with these, learn a little what it is to love. First, a leaf, a fall of rain, then someone to receive what a leaf has taught you, what a fall of rain has ripened. No easy process, understand; it could take a lifetime, it has mine, and still I've never mastered it—I only know how true it is: that love is a chain of love, as nature is a chain of life."

"Then," said Dolly with an intake of breath, "I've been in

love all my life." She sank down into the quilt. "Well, no,"
and her voice fell off, "I guess not. I've never loved a'," while
she searched for the word wind frolicked her veil, "gentleman.
You might say that I've never had the opportunity. Except
Papa," she paused, as though she'd said too much. A gauze of
starlight wrapped her closely as the quilt; something, the reciting frogs, the string of voices stretching from the field of
grass, lured, impelled her: "But I have loved everything else.
Like the color pink; when I was a child I had one colored
crayon, and it was pink; I drew pink cats, pink trees—for
thirty-four years I lived in a pink room. And the box I kept,
it's somewhere in the attic now, I must ask Verena please to
give it to me, it would be nice to see my first loves again:
what is there? a dried honeycomb, an empty hornet's nest,
other things, or an orange stuck with cloves and a jaybird's
egg—when I loved those love collected inside me so that it
went flying about like a bird in a sunflower field. But it's best
not to show such things, it burdens people and makes them, I
don't know why, unhappy. Verena scolds at me for what she
calls hiding in corners, but I'm afraid of scaring people if I
show that I care for them. Like Paul Jimson's wife; after he
got sick and couldn't deliver the papers any more, remember
she took over his route? poor thin little thing just dragging herself with that sack of papers. It was one cold afternoon, she
came up on the porch her nose running and tears of cold
hanging in her eyes—she put down the paper, and I said wait,
hold on, and took my handkerchief to wipe her eyes: I wanted
to say, if I could, that I was sorry and that I loved her—my
hand grazed her face, she turned with the smallest shout and
ran down the steps. Then on, she always tossed the papers from
the street, and whenever I heard them hit the porch it sounded
in my bones."

"Paul Jimson's wife: worrying yourself over trash like that!"
said Catherine, rinsing her mouth with the last of the wine.
"I've got a bowl of goldfish, just 'cause I like them don't make
me love the world. Love a lot of mess, my foot. You can talk
what you want, not going to do anything but harm, bringing
up what's best forgot. People ought to keep more things to
themselves. The deepdown ownself part of you, that's the good
part: what's left of a human being that goes around speaking
his privates? The Judge, he say we all up here 'cause of
trouble some kind. Shoot! We here for very plain reasons. One
is, this our tree-house, and two, That One and the Jew's trying
to steal what belongs to us. Three: you here, every one of you,

'cause you want to be: the deepdown part of you tells you so. This last don't apply to me. I like a roof over my own head. Dollyheart, give the Judge a portion of that quilt: man's shivering like was Halloween."

Shyly Dolly lifted a wing of the quilt and nodded to him; the Judge, not at all shy, slipped under it. The branches of the China tree swayed like immense oars dipping into a sea rolling and chilled by the far far stars. Left alone, Riley sat hunched up in himself like a pitiful orphan. "Snuggle up, hard head: you cold like anybody else," said Catherine, offering him the position on her right that I occupied on her left. He didn't seem to want to; maybe he noticed that she smelled like bitterweed, or maybe he thought it was sissy; but I said come on, Riley, Catherine's good and warm, better than a quilt. After a while Riley moved over to us. It was quiet for so long I thought everyone had gone to sleep. Then I felt Catherine stiffen. "It's just come to me who it was sent my letter: Bill Nobody. That One, that's who. Sure as my name's Catherine Creek she got some nigger in Miami to mail me a letter, thinking I'd scoot off there never to be heard from again." Dolly sleepily said hush now hush, shut your eyes: "Nothing to be afraid of; we've men here to watch out for us." A branch swung back, moonlight ignited the tree: I saw the Judge take Dolly's hand. It was the last thing I saw.

Four

RILEY was the first to wake, and he wakened me. On the skyline three morning stars swooned in the flush of an arriving sun; dew tinseled the leaves, a jet chain of blackbirds swung out to meet the mounting light. Riley beckoned for me to come with him; we slid silently down through the tree. Catherine, snoring with abandon, did not hear us go; nor did Dolly and the Judge who, like two children lost in a witch-ruled forest, were asleep with their cheeks together.

We headed toward the river, Riley leading the way. The legs of his canvas trousers whispered against each other. Every little bit he stopped and stretched himself, as though he'd been riding on a train. Somewhere we came to a hill of already about and busy red ants. Riley unbuttoned his fly and began to flood them; I don't know that it was funny, but I laughed to keep him company. Naturally I was insulted when he switched around and peed on my shoe. I thought it meant he had no respect for me. I said to him why would he want to do a thing like that? Don't you know a joke? he said, and threw a hugging arm around my shoulder.

If such events can be dated, this I would say was the moment Riley Henderson and I became friends, the moment, at least, when there began in him an affectionate feeling for me that supported my own for him. Through brown briars under brown trees we walked deep in the woods down to the river.

Leaves like scarlet hands floated on the green slow water. A poking end of a drowned log seemed the peering head of some river-beast. We moved on to the old houseboat, where the water was clearer. The houseboat was slightly tipped over; drifts of waterbay sheddings were like a rich rust on its roof and declining deck. The inside cabin had a mystifying tended-to look. Scattered around were issues of an adventure magazine, there was a kerosene lamp and a line of beer empties ranged on a table; the bunk sported a blanket, a pillow, and the pillow was colored with pink markings of lipstick. In a rush I realized the houseboat was someone's hide-out; then, from the grin taking over Riley's homely face, I knew whose it was. "What's more," he said, "you can get in a little fishing on the side. Don't you tell anybody." I crossed an admiring heart.

While we were undressing I had a kind of dream. I dreamed the houseboat had been launched on the river with the five of us aboard: our laundry flapped like sails, in the pantry a coconut cake was cooking; a geranium bloomed on the windowsill —together we floated over changing rivers past varying views.

The last of summer warmed the climbing sun, but the water, at first plunge, sent me chattering and chicken-skinned back to the deck where I stood watching Riley unconcernedly propel himself to and fro between the banks. An island of bamboo reeds, standing like the legs of cranes, shivered in a shallow patch, and Riley waded out among them with lowered, hunting eyes. He signaled to me. Though it hurt, I eased down into the cold river and swam to join him. The water bending the bamboo was clear and divided into knee-deep basins—Riley hovered above one: in the thin pool a coal-black catfish lay dozingly trapped. We closed in upon it with fingers tense as fork-prongs: thrashing backwards, it flung itself straight into my hands. The flailing razory whiskers made a gash across my palm, still I had the sense to hold on—thank goodness, for it's the only fish I ever caught. Most people don't believe it when I tell about catching a catfish barehanded; I say well ask Riley Henderson. We drove a spike of bamboo through its gills and swam back to the houseboat holding it aloft. Riley said it was one of the fattest catfish he'd ever seen: we would take it back to the tree and, since he'd bragged what a great hand he was at frying a catfish, let the Judge fix it for breakfast. As it turned out, that fish never got eaten.

All this time at the tree-house there was a terrible situation. During our absence Sheriff Candle had returned backed by deputies and a warrant of arrest. Meanwhile, unaware of what was in store, Riley and I lazed along kicking over toadstools, sometimes stopping to skip rocks on the water.

We still were some distance away when rioting voices reached us; they rang in the trees like axe-blows. I heard Catherine scream: roar, rather. It made such soup of my legs I couldn't keep up with Riley, who grabbed a stick and began to run. I zigged one way, zagged another, then, having made a wrong turn, came out on the grass-field's rim. And there was Catherine.

Her dress was ripped down the front: she was good as naked. Ray Oliver, Jack Mill, and Big Eddie Stover, three grown men, cronies of the Sheriff, were dragging and slapping her through the grass. I wanted to kill them; and Catherine was trying to: but she didn't stand a chance—though she butted them with her head, bounced them with her elbows. Big Eddie Stover was legally born a bastard; the other two made the grade on their own. It was Big Eddie that went for me, and I slammed my catfish flat in his face. Catherine said, "You leave my baby be, he's an orphan"; and, when she saw that he had me around the waist: "In the booboos, Collin, kick his old booboos." So I did. Big Eddie's face curdled like clabber. Jack Mill (he's the one who a year later got locked in the ice-plant and froze to death: served him right) snatched at me, but I bolted across the field and crouched down in the tallest grass. I don't think they bothered to look for me, they had their hands so full with Catherine; she fought them the whole way, and I watched her, sick with knowing there was no help to give, until they passed out of sight over the ridge into the cemetery.

Overhead two squawking crows crossed, recrossed, as though making an evil sign. I crept toward the woods—near me, then, I heard boots cutting through the grass. It was the Sheriff; with him was a man called Will Harris. Tall as a door, buffalo-shouldered, Will Harris had once had his throat eaten out by a mad dog; the scars were bad enough, but his damaged voice was worse: it sounded giddy and babyfied, like a midget's. They passed so close I could have untied Will's shoes. His tiny voice, shrilling at the Sheriff, jumped with Morris Ritz's name and Verena's: I couldn't make out exactly, except something had happened about Morris Ritz and Verena had sent Will to bring back the Sheriff. The Sheriff said: "What in hell does the woman want, an army?" When they were gone I sprang up and ran into the woods.

In sight of the China tree I hid behind a fan of fern: I thought one of the Sheriff's men might still be hanging around. But there was nothing, simply a lonely singing bird. And no one in the tree-house: smoky as ghosts, streamers of sunlight illuminated its emptiness. Numbly I moved into view and leaned my head against the tree's trunk; at this, the vision of the houseboat returned: our laundry flapped, the geranium bloomed, the carrying river carried us out to sea into the world.

"Collin." My name fell out of the sky. "Is that you I hear? are you crying?"

It was Dolly, calling from somewhere I could not see—until, climbing to the tree's heart, I saw in the above distance Dolly's dangling childish shoe. "Careful boy," said the Judge, who was beside her, "you'll shake us out of here." Indeed, like gulls resting on a ship's mast, they were sitting in the absolute tower of the tree; afterwards, Dolly was to remark that the view afforded was so enthralling she regretted not having visited there before. The Judge, it developed, had seen the approach of the Sheriff and his men in time for them to take refuge in those heights. "Wait, we're coming," she said; and, with one arm steadied by the Judge, she descended like a fine lady sweeping down a flight of stairs.

We kissed each other; she continued to hold me. "She went to look for you—Catherine; we didn't know where you were, and I was so afraid, I . . ." Her fear tingled my hands: she felt like a shaking small animal, a rabbit just taken from the trap. The Judge looked on with humbled eyes, fumbling hands; he seemed to feel in the way, perhaps because he thought he'd failed us in not preventing what had happened to Catherine. But then, what could he have done? Had he gone to her aid he would only have got himself caught: they weren't fooling, the Sheriff, Big Eddie Stover and the others. I was the one to feel guilty. If Catherine hadn't gone to look for me they probably never would have caught her. I told of what had taken place in the field of grass.

But Dolly really wanted not to hear. As thought scattering a dream she brushed back her veil. "I want to believe Catherine is gone: and I can't. If I could I would run to find her. I want to believe Verena has done this: and I can't. Collin, what do you think: is it that after all the world is a bad place? Last night I saw it so differently."

The Judge focused his eyes on mine: he was trying, I think, to tell me how to answer. But I knew myself. No matter what passions compose them, all private worlds are good, they are never vulgar places: Dolly had been made too civilized by her own, the one she shared with Catherine and me, to feel the winds of wickedness that circulate elsewhere: No, Dolly, the world is not a bad place. She passed a hand across her forehead: "If you are right, then in a moment Catherine will be walking under the tree— she won't have found you or Riley, but she will have come back."

"By the way," said the Judge, "where *is* Riley?"

He'd run ahead of me, that was the last I'd seen of him; with an anxiety that struck us simultaneously, the Judge and I stood up and started yelling his name. Our voices, curving slowly around the woods, again, again swung back on silence. I knew what had happened: he'd fallen into an old Indian well —many's the case I could tell you of. I was about to suggest this when abruptly the Judge put a finger to his lips. The man must have had ears like a dog: I couldn't hear a sound. But he was right, there was someone on the path. It turned out to be Maude Riordan and Riley's older sister, the smart one, Elizabeth. They were very dear friends and wore white matching sweaters. Elizabeth was carrying a violin case.

"Look here, Elizabeth," said the Judge, startling the girls, for as yet they had not discovered us. "Look here, child, have you seen your brother?"

Maude recovered first, and it was she who answered. "We sure have," she said emphatically. "I was walking Elizabeth home from her lesson when Riley came along doing ninety miles an hour; nearly ran us over. You should speak to him, Elizabeth. Anyway, he asked us to come down here and tell you not to worry, said he'd explain everything later. Whatever that means."

Both Maude and Elizabeth had been in my class at school; they'd jumped a grade and graduated the previous June. I knew Maude especially well because for a summer I'd taken piano lessons from her mother; her father taught violin, and Elizabeth Henderson was one of his pupils. Maude herself played the violin beautifully; just a week before I'd read in the town paper where she'd been invited to play on a radio program in Birmingham: I was glad to hear it. The Riordans were nice people, considerate and cheerful. It was not because I wanted to learn piano that I took lessons with Mrs. Riordan— rather, I liked her blond largeness, the sympathetic, educated talk that went on while we sat before the splendid upright that smelled of polish and attention; and what I particularly liked was afterwards, when Maude would ask me to have a lemonade on the cool back porch. She was snub-nosed and elfineared, a skinny excitable girl who from her father had inherited Irish black eyes and from her mother platinum hair pale as morning—not the least like her best friend, the soulful and shadowy Elizabeth. I don't know what those two talked about, books and music maybe. But with me Maude's subjects were boys, dates, drugstore slander: didn't I think it was terrible, the awful girls Riley Henderson chased around with? she felt so sorry for Elizabeth, and thought it wonderful how, despite all, Elizabeth held up her head. It didn't take a genius to see that Maude was heartset on Riley; nevertheless, I imagined for a while that I was in love with her. At home I kept mentioning her until finally Catherine said Oh Maude Riordan, she's too scrawny—nothing on her to pinch, a man's crazy to give her the time of day. Once I showed Maude a big evening, made for her with my own hands a sweet-pea corsage, then took her to Phil's Café where we had Kansas City steaks; afterwards, there was a dance at the Lola Hotel. Still she behaved as though she hadn't expected to be kissed good night. "I don't think that's necessary, Collin—though it was cute of you to take me out." I was let down, you can see why; but as I didn't allow myself to brood over it our friendship went on little changed. One day, at the end of a lesson, Mrs. Riordan omitted the usual new piece for home practice; instead, she kindly informed me that she preferred not to continue with my lessons: "We're very fond of you, Collin, I don't have to say that you're welcome in this house at any time. But dear, the truth is you have no ability for music; it happens that way occasionally, and I don't think it's fair on either of us to pretend otherwise." She was right, all the same my pride was hurt, I couldn't help feeling pushed-out, it made me miserable to think of the Riordans, and gradually, in about the time it took to forget my few hard-learned tunes, I drew a curtain on them. At first Maude used to stop me after school and ask me over to her house; one way or another I always got out of it; furthermore, it was winter then and I liked to stay in the kitchen with Dolly and Catherine. Catherine wanted to know: How come you don't talk any more about Maude Riordan? I said because I don't, that's all. But while I didn't talk, I must have been thinking; at least, seeing her there under the tree, old feelings squeezed my chest. For the first time I considered the circumstances self-consciously: did we, Dolly, the Judge and I, strike Maude and Elizabeth as a ludicrous sight? I could be judged by them, they were my own age. But from their manner we might just have met on the street or at the drugstore.

The Judge said, "Maude, how's your daddy? Heard he hasn't been feeling too good."

"He can't complain. You know how men are, always looking for an ailment. And yourself, sir?"

"That's a pity," said the Judge, his mind wandering. "You give your daddy my regards, and tell him I hope he feels better."

Maude submitted agreeably: "I will, sir, thank you. I know he'll appreciate your concern." Draping her skirt, she dropped on the moss and settled beside her an unwilling Elizabeth. For Elizabeth no one used a nickname; you might begin by calling her Betty, but in a week it would be Elizabeth again: that was her effect. Languid, banana-boned, she had dour black hair and an apathetic, at moments saintly face—in an enamel locket worn around her lily-stalk neck she preserved a miniature of her missionary father. "Look, Elizabeth, isn't that a becoming hat Miss Dolly has on? Velvet, with a veil."

Dolly roused herself; she patted her head. "I don't generally wear hats—we intended to travel."

"We heard you'd left home," said Maude; and, proceeding more frankly: "In fact that's all anyone talks about, isn't it, Elizabeth?" Elizabeth nodded without enthusiasm. "Gracious, there are some peculiar stories going around. I mean, on the way here we met Gus Ham and he said that colored woman Catherine Crook (is that her name?) had been arrested for hitting Mrs. Buster with a mason jar."

In sloping tones, Dolly said, "Catherine—had nothing to do with it."

"I guess someone did," said Maude. "We saw Mrs. Buster in the post office this morning; she was showing everybody a bump on her head, quite large. It looked genuine to us, didn't it Elizabeth?" Elizabeth yawned. "To be sure, I don't care who hit her, I think they ought to get a medal."

"No," sighed Dolly, "it isn't proper, it shouldn't have happened. We all will have a lot to be sorry for."

At last Maude took account of me. "I've been wanting to see you, Collin," she said hurrying as though to hide an embarrassment: mine, not hers. "Elizabeth and I are planning a Halloween party, a real scary one, and we thought it would be grand to dress you in a skeleton suit and sit you in a dark room to tell people's fortunes: because you're so good at . . ."

"Fibbing," said Elizabeth disinterestedly.

"Which is what fortune-telling is," Maude elaborated.

I don't know what gave them the idea I was such a story-teller, unless it was at school I'd shown a superior talent for alibis. I said it sounded fine, the party. "But you better not count on me. We might be in jail by then."

"Oh well, in that case," said Maude, as if accepting one of my old and usual excuses for not coming to her house.

"Say, Maude," said the Judge, helping us out of the silence that had fallen, "you're getting to be a celebrity: I saw in the paper where you're going to play on the radio."

As though dreaming aloud, she explained the broadcast was the finals of a state competition; if she won, the prize was a musical scholarship at the University: even second prize meant a half-scholarship. "I'm going to play a piece of daddy's, a serenade: he wrote it for me the day I was born. But it's a surprise, I don't want him to know."

"Make her play it for you," said Elizabeth, unclasping her violin case.

Maude was generous, she did not have to be begged. The wine-colored violin, coddled under her chin, trilled as she tuned it; a brazen butterfly, lighting on the bow, was spiraled away as the bow swept across the strings singing a music that seemed a blizzard of butterflies flying, a sky-rocket of spring sweet to hear in the gnarled fall woods. It slowed, saddened, her silver hair drooped across the violin. We applauded; after we'd stopped there went on sounding a mysterious extra pair of hands. Riley stepped from behind a bank of fern, and when she saw him Maude's cheeks pinked. I don't think she would have played so well if she'd known he was listening.

Riley sent the girls home; they seemed reluctant to go, but Elizabeth was not used to disobeying her brother. "Lock the doors," he told her, "and Maude, I'd appreciate it if you'd spend the night at our place: anybody comes by asking for me, say you don't know where I am."

I had to help him into the tree, for he'd brought back his gun and a knapsack heavy with provisions—a bottle of rose and raisin wine, oranges, sardines, wieners, rolls from the Katydid Bakery, a jumbo box of animal crackers: each item appearing stepped up our spirits, and Dolly, overcome by the animal crackers, said Riley ought to have a kiss.

But it was with grave face that we listened to his report.

When we'd separated in the woods it was toward the sound of Catherine that he'd run. This had brought him to the grass: he'd been watching when I had my encounter with Big Eddie Stover. I said well why didn't you help me? "You were doing all right: I don't figure Big Eddie's liable to forget you too soon: poor fellow limped along doubled over." Besides, it occurred to him that no one knew he was one of us, that he'd joined us in the tree: he was right to have stayed hidden, it made it possible for him to follow Catherine and the deputies into town. They'd stuffed her into the rumble-seat of Big Eddie's old coupé and driven straight to jail: Riley trailed them in his car. "By the time we reached the jail she seemed to have got quieted down; there was a little crowd hanging around, kids, some old farmers—you would have been proud of Catherine, she walked through them holding her dress together and her head like this." He tilted his head at a royal angle. How often I'd seen Catherine do that, especially when anyone criticized her (for hiding puzzle pieces, spreading misinformation, not having her teeth fixed); and Dolly, recognizing it too, had to blow her nose. "But," said Riley, "as soon as she was inside the jail she kicked up another fuss." In the jail there are only four cells, two for colored and two for white. Catherine had objected to being put in a colored people's cell.

The Judge stroked his chin, waved his head. "You didn't get a chance to speak to her? She ought to have had the comfort of knowing one of us was there."

"I stood around hoping she'd come to the window. But then I heard the other news."

Thinking back, I don't see how Riley could have waited so long to tell us. Because, my God: our friend from Chicago, that hateful Dr. Morris Ritz, had skipped town after rifling Verena's safe of twelve thousand dollars in negotiable bonds and more than seven hundred dollars in cash: that, as we later learned, was not half his loot. But wouldn't you know? I realized this was what baby-voiced Will Harris had been recounting to the Sheriff: no wonder Verena had sent a hurry call: her troubles with us must have become quite a side issue. Riley had a few details: he knew that Verena, upon discovering the safe door swung open (this happened in the office she kept above her drygoods store) had whirled around the corner to the Lola Hotel, there to find that Morris Ritz had checked out the previous evening: she fainted: when they revived her she fainted all over again.

Dolly's soft face hollowed; an urge to go to Verena was rising, at the same moment some sense of self, a deeper will, held her. Regretfully she gazed at me. "It's better you know it now, Collin; you shouldn't have to wait until you're as old as I am: the world is a bad place."

A change, like a shift of wind, overcame the Judge: he looked at once his age, autumnal, bare, as though he believed that Dolly, by accepting wickedness, had forsaken him. But I knew she had not: he'd called her a spirit, she was really a woman. Uncorking the rose and raisin wine, Riley spilled its topaz color into four glasses; after a moment he filled a fifth, Catherine's. The Judge, raising the wine to his lips, proposed a toast: "To Catherine, give her trust." We lifted our glasses, and "Oh Collin," said Dolly, a sudden stark thought widening her eyes, "you and I, we're the only ones that can understand a word she says!"

Five

THE following day, which was the first of October, a Wednesday, is one day I won't forget.

First off, Riley woke me by stepping on my fingers. Dolly, already awake, insisted I apologize for cursing him. Courtesy, she said, is more important in the morning than at any other time: particularly when one is living in such close quarters. The Judge's watch, still bending the twig like a heavy gold apple, gave the time as six after six. I don't know whose idea it was, but we breakfasted on oranges and animal crackers and cold hotdogs. The Judge grouched that a body didn't feel human till he'd had a pot of hot coffee. We agreed that coffee was what we all most missed. Riley volunteered to drive into town and get some; also, he would have a chance to scout around, find out what was going on. He suggested I come with him: "Nobody's going to see him, not if he stays down in the seat." Although the Judge objected, saying he thought it foolhardy, Dolly could tell I wanted to go: I'd yearned so much for a ride in Riley's car that now the opportunity presented itself nothing, even the prospect that no one might see me, could have thinned my excitement. Dolly said, "I can't see there's any harm. But you ought to have a clean shirt: I could plant turnips in the collar of that one."

The field of grass was without voice, no pheasant rustle,

furtive flurry; the pointed leaves were sharp and blood-red as
the aftermath arrows of a massacre; their brittleness broke
beneath our feet as we waded up the hill into the cemetery.
The view from there is very fine: the limitless trembling surface of River Woods, fifty unfolding miles of ploughed, wind-
milled farmland, far-off the spired courthouse tower, smoking chimneys of town. I stopped by the graves of my mother
and father. I had not often visited them, it depressed me, the
tomb-cold stone—so unlike what I remembered of them, their
aliveness, how she'd cried when he went away to sell his frigidaires, how he'd run naked into the street. I wanted flowers for
the terracotta jars sitting empty on the streaked and muddied
marble. Riley helped me; he tore beginning buds off a japonica
tree, and watching me arrange them, said: "I'm glad your ma
was nice. Bitches, by and large." I wondered if he meant his
own mother, poor Rose Henderson, who used to make him
hop around the yard reciting the multiplication table. It did
seem to me, though, that he'd made up for those hard days.
After all, he had a car that was supposed to have cost three
thousand dollars. Second-hand, mind you. It was a foreign
car, an Alfa-Romeo roadster (Romeo's Alfa, the joke was)
he'd bought in New Orleans from a politician bound for the
penitentiary.

As we purred along the unpaved road toward town I kept
hoping for a witness: there were certain persons it would have
done my heart good to have seen me sailing by in Riley Henderson's car. But it was too early for anyone much to be about;
breakfast was still on the stove, and smoke soared out the
chimneys of passing houses. We turned the corner by the
church, drove around the square and parked in the dirt lane
that runs between Cooper's Livery and the Katydid Bakery.
There Riley left me with orders to stay put: he wouldn't be
more than an hour. So, stretching out on the seat, I listened
to the chicanery of thieving sparrows in the livery stable's hay-
stacks, breathed the fresh bread, tart as currant odors escap-
ing from the bakery. The couple who owned this bakery,
County was their name, Mr. and Mrs. C. C. County, had to
begin their day at three in the morning to be ready by opening
time, eight o'clock. It was a clean prosperous place. Mrs.
County could afford the most expensive clothes at Verena's
drygoods store. While I lay there smelling the good things, the
back door of the bakery opened and Mr. County, broom in
hand, swept flour dust into the lane. I guess he was surprised
to see Riley's car, and surprised to find me in it.

"What you up to, Collin?"

"Up to nothing, Mr. County," I said, and asked myself if he knew about our trouble.

"Sure am happy October's here," he said, rubbing the air with his fingers as though the chill woven into it was a material he could feel. "We have a terrible time in the summer: ovens and all make it too hot to live. See here, son, there's a gingerbread man waiting for you—come on in and run him down."

Now he was not the kind of man to get me in there and then call the Sheriff.

His wife welcomed me into the spiced heat of the oven room as though she could think of nothing pleasanter than my being there. Most anyone would have liked Mrs. County. A chunky woman with no fuss about her, she had elephant ankles, developed arms, a muscular face permanently fire-flushed; her eyes were like blue cake-icing, her hair looked as if she'd mopped it around in a flour barrel, and she wore an apron that trailed to the tips of her toes. Her husband also wore one; sometimes, with the fulsome apron still tied around him, I'd seen him crossing the street to have a time-off beer with the men that lean around the corner at Phil's Café: he seemed a painted clown, flopping, powdered, elegantly angular.

Clearing a place on her work table, Mrs. County set me down to a cup of coffee and a warm tray of cinnamon rolls, the kind Dolly relished. Mr. County suggested I might prefer something else: "I promised him, what did I promise? a gingerbread man." His wife socked a lump of dough: "Those are for kids. He's a grown man; or nearly. Collin, just how old are you?"

"Sixteen."

"Same as Samuel," she said, meaning her son, whom we all called Mule: inasmuch as he was not much brighter than one. I asked what was their news of him? because the previous autumn, after having been left back in the eighth grade three years running, Mule had gone to Pensacola and joined the Navy. "He's in Panama, last we heard," she said, flattening the dough into a piecrust. "We don't hear often. I wrote him once, I said Samuel you do better about writing home or I'm going to write the President exactly how old you are. Because you know he joined up under false pretenses. I was darned mad at the time—blamed Mr. Hand up at the schoolhouse: that's why Samuel did it, he just couldn't tolerate always being left behind in the eighth grade, him getting so tall and the other children so little. But now I can see Mr. Hand was right: it wouldn't be fair to the rest of you boys if they promoted Samuel when he didn't do his work proper. So maybe it turned out for the best. C. C., show Collin the picture."

Photographed against a background of palms and real sea, four smirking sailors stood with their arms linked together; underneath was written, God Bless Mom and Pop, Samuel. It rankled me. Mule, off seeing the world, while I, well, maybe I deserved a gingerbread man. As I returned the picture, Mr. County said: "I'm all for a boy serving his country. But the bad part of it is, Samuel was just getting where he could give us a hand around here. I sure hate to depend on nigger help. Lying and stealing, never know where you are."

"It beats me why C.C. carries on like that," said his wife, knotting her lips. "He knows it irks me. Colored people are no worse than white people: in some cases, better. I've had occasion to say so to other people in this town. Like this business about old Catherine Creek. Makes me sick. Cranky she may be, and peculiar, but there's as good a woman as you'll find. Which reminds me, I mean to send her a dinner-tray up to the jail, for I'll wager the Sheriff doesn't set much of a table."

So little, once it has changed, changes back: the world knew us: we would never be warm again: I let go, saw winter coming toward a cold tree, cried, cried, came apart like a rain-rotted rag. I'd wanted to since we left the house. Mrs. County begged pardon if she'd said anything to upset me; with her kitchen-slopped apron she wiped my face, and we laughed, had to, at the mess it made, the paste of flour and tears, and I felt, as they say, a lot better, kind of lighthearted. For manly reasons I understood, but which made me feel no shame, Mr. County had been mortified by the outburst: he retired to the front of the shop.

Mrs. County poured coffee for herself and sat down. "I don't pretend to follow what's going on," she said. "The way I hear it, Miss Dolly broke up housekeeping because of some disagreement with Verena?" I wanted to say the situation was more complicated than that, but wondered, as I tried to array events, if really it was. "Now," she continued thoughtfully, "it may sound as though I'm talking against Dolly: I'm not. But this is what I feel—you people should go home, Dolly ought to make her peace with Verena: that's what she's always done, and you can't turn around at her time of life. Also, it sets a poor example for the town, two sisters quarreling, one of them sitting in a tree; and Judge Charlie Cool, for the first time in my life I feel sorry for those sons of his. Leading citizens have to behave themselves; otherwise the entire place goes to pieces. For instance, have you seen that wagon in the square? Well then, you better go have a look. Family of cowboys, they are. Evangelists, C.C. says—all I know is there's been a great racket over them and something to do with Dolly." Angrily she puffed up a paper sack. "I want you to tell her what I said: go home. And here, Collin, take along some cinnamon rolls. I know how Dolly dotes on them."

As I left the bakery the bells of the courthouse clock were ringing eight, which meant that it was seven-thirty. This clock has always run a half-hour fast. Once an expert was imported to repair it; at the end of almost a week's tinkering he recommended, as the only remedy, a stick of dynamite; the town council voted he be paid in full, for there was a general feeling of pride that the clock had proved so incorrigible. Around the square a few store-keepers were preparing to open; broom-sweepings fogged doorways, rolled trashbarrels berated the cool cat-quiet streets. At the Early Bird, a better grocery store than Verena's Jitney Jungle, two colored boys were fancying the window with cans of Hawaiian pineapple. On the south side of the square, beyond the cane benches where in all seasons sit the peaceful, perishing old men, I saw the wagon Mrs. County had spoken of—in reality an old truck contrived with tarpaulin covering to resemble the western wagons of history. It looked forlorn and foolish standing alone in the empty square. A homemade sign, perhaps four feet high, crested the cab like a shark's fin. Let Little Homer Honey Lasso Your Soul For The Lord. Painted on the other side there was a blistered greenish grinning head topped by a ten-gallon hat. I would not have thought it a portrait of anything human, but, according to a notice, this was: Child Wonder Little Homer Honey. With nothing more to see, for there was no one around the truck, I took myself toward the jail, which is a box-shaped brick building next door to the Ford Motor Company. I'd been inside it once. Big Eddie Stover had taken me there, along with a dozen other boys and men; he'd walked into the drugstore and said come over to the jail if you want to see something. The attraction was a thin handsome gipsy boy they'd taken off a freight train; Big Eddie gave him a quarter and told him to let down his pants; nobody could believe the size of it, and one of the men said, "Boy, how come they keep you locked up when you got a crowbar like that?" For weeks you could tell girls who had heard that joke: they giggled every time they passed the jail.

There is an unusual emblem decorating a side wall of the jail. I asked Dolly, and she said that in her youth she remembers it as a candy advertisement. If so, the lettering has vanished; what remains is a chalky tapestry: two flamingo-pink trumpeting angels swinging, swooping above a huge horn filled with fruit like a Christmas stocking; embroidered on the brick, it seems a faded mural, a faint tattoo, and sunshine flutters the imprisoned angels as though they were the spirits of thieves. I knew the risk I was taking, parading around in plain sight; but I walked past the jail, then back, and whistled, later whispered Catherine, Catherine, hoping this would bring her to the window. I realized which was her window: on the sill, reflecting beyond the bars, I saw a bowl of goldfish, the one thing, as subsequently we learned, she'd asked to have brought her. Orange flickerings of the fish fanned around the coral castle, and I thought of the morning I'd helped Dolly find it, the castle, the pearl pebbles. It had been the beginning and, chilled suddenly by a thought of what the end could be, Catherine coldly shadowed and peering downward, I prayed she would not come to the window: she would have seen no one, for I turned and ran.

Riley kept me waiting in the car more than two hours. By the time he showed up he was himself in such a temper I didn't dare show any of my own. It seems he'd gone home and found his sisters, Anne and Elizabeth, and Maude Riordan, who had spent the night, still lolling abed: not just that, but Coca-Cola bottles and cigarette butts all over the parlor. Maude took the blame: she confessed to having invited some boys over to listen to the radio and dance; but it was the sisters who got punished. He'd dragged them out of bed and whipped them. I asked what did he mean, whipped them? Turned them over my knee, he said, and whipped them with a tennis shoe. I couldn't picture this; it conflicted with my sense of Elizabeth's dignity. You're too hard on those girls, I said, adding vindictively: Maude, now there's the bad one. He took me seriously, said yes he'd intended to whip her if only because she'd called him the kind of names he wouldn't take off anybody; but before he could catch her she'd bolted out the back door. I thought to myself maybe at last Maude's had her bait of you.

Riley's ragged hair was glued down with brilliantine; he

smelled of lilac water and talcum. He didn't have to tell me he'd been to the barber's; or why.

Though he has since retired, there was in those days an exceptional fellow running the barbershop. Amos Legrand. Men like the Sheriff, for that matter Riley Henderson, oh everybody come to think of it, said: that old sis. But they didn't mean any harm; most people enjoyed Amos and really wished him well. A little monkeyman who had to stand on a box to cut your hair, he was agitated and chattery as a pair of castanets. All his steady customers he called honey, men and women alike, it made no difference to him. "Honey," he'd say, "it's about time you got this hair cut: was about to buy you a package of bobby-pins." Amos had one tremendous gift: he could tattle along on matters of true interest to businessmen and girls of ten—everything from what price Ben Jones got for his peanut crop to who would be invited to Mary Simpson's birthday party.

It was natural that Riley should have gone to him to get the news. Of course he repeated it straightforwardly; but I could imagine Amos, hear his hummingbird whirr: "There you are, honey, that's how it turns out when you leave money lying around. And of all people, Verena Talbo: here we thought she trotted to the bank with every dime came her way. Twelve thousand seven hundred dollars. But don't think it stops there. Seems Verena and this Dr. Ritz were going into business together, that's why she bought the old canning factory. Well get this: she gave Ritz over ten thousand to buy machinery, mercy knows what, and now it turns out he never bought one blessed penny's worth. Pocketed the whole thing. As for him, they've located not hide nor hair; South America, that's where they'll find him when and if. I never was somebody to insinuate any monkeyshines went on between him and her; I said Verena Talbo's too particular: honey, that Jew had the worst case of dandruff I've ever seen on a human head. But a smart woman like her, maybe she *was* stuck on him. Then all this to-do with her sister, the uproar over that. I don't wonder Doc Carter's giving her shots. But Charlie Cool's the one kills me: what do you make of him out there catching his death?"

We cleared town on two wheels; pop, pulp, insects spit against the windshield. The dry starched blue day whistled round us, there was not a cloud. And yet I swear storms foretell themselves in my bones. This is a nuisance common to old people, but fairly rare with anyone young. It's as though a

damp rumble of thunder had sounded in your joints. The way
I hurt, I felt nothing less than a hurricane could be headed
our way, and said so to Riley, who said go on, you're crazy,
look at the sky. We were making a bet about it when, rounding
that bad curve so convenient to the cemetery, Riley winced
and froze his brakes; we skidded long enough for a detailed
review of our lives.

It was not Riley's fault: square in the road and struggling
along like a lame cow was the Little Homer Honey wagon.
With a clatter of collapsing machinery it came to a dead halt.
In a moment the driver climbed out, a woman.

She was not young, but there was a merriness in the seesaw of her hips, and her breasts rubbed and nudged against
her peach-colored blouse in such a coaxing way. She wore a
fringed chamois skirt and knee-high cowboy boots, which was
a mistake, for you felt that her legs, if fully exposed, would
have been the best part. She leaned on the car door. Her eyelids drooped as though the lashes weighed intolerably; with the
tip of her tongue she wettened her very red lips. "Good morning, fellows," she said, and it was a dragging slow-fuse voice.
"I'd appreciate a few directions."

"What the hell's wrong with you?" said Riley, asserting himself. "You nearly made us turn over."

"I'm surprised you mention it," said the woman, amiably
tossing her large head; her hair, an invented apricot color,
was meticulously curled, and the curls, shaken out, were like
bells with no music in them. "You were speeding, dear," she
reproved him complacently. "I imagine there's a law against
it; there are laws against everything, especially here."

Riley said, "There should be a law against that truck. A
broken-down pile like that, it oughtn't to be allowed."

"I know, dear," the woman laughed. "Trade with you.
Though I'm afraid we couldn't all fit into this car; we're even
a bit squeezed in the wagon. Could you help me with a cigarette? That's a doll, thanks." As she lighted the cigarette I
noticed how gaunt her hands were, rough; the nails were un-
painted and one of them was black as though she'd crushed
it in a door. "I was told that out this way we'd find a Miss
Talbo. Dolly Talbo. She seems to be living in a tree. I wish
you'd kindly show us where . . ."

Back of her there appeared to be an entire orphanage empty-
ing out of the truck. Babies barely able to toddle on their
rickety bowlegs, towheads dribbling ropes of snot, girls old
enough to wear brassieres, and a ladder of boys, man-sized

some of them. I counted up to ten, this including a set of
crosseyed twins and a diapered baby being lugged by a child
not more than five. Still, like a magician's rabbits, they kept
coming, multiplied until the road was thickly populated.

"These all yours?" I said, really anxious; in another count
I'd made a total of fifteen. One boy, he was about twelve and
had tiny steel-rimmed glasses, flopped around in a ten-gallon
hat like a walking mushroom. Most of them wore a few cowboy items, boots, at least a rodeo scarf. But they were a dis-
couraged-looking lot, and sickly too, as though they'd lived
years off boiled potatoes and onions. They pressed around the
car, ghostly quiet except for the youngest who thumped the
headlights and bounced on the fenders.

"Sure enough, dear: all mine," she answered, swatting at a
mite of a girl playing maypole on her leg. "Sometimes I figure
we've picked up one or two that don't belong," she added with
a shrug, and several of the children smiled. They seemed to
adore her. "Some of their daddies are dead; I guess the rest
are living—one way and another: either case it's no concern
of ours. I take it you weren't at our meeting last night. I'm
Sister Ida, Little Homer Honey's mother." I wanted to know
which one was Little Homer. She blinked around and singled
out the spectacled boy who, wobbling up under his hat, saluted
us: "Praise Jesus. Want a whistle?" and, swelling his cheeks,
blasted a tin whistle.

"With one of those," explained his mother, tucking up her
back hairs, "you can give the devil a scare. They have a number of practical uses as well."

"Two bits," the child bargained. He had a worried little
face white as cold cream. The hat came down to his eyebrows.

I would have bought one if I'd had the money. You could
see they were hungry. Riley felt the same, at any rate he produced fifty cents and took two of the whistles. "Bless you,"
said Little Homer, slipping the coin between his teeth and
biting hard. "There's so much counterfeit going around these
days," his mother confided apologetically. "In our branch of
endeavor you wouldn't expect that kind of trouble," she said,
sighing. "But if you kindly would show us—we can't go on
much more, just haven't got the gas."

Riley told her she was wasting her time. "Nobody there
any more," he said, racing the motor. Another driver, block-
aded behind us, was honking his horn.

"Not in the tree?" Her voice was plaintive above the motor's

impatient roar. "But where will we find her then?" Her hands
were trying to hold back the car. "We've important business,
we . . ."

Riley jumped the car forward. Looking back, I saw them
watching after us in the raised and drifting road dust. I said
to Riley, and was sullen about it, that we ought to have found
out what they wanted.

And he said: "Maybe I know."

He did know a great deal, Amos Legrand having informed
him thoroughly on the subject of Sister Ida. Although she'd
not previously been to our town, Amos, who does a little
traveling now and then, claimed to have seen her once at a
fair in Bottle, which is a county town not far from here. Nor,
apparently, was she a stranger to the Reverend Buster who,
the instant she arrived, had hunted out the Sheriff and demanded an injunction to prevent the Little Homer Honey
troupe from holding any meetings. Racketeers, he called them;
and argued that the so-called Sister Ida was known throughout
six states as an infamous trollop: think of it, fifteen children
and no sign of a husband! Amos, too, was pretty sure she'd
never been married; but in his opinion a woman so industrious
was entitled to respect. The Sheriff said didn't he have enough
problems? and said: Maybe those fools have the right idea, sit
in a tree and mind your own business—for five cents he'd go
out there and join them. Old Buster told him in that case he
wasn't fit to be Sheriff and ought to hand in his badge. Meanwhile, Sister Ida had, without legal interference, called an evening of prayers and shenanigans under the oak trees in the
square. Revivalists are popular in this town; it's the music, the
chance to sing and congregate in the open air. Sister Ida and
her family made a particular hit; even Amos, usually so criti-
cal, told Riley he'd missed something: those kids really could
shout, and that Little Homer Honey, he was cute as a button
dancing and twirling a rope. Everybody had a grand time except the Reverend and Mrs. Buster, who had come to start a
fuss. What got their goat was when the children started haul-
ing in God's Washline, a rope with clothespins to which you
could attach a contribution. People who never dropped a dime
in Buster's collection plate were hanging up dollar bills. It was
more than he could stand. So he'd skipped off to the house on
Talbo Lane and had a small shrewd talk with Verena, whose
support, he realized, was necessary if he were going to get action. According to Amos, he'd incited Verena by telling her

some hussy of a revivalist was describing Dolly as an infidel, an enemy of Jesus, and that Verena owed it to the Talbo name to see this woman was run out of town. It was unlikely that at the time Sister Ida had ever heard the name Talbo. But sick as she was, Verena went right to work; she rang up the Sheriff and said now look here Junius, I want these tramps run clear across the county line. Those were orders; and old Buster made it his duty to see they were carried out. He accompanied the Sheriff to the square where Sister Ida and her brood were cleaning up after the meeting. It had ended in a real scuffle, mainly because Buster, charging illegal gain, had insisted on confiscating the money gathered off God's Washline. He got it, too—along with a few scratches. It made no difference that many bystanders had taken Sister Ida's side: the Sheriff told them they'd better be out of town by noon the next day. Now after I'd heard all this I said to Riley why, when these people had been wrongly treated, hadn't he wanted to be more helpful? You'd never guess the answer he gave me. In dead earnest he said a loose woman like that was no one to associate with Dolly.

A twig fire fizzed under the tree; Riley collected leaves for it, while the Judge, his eyes smarting with smoke, set about the business of our midday meal. We were the indolent ones, Dolly and I. "I'm afraid," she said, dealing a game of Rook, "really afraid Verena's seen the last of that money. And you know, Collin, I doubt if it's losing the money that hurts her most. For whatever reason, she trusted him: Dr. Ritz, I mean. I keep remembering Maudie Laura Murphy. The girl who worked in the post office. She and Verena were very close. Lord, it was a great blow when Maudie Laura took up with that whiskey salesman, married him. I couldn't criticize her; 'twas only fitting if she loved the man. Just the same, Maudie Laura and Dr. Ritz, maybe those are the only two Verena ever trusted, and both of them—well, it could take the heart out of anyone." She thumbed the Rook cards with wandering attention. "You said something before—about Catherine."

"About her goldfish. I saw them in the window."

"But not Catherine?"

"No, the goldfish, that's all. Mrs. County was awfully nice: she said she was going to send some dinner around to the jail."

She broke one of Mrs. County's cinnamon rolls and picked out the raisins. "Collin, suppose we let them have their way,

gave up, that is: they'd have to let Catherine go, wouldn't
they?" Her eyes tilted toward the heights of the tree, searching, it seemed, a passage through the braided leaves. "Should
I—let myself lose?"

"Mrs. County thinks so: that we should go home."

"Did she say why?"

"Because—she did run on. Because you always have. Always made your peace, she said."

Dolly smiled, smoothed her long skirt; sifting rays placed
rings of sun upon her fingers. "Was there ever a choice? It's
what I want, a choice. To know I could've had another life,
all made of my own decisions. That would be making my
peace, and truly." She rested her eyes on the scene below,
Riley cracking twigs, the Judge hunched over a steaming pot.
"And the Judge, Charlie, if we gave up it would let him down
so badly. Yes," she tangled her fingers with mine, "he is very
dear to me," and an immeasurable pause lengthened the moment, my heart reeled, the tree closed inward like a folding
umbrella.

"This morning, while you were away, he asked me to marry
him."

As if he'd heard her, the Judge straightened up, a schoolboy
grin reviving the youthfulness of his countrified face. He
waved: and it was difficult to disregard the charm of Dolly's
expression as she waved back. It was as though a familiar
portrait had been cleaned and, turning to it, one discovered a
fleshy luster, clearer, till then unknown colors: whatever else,
she could never again be a shadow in the corner.

"And now—don't be unhappy, Collin," she said, scolding me,
I thought, for what she must have recognized as my resent-
ment.

"But are you . . .?"

"I've never earned the privilege of making up my own mind;
when I do, God willing, I'll know what is right. Who else,"
she said, putting me off further, "did you see in town?"

I would have invented someone, a story to retrieve her, for
she seemed to be moving forward into the future, while I,
unable to follow, was left with my sameness. But as I described Sister Ida, the wagon, the children, told the wherefores
of their run-in with the Sheriff and how we'd met them on the
road inquiring after the lady in the tree, we flowed together
again like a stream that for an instant an island had separated.
Though it would have been too bad if Riley had heard me be-
traying him, I went so far as to repeat what he'd said about a

woman of Sister Ida's sort not being fit company for Dolly. She had a proper laugh over this; then, with sudden soberness: "But it's wicked—taking the bread out of children's mouths and using my name to do it. Shame on them!" She straightened her hat determinedly. "Collin, lift yourself; you and I are going for a little walk. I'll bet those people are right where you left them. Leastways, we'll see."

The Judge tried to prevent us, or at any rate maintained that if Dolly wanted a stroll he would have to accompany us. It went a long way toward mollifying my jealous rancor when Dolly told him he'd best tend to his chores: with Collin along she'd be safe enough—it was just to stretch our legs a bit.

As usual, Dolly could not be hurried. It was her habit, even when it rained, to loiter along an ordinary path as though she were dallying in a garden, her eyes primed for the sight of precious medicine flavorings, a sprig of penny-royal, sweet-mary and mint, useful herbs whose odor scented her clothes. She saw everything first, and it was her one real vanity to prefer that she, rather than you, point out certain discoveries: a birdtrack bracelet, an eave of icicles—she was always calling come see the cat-shaped cloud, the ship in the stars, the face of frost. In this slow manner we crossed the grass, Dolly amassing a pocketful of withered dandelions, a pheasant's quill: I thought it would be sundown before we reached the road.

Fortunately we had not that far to go: entering the cemetery, we found Sister Ida and all her family encamped among the graves. It was like a lugubrious playground. The crosseyed twins were having their hair cut by older sisters, and Little Homer was shining his boots with spit and leaves; a nearly grown boy, sprawled with his back against a tombstone, picked melancholy notes on a guitar. Sister Ida was suckling the baby; it lay curled against her breasts like a pink ear. She did not rise when she realized our presence, and Dolly said, "I do believe you're sitting on my father."

For a fact it was Mr. Talbo's grave, and Sister Ida, addressing the headstone (Uriah Fenwick Talbo, 1844-1922, Good Soldier, Dear Husband, Loving Father) said, "Sorry, soldier." Buttoning her blouse, which made the baby wail, she started to her feet.

"Please don't; I only meant—to introduce myself."

Sister Ida shrugged, "He was beginning to hurt me anyway," and rubbed herself appropriately. "You again," she said, eyeing me with amusement. "Where's your friend?"

"I understand . . ." Dolly stopped, disconcerted by the maze of children drawing in around her; "Did you," she went on, attempting to ignore a boy no bigger than a jackrabbit who, having raised her skirt, was sternly examining her shanks, "wish to see me? I'm Dolly Talbo."

Shifting the baby, Sister Ida threw an arm around Dolly's waist, embraced her, actually, and said, as though they were the oldest friends, "I knew I could count on you, Dolly. Kids," she lifted the baby like a baton, "tell Dolly we never said a word against her!"

The children shook their heads, mumbled, and Dolly seemed touched. "We can't leave town, I kept telling them," said Sister Ida, and launched into the tale of her predicament. I wished that I could have a picture of them together, Dolly, formal, as out of fashion as her old face-veil, and Sister Ida with her fruity lips, fun-loving figure. "It's a matter of cash; they took it all. I ought to have them arrested, that puke-faced Buster and what's-his-name, the Sheriff: thinks he's King Kong." She caught her breath; her cheeks were like a raspberry patch. "The plain truth is, we're stranded. Even if we'd ever heard of you, it's not our policy to speak ill of anyone. Oh I know that was just the excuse; but I figured you could straighten it out and . . ."

"I'm hardly the person—dear me," said Dolly.

"But what would you do? with a half gallon of gas, maybe not that, fifteen mouths and a dollar ten? We'd be better off in jail."

Then, "I have a friend," Dolly announced proudly, "a brilliant man, he'll know an answer," and I could tell by the pleased conviction of her voice that she believed this one hundred per cent. "Collin, you scoot ahead and let the Judge know to expect company for dinner."

Licketysplit across the field with the grass whipping my legs: couldn't wait to see the Judge's face. It was not a disappointment. "Lordylaw!" he said, raring back, rocking forward; "Sixteen people," and, observing the meager stew simmering on the fire, struck his head. For Riley's benefit I tried to make out it was none of my doing, Dolly's meeting Sister Ida; but he just stood there skinning me with his eyes: it could have led to bitter words if the Judge hadn't sent us scurrying. He fanned up his fire, Riley fetched more water, and into the stew we tossed sardines, hotdogs, green bay-leaves, in fact whatever lay at hand, including an entire box of Saltines which the Judge claimed would help thicken it: a few stuffs got mixed in by mistake—coffee grounds, for instance. Having reached that

overwrought hilarious state achieved by cooks at family re-
unions, we had the gall to stand back and congratulate ourselves: Riley gave me a forgiving, comradely punch, and as the
first of the children appeared the Judge scared them with the
vigor of his welcome.

None of them would advance until the whole herd had assembled. Whereupon Dolly, apprehensive as a woman exhibit-
ing the results of an afternoon at an auction, brought them
forward to be introduced. The children made a rollcall of
their names: Beth, Laurel, Sam, Lillie, Ida, Cleo, Kate, Homer,
Harry—here the melody broke because one small girl refused
to give her name. She said it was a secret. Sister Ida agreed
that if she thought it a secret, then so it should remain.

"They're all so fretful," she said, favorably affecting the
Judge with her smoky voice and grasslike eyelashes. He pro-
longed their handshake and overdid his smile, which struck me
as peculiar conduct in a man who, not three hours before, had
asked a woman to marry him, and I hoped that if Dolly
noticed it would give her pause. But she was saying, "Why
certain they're fretful: hungry as they can be," and the Judge,
with a hearty clap and a boastful nod towards the stew, promised he'd fix that soon enough. In the meantime, he thought it
would be a good idea if the children went to the creek and
washed their hands. Sister Ida vowed they'd wash more than
that. They needed to, I'll tell you.

There was trouble with the little girl who wanted her name
a secret; she wouldn't go, not unless her papa rode her piggy-
back. "You are too my papa," she told Riley, who did not
contradict her. He lifted her onto his shoulders, and she was
tickled to death. All the way to the creek she acted the cut-up,
and when, with her hands thrust over his eyes, Riley stumbled
blindly into a bullis vine, she ripped the air with in-heaven
shrieks. He said he'd had enough of that and down you go.
"Please: I'll whisper you my name." Later on I remembered to
ask him what the name had been. It was Texaco Gasoline;
because those were such pretty words.

The creek is nowhere more than knee-deep; glossy beds of
moss green the banks, and in the spring snowy dew-drops and
dwarf violets flourish there like floral crumbs for the new bees
whose hives hang in the waterbays. Sister Ida chose a place
on the bank from which she could supervise the bathing. "No
cheating now—I want to see a lot of commotion." We did.
Suddenly girls old enough to be married were trotting around
and not a stitch on; boys, too, big and little all in there to-

gether naked as jaybirds. It was as well that Dolly had stayed behind with the Judge; and I wished Riley had not come either, for he was embarrassing in his embarrassment. Seriously, though, it's only now, seeing the kind of man he turned out to be, that I understand the paradox of his primness: he wanted so to be respectable that the defections of others somehow seemed to him backsliding on his own part.

Those famous landscapes of youth and woodland water—in after years how often, trailing through the cold rooms of museums, I stopped before such a picture, stood long haunted moments having it recall that gone scene, not as it was, a band of goose-fleshed children dabbling in an autumn creek, but as the painting presented it, husky youths and wading water-diamonded girls; and I've wondered then, wonder now, how they fared, where they went in this world, that extraordinary family.

"Beth, give your hair a douse. Stop splashing Laurel, I mean you Buck, you quit that. All you kids get behind your ears, mercy knows when you'll have the chance again." But presently Sister Ida relaxed and left the children at liberty. "On such a day as this . . ." she sank against the moss; with the full light of her eyes she looked at Riley, "There is something: the mouth, the same jug ears—cigarette, dear?" she said, impervious to his distaste for her. A smoothing expression suggested for a moment the girl she had been. "On such a day as this . . .

". . . but in a sorrier place, no trees to speak of, a house in a wheatfield and all alone like a scarecrow. I'm not complaining: there was mama and papa and my sister Geraldine, and we were sufficient, had plenty of pets and a piano and good voices every one of us. Not that it was easy, what with all the heavy work and only the one man to do it. Papa was a sickly man besides. Hired hands were hard to come by, nobody liked it way out there for long: one old fellow we thought a heap of, but then he got drunk and tried to burn down the house. Geraldine was going on sixteen, a year older than me, and nice to look at, both of us were that, when she got it into her head to marry a man who'd run the place with papa. But where we were there wasn't much to choose from. Mama gave us our schooling, what of it we had, and the closest town was ten miles. That was the town of Youfry, called after a family; the slogan was You Won't Fry In Youfry: because it was up a mountain and well-to-do people went there in the summer. So the summer I'm thinking of Geraldine got waitress work

at the Lookout Hotel in Youfry. I used to hitch a ride in on
Saturdays and stay the night with her. This was the first either
of us had ever been away from home. Geraldine didn't care
about it particular, town life, but as for me I looked toward
those Saturdays like each of them was Christmas and my
birthday rolled into one. There was a dancing pavilion, it didn't
cost a cent, the music was free and the colored lights. I'd
help Geraldine with her work so we could go there all the
sooner; we'd run hand in hand down the street, and I used to
start dancing before I got my breath—never had to wait for
a partner, there were five boys to every girl, and we were the
prettiest girls anyway. I wasn't boy-crazy especially, it was
the dancing—sometimes everyone would stand still to watch
me waltz, and I never got more than a glimpse of my partners,
they changed so fast. Boys would follow us to the hotel, then
call under our window Come out! Come out! and sing, so silly
they were—Geraldine almost lost her job. Well we'd lie awake
considering the night in a practical way. She was not romantic,
my sister; what concerned her was which of our beaux was
surest to make things easier out home. It was Dan Rainey she
decided on. He was older than the others, twenty-five, a man,
not handsome in the face, he had jug ears and freckles and not
much chin, but Dan Rainey, oh he was smart in his own steady
way and strong enough to lift a keg of nails. End of summer
he came out home and helped bring in the wheat. Papa liked
him from the first, and though mama said Geraldine was too
young, she didn't make any ruckus about it. I cried at the wedding, and thought it was because the nights at the dancing
pavilion were over, and because Geraldine and I would never
lie cozy in the same bed again. But as soon as Dan Rainey
took over everything seemed to go right; he brought out the
best in the land and maybe the best in us. Except when winter
came on, and we'd be sitting round the fire, sometimes the heat,
something made me feel just faint. I'd go stand in the yard
with only my dress on, it was like I couldn't feel the cold because I'd become a piece of it, and I'd close my eyes, waltz
round and round, and one night, I didn't hear him sneaking
up, Dan Rainey caught me in his arms and danced me for a
joke. Only it wasn't such a joke. He had feelings for me; way
back in my head I'd known it from the start. But he didn't
say it, and I never asked him to; and it wouldn't have come
to anything provided Geraldine hadn't lost her baby. That was
in the spring. She was mortally afraid of snakes, Geraldine,
and it was seeing one that did it; she was collecting eggs, it

was only a chicken snake, but it scared her so bad she dropped her baby four months too soon. I don't know what happened to her—got cross and mean, got where she'd fly out about anything. Dan Rainey took the worst of it; he kept out of her way as much as he could; used to roll himself in a blanket and sleep down in the wheatfield. I knew if I stayed there—so I went to Youfry and got Geraldine's old job at the hotel. The dancing pavilion, it was the same as the summer before, and I was even prettier: one boy nearly killed another over who was going to buy me an orangeade. I can't say I didn't enjoy myself, but my mind wasn't on it; at the hotel they asked where was my mind—always filling the sugar bowl with salt, giving people spoons to cut their meat. I never went home the whole summer. When the time came—it was such a day as this, a fall day blue as eternity—I didn't let them know I was coming, just got out of the coach and walked three miles through the wheat stacks till I found Dan Rainey. He didn't speak a word, only plopped down and cried like a baby. I was that sorry for him, and loved him more than tongue can tell."

Her cigarette had gone out. She seemed to have lost track of the story; or worse, thought better of finishing it. I wanted to stamp and whistle, the way rowdies do at the picture-show when the screen goes unexpectedly blank; and Riley, though less bald about it, was impatient too. He struck a match for her cigarette: starting at the sound, she remembered her voice again, but it was as if, in the interval, she'd traveled far ahead.

"So papa swore he'd shoot him. A hundred times Geraldine said tell us who it was and Dan here'll take a gun after him. I laughed till I cried; sometimes the other way round. I said well I had no idea; there were five or six boys in Youfry could be the one, and how was I to know? Mama slapped my face when I said that. But they believed it; even after a while I think Dan Rainey believed it—wanted to anyway, poor unhappy fellow. All those months not stirring out of the house; and in the middle of it papa died. They wouldn't let me go to the funeral, they were so ashamed for anyone to see. It happened this day, with them off at the burial and me alone in the house and a sandy wind blowing rough as an elephant, that I got in touch with God. I didn't by any means deserve to be Chosen: up till then, mama'd had to coax me to learn my Bible verses; afterwards, I memorized over a thousand in less than three months. Well I was practicing a tune on the piano, and suddenly a window broke, the whole room turned topsy-turvy, then fell together again, and someone was with me, papa's spirit I thought; but the wind died down peaceful as spring—He was there, and standing as He made me, straight, I opened my arms to welcome Him. That was twenty-six years ago last February the third; I was sixteen, I'm forty-two now, and I've never wavered. When I had my baby I didn't call Geraldine or Dan Rainey or anybody, only lay there whispering my verses one after the other and not a soul knew Danny was born till they heard him holler. It was Geraldine named him that. He was hers, everyone thought so, and people round the countryside rode over to see her new baby, brought presents, some of them, and the men hit Dan Rainey on the back and told him what a fine son he had. Soon as I was able I moved thirty miles away to Stoneville, that's a town double the size of Youfry and where they have a big mining camp. Another girl and I, we started a laundry, and did a good business on account of in a mining town there's mostly bachelors. About twice a month I went home to see Danny; I was seven years going back and forth; it was the only pleasure I had, and a strange one, considering how it tore me up every time: such a beautiful boy, there's no describing. But Geraldine died for me to touch him: if I kissed him she'd come near to jumping out of her skin; Dan Rainey wasn't much different, he was so scared I wouldn't leave well enough alone. The last time I ever was home I asked him would he meet me in Youfry. Because for a crazy long while I'd had an idea, which was: if I could live it again, if I could bear a child that would be a twin to Danny. But I was wrong to think it could have the same father. It would've been a dead child, born dead: I looked at Dan Rainey (it was the coldest day, we sat by the empty dancing pavilion, I remember he never took his hands out of his pockets) and sent him away without saying why it was I'd asked him to come. Then years spent hunting the likeness of him. One of the miners in Stoneville, he had the same freckles, yellow eyes; a goodhearted boy, he obliged me with Sam, my oldest. As best I recall, Beth's father was a dead ringer for Dan Rainey; but being a girl, Beth didn't favor Danny. I forget to tell you that I'd sold my share of the laundry and gone to Texas—had restaurant work in Amarillo and Dallas. But it wasn't until I met Mr. Honey that I saw why the Lord had chosen me and what my task was to be. Mr. Honey possessed the True Word; after I heard him preach that first time I went round to see him: we hadn't talked twenty minutes than he said I'm going to marry you provided you're not married a'ready. I said no I'm not married, but I've got some family; fact is, there was five by then. Didn't faze him a bit. We got married a week later on Valentine's Day. He wasn't a young man, and he didn't look a particle like Dan Rainey; stripped of his boots he couldn't make it to my shoulder; but when the Lord brought us together He knew certain what He was doing: we had Roy, then Pearl and Kate and Cleo and Little Homer —most of them born in that wagon you saw up there. We traveled all over the country carrying His Word to folks who'd never heard it before, not the way my man could tell it. Now I must mention a sad circumstance, which is: I lost Mr. Honey. One morning, this was in a queer part of Louisiana, Cajun parts, he walked off down the road to buy some groceries: you know we never saw him again. He disappeared right into thin air. I don't give a hoot what the police say; he wasn't the kind to run out on his family; no sir it was foul play."

"Or amnesia," I said. "You forget everything, even your own name."

"A man with the whole Bible on the tip of his tongue— would you say he was liable to forget something like his name? One of them Cajuns murdered him for his amethyst ring. Naturally I've known men since then; but not love. Lillie Ida, Laurel, the other kids, they happened like. Seems somehow I can't get on without another life kicking under my heart: feel so sluggish otherwise."

When the children were dressed, some with their clothes inside out, we returned to the tree where the older girls, bending over the fire, dried and combed their hair. In our absence Dolly had cared for the baby; she seemed now not to want to give it back: "I wish one of us had had a baby, my sister or Catherine," and Sister Ida said yes, it was entertaining and a satisfaction too. We sat finally in a circle around the fire. The stew was too hot to taste, which perhaps accounted for its thorough success, and the Judge, who had to serve it in rotation, for there were only three cups, was full of gay stunts and nonsense that exhilarated the children: Texaco Gasoline decided she'd made a mistake—the Judge, not Riley, was her papa, and the Judge rewarded her with a trip to the moon, swung her, that is, high over his head: *Some flocked south, Some flocked west, You go flying after the rest, Away! Awhee!* Sister Ida said say you're pretty strong. Of course he lapped it up, all but asked her to feel his muscles. Every quarter-minute he peeked to see if Dolly were admiring him. She was.

The croonings of a ringdove wavered among the long last lances of sunlight. Chill green, blues filtered through the air as though a rainbow had dissolved around us. Dolly shivered: "There's a storm nearby. I've had the notion all day." I looked at Riley triumphantly: hadn't I told him?

"And it's getting late," said Sister Ida. "Buck, Homer—you boys chase up to the wagon. Gracious knows who's come along and helped themselves. Not," she added, watching her sons vanish on the darkening path, "that there's a whole lot to take, nothing much except my sewing machine. So, Dolly? Have you ..."

"We've discussed it," said Dolly turning to the Judge for confirmation.

"You'd win your case in court, no question of it," he said, very professional. "For once the law would be on the right side. As matters stand, however ..."

Dolly said, "As matters stand," and pressed into Sister Ida's hand the forty-seven dollars which constituted our cash asset; in addition, she gave her the Judge's big gold watch. Contemplating these gifts, Sister Ida shook her head as though she should refuse them. "It's wrong. But I thank you."

A light thunder rolled through the woods, and in the perilous quiet of its wake Buck and Little Homer burst upon the path like charging cavalry. "They're coming! They're coming!" both got out at once, and Little Homer, pushing back his hat, gasped: "We ran all the way."

"Make sense, boy: who?"

Little Homer swallowed. "Those fellows. The Sheriff one, and I don't know how many more. Coming down through the grass. With guns, too."

Thunder rumbled again; tricks of wind rustled our fire.

"All right now," said the Judge, assuming command. "Everybody keep their heads." It was as though he'd planned for this moment, and he rose to it, I do concede, gloriously. "The women, you little kids, get up in the treehouse. Riley, see that the rest of you scatter out, shinny up those other trees and take a load of rocks." When we'd followed these directions, he alone remained on the ground; firm-jawed, he stayed there guarding the tense twilighted silence like a captain who will not abandon his drowning ship.

Six

FIVE of us roosted in the sycamore tree that overhung the path. Little Homer was there, and his brother Buck, a scowling boy with rocks in either hand. Across the way, straddling the limbs of a second sycamore, we could see Riley surrounded by the older girls: in the deepening burnished light their white faces glimmered like candle-lanterns. I thought I felt a raindrop: it was a bead of sweat slipping along my cheek; still, and though the thunder lulled, a smell of rain intensified the odor of leaves and woodsmoke. The overloaded tree-house gave an evil creak; from my vantage point, its tenants seemed a single creature, a many-legged, many-eyed spider upon whose head Dolly's hat sat perched like a velvet crown.

In our tree everybody pulled out the kind of tin whistles Riley had bought from Little Homer: good to give the devil a scare, Sister Ida had said. Then Little Homer took off his huge hat and, removing from its vast interior what was perhaps God's Washline, a thick long rope, at any rate, proceeded to make a sliding noose. As he tested its efficiency, stretched and tightened the knot, his steely miniature spectacles cast such a menacing sparkle that, edging away, I put the distance of another branch between us. The Judge, patrolling below, hissed

78

to stop moving around up there; it was his last order before the invasion began.

The invaders themselves made no pretense at stealth. Swinging their rifles against the undergrowth like canecutters, they swaggered up the path, nine, twelve, twenty strong. First, Junius Candle, his Sheriff's star winking in the dusk; and after him, Big Eddie Stover, whose squint-eyed search of our hiding places reminded me of those newspaper picture puzzles; find five boys and an owl in this drawing of a tree. It requires someone cleverer than Big Eddie Stover. He looked straight at me, and through me. Not many of that gang would have troubled you with their braininess: good for nothing but a lick of salt and swallow of beer most of them. Except I recognized Mr. Hand, the principal at school, a decent enough fellow taken all around, no one, you would have thought, to involve himself in such shabby company on so shameful an errand. Curiosity explained the attendance of Amos Legrand; he was there, and silent for once: no wonder: as though he were a walking-stick, Verena was leaning a hand on his head, which came not quite to her hip. A grim Reverend Buster ceremoniously supported her other arm. When I saw Verena I felt a numbed reliving of the terror I'd known when, after my mother's death, she'd come to our house to claim me. Despite what seemed a lameness, she moved with her customary tall authority and, accompanied by her escorts, stopped under our sycamore.

The Judge didn't give an inch; toe to toe with the Sheriff, he stood his ground as if there were a drawn line he dared the other to cross.

It was at this crucial moment that I noticed Little Homer. He gradually was lowering his lasso. It crawled, dangled like a snake, the wide noose open as a pair of jaws, then fell, with an expert snap, around the neck of the Reverend Buster, whose strangling outcry Little Homer stifled by giving the rope a mighty tug.

His friends hadn't long to consider old Buster's predicament, his blood-gorged face and flailing arms; for Little Homer's success inspired an all-out attack: rocks flew, whistles shrilled like the shriekings of savage birds, and the men, pummeling each other in the general rout, took refuge where they could, principally under the bodies of comrades already fallen. Verena had to box Amos Legrand's ears: he tried to sneak up under her skirt. She alone, you might say, behaved like a real man: shook her fists at the trees and cursed us blue.

At the height of the din, a shot slammed like an iron door. It quelled us all, the serious endless echo of it; but in the hush that followed we heard a weight come crashing through the opposite sycamore.

It was Riley, falling; and falling: slowly, relaxed as a killed cat. Covering their eyes, the girls screamed as he struck a branch and splintered it, hovered, like the torn leaves, then in a bleeding heap hit the ground. No one moved toward him.

Until at last the Judge said, "Boy, my boy," and in a trance sank to his knees; he caressed Riley's limp hands. "Have mercy. Have mercy, son: answer." Other men, sheepish and frightened, closed round; some offered advice which the Judge seemed unable to comprehend. One by one we dropped down from the trees, and the children's gathering whisper is he dead? is he dead? was like the moan, the delicate roar of a sea-trumpet. Doffing their hats respectfully, the men made an aisle for Dolly; she was too stunned to take account of them, or of Verena, whom she passed without seeing.

"I want to know," said Verena, in tones that summoned attention, ". . . which of you fools fired that gun?"

The men guardedly looked each other over: too many of them fixed on Big Eddie Stover. His jowls trembled, he licked his lips: "Hell, I never meant to shoot nobody; was doing my duty, that's all."

"Not all," Verena severely replied. "I hold you responsible, Mr. Stover."

At this Dolly turned round; her eyes, vague beyond the veiling, seemed to frame Verena in a gaze that excluded everyone else. "Responsible? No one is that; except ourselves."

Sister Ida had replaced the Judge at Riley's side; she completely stripped off his shirt. "Thank your stars, it's his shoulder," she said, and the relieved sighs, Big Eddie's alone, would have floated a kite. "He's fairly knocked out, though. Some of you fellows better get him to a doctor." She stopped Riley's bleeding with a bandage torn off his shirt. The Sheriff and three of his men locked arms, making a litter on which to carry him. He was not the only one who had to be carried; the Reverend Buster had also come to considerable grief: loose-limbed as a puppet, and too weak to know the noose still hung around his neck, he needed several assistants to get up the path. Little Homer chased after him: "Hey, hand me back my rope!"

Amos Legrand waited to accompany Verena; she told him to go without her as she had no intention of leaving unless

Dolly—hesitating, she looked at the rest of us, Sister Ida in particular: "I would like to speak with my sister alone."

With a wave of her hand that quite dismissed Verena, Sister Ida said, "Never mind, lady. We're on our way." She hugged Dolly. "Bless us, we love you. Don't we, kids?" Little Homer said, "Come with us, Dolly. We'll have such good times. I'll give you my sparkle belt." And Texaco Gasoline threw herself upon the Judge, pleading for him to go with them, too. Nobody seemed to want me.

"I'll always remember that you asked me," said Dolly, her eyes hurrying as though to memorize the children's faces. "Good luck. Good-bye. Run now," she raised her voice above new and nearer thunder, "run, it's raining."

It was a tickling feathery rain fine as a gauze curtain, and as they faded into the folds of it, Sister Ida and her family, Verena said: "Do I understand you've been conniving with that—woman? After she made a mockery of our name?"

"I don't think you can accuse me of conniving with anyone," Dolly answered serenely. "Especially not with bullies who," she a little lost control, "steal from children and drag old women into jail. I can't set much store by a name that endorses such methods. It ought to be a mockery."

Verena received this without flinching. "You're not yourself," she said, as if it were a clinical opinion.

"You'd best look again: I am myself." Dolly seemed to pose for inspection. She was as tall as Verena, as assured; nothing about her was incomplete or blurred. "I've taken your advice: stopped hanging my head, I mean. You told me it made you dizzy. And not many days ago," she continued, "you told me that you were ashamed of me. Of Catherine. So much of our lives had been lived for you; it was painful to realize the waste that had been. Can you know what it is, such a feeling of waste?"

Scarcely audible, Verena said, "I do know," and it was as if her eyes crossed, peered inward upon a stony vista. It was the expression I'd seen when, spying from the attic, I'd watched her late at night brooding over the Kodak pictures of Maudie Laura Murphy, Maudie Laura's husband and children. She swayed, she put a hand on my shoulder; except for that, I think she might have fallen.

"I imagined I would go to my dying day with the hurt of it. I won't. But it's no satisfaction, Verena, to say that I'm ashamed of you, too."

It was night now; frogs, sawing insects celebrated the slow-falling rain. We dimmed as though the wetness had snuffed the light of our faces. Verena sagged against me. "I'm not well," she said in a skeleton voice. "I'm a sick woman, I am, Dolly."

Somewhat unconvinced, Dolly approached Verena, presently touched her, as though her fingers could sense the truth. "Collin," she said, "Judge, please help me with her into the tree." Verena protested that she couldn't go climbing trees; but once she got used to the idea she went up easily enough. The raftlike tree-house seemed to be floating over shrouded vaporish waters; it was dry there, however, for the mild rain had not penetrated the parasol of leaves. We drifted in a current of silence until Verena said, "I have something to say, Dolly. I could say it more easily if we were alone."

The Judge crossed his arms. "I'm afraid you'll have to put up with me, Miss Verena." He was emphatic, though not belligerent. "I have an interest in the outcome of what you might have to say."

"I doubt that: how so?" she said, recovering to a degree her exalted manner.

He lighted a stub of candle, and our sudden shadows stooped over us like four eavesdroppers. "I don't like talking in the dark," he said. There was a purpose in the proud erectness of his posture: it was, I thought, to let Verena know she was dealing with a man, a fact too few men in her experience had enough believed to assert. She found it unforgivable. "You don't remember, do you, Charlie Cool? Fifty years ago, more maybe. Some of you boys came blackberry stealing out at our place. My father caught your cousin Seth, and I caught you. It was quite a licking you got that day."

The Judge did remember; he blushed, smiled, said: "You didn't fight fair, Verena."

"I fought fair," she told him drily. "But you're right—since neither of us like it, let's not talk in the dark. Frankly, Charlie, you're not a welcome sight to me. My sister couldn't have gone through such tommyrot if you hadn't been goading her on. So I'll thank you to leave us; it can be no further affair of yours."

"But it is," said Dolly. "Because Judge Cool, Charlie . . ." she dwindled, appeared for the first time to question her boldness.

"Dolly means that I have asked her to marry me."

"That," Verena managed after some suspenseful seconds, "is," she said, regarding her gloved hands, "remarkable. Very. I wouldn't have credited either of you with so much imagination. Or is it that I am imagining? Quite likely I'm dreaming of myself in a wet tree on a thundery night. Except I never have dreams, or perhaps I only forget them. This one I suggest we all forget."

"I'll own up: I think it is a dream, Miss Verena. But a man who doesn't dream is like a man who doesn't sweat: he stores up a lot of poison."

She ignored him; her attention was with Dolly, Dolly's with her: they might have been alone together, two persons at far ends of a bleak room, mutes communicating in an eccentric sign-language, subtle shifting of the eye; and it was as though, then, Dolly gave an answer, one that sapped all color from Verena's face. "I see. You've accepted him, have you?"

The rain had thickened, fish could have swum through the air; like a deepening scale of piano notes, it struck its blackest chord, and drummed into a downpour that, though it threatened, did not at once reach us: drippings leaked through the leaves, but the tree-house stayed a dry seed in a soaking plant. The Judge put a protective hand over the candle; he waited as anxiously as Verena for Dolly's reply. My impatience equaled theirs, yet I felt exiled from the scene, again a spy peering from the attic, and my sympathies, curiously, were nowhere; or rather, everywhere: a tenderness for all three ran together like raindrops, I could not separate them, they expanded into a human oneness.

Dolly, too. She could not separate the Judge from Verena. At last, excruciatingly, "I can't," she cried, implying failures beyond calculation. "I said I would know what was right. But it hasn't happened; I don't know: do other people? A choice, I thought: to have had a life made of my own decisions . . ."

"But we have had our lives," said Verena. "Yours has been nothing to despise, I don't think you've required more than you've had; I've envied you always. Come home, Dolly. Leave decisions to me: that, you see, has been my life."

"Is it true, Charlie?" Dolly asked, as a child might ask where do falling stars fall? and: "Have we had our lives?"

"We're not dead," he told her; but it was as if, to the questioning child, he'd said stars fall into space: an irrefutable, still unsatisfactory answer. Dolly could not accept it: "You don't have to be dead. At home, in the kitchen, there is a geranium that blooms over and over. Some plants, though, they bloom just the once, if at all, and nothing more happens to them. They live, but they've had their life."

"Not you," he said, and brought his face nearer hers, as

though he meant their lips to touch, yet wavered, not daring it. Rain had tunneled through the branches, it fell full weight; rivulets of it streamed off Dolly's hat, the veiling clung to her cheeks; with a flutter the candle failed. "Not me."

Successive strokes of lightning throbbed like veins of fire, and Verena, illuminated in that sustained glare, was not anyone I knew; but some woman woebegone, wasted—with eyes once more drawn toward each other, their stare settled on an inner territory, a withered country; as the lightning lessened, as the hum of rain sealed us in its multiple sounds, she spoke, and her voice came so weakly from so very far, not expecting, it seemed, to be heard at all. "Envied you, Dolly. Your pink room. I've only knocked at the doors of such rooms, not often —enough to know that now there is no one but you to let me in. Because little Morris, little Morris—help me, I loved him, I did. Not in a womanly way; it was, oh I admit it, that we were kindred spirits. We looked each other in the eye, we saw the same devil, we weren't afraid; it was—merry. But he outsmarted me; I'd known he could, and hoped he wouldn't, and he did, and now: it's too long to be alone, a lifetime. I walk through the house, nothing is mine: your pink room, your kitchen, the house is yours, and Catherine's too, I think. Only don't leave me, let me live with you. I'm feeling old, I want my sister."

The rain, adding its voice to Verena's, was between them, Dolly and the Judge, a transparent wall through which he could watch her losing substance, recede before him as earlier she had seemed to recede before me. More than that, it was as if the tree-house were dissolving. Lunging wind cast overboard the soggy wreckage of our Rook cards, our wrapping papers; animal crackers crumbled, the rain-filled mason jars spilled over like fountains; and Catherine's beautiful scrapquilt was ruined, a puddle. It was going: like the doomed houses rivers in flood float away; and it was as though the Judge were trapped there—waving to us as we, the survivors, stood ashore. For Dolly had said, "Forgive me; I want my sister, too," and the Judge could not reach her, not with his arms, not with his heart: Verena's claim was too final.

Somewhere near midnight the rain slackened, halted; wind barreled about wringing out the trees. Singly, like delayed guests arriving at a dance, appearing stars pierced the sky. It was time to leave. We took nothing with us: left the quilt to rot, spoons to rust; and the tree-house, the woods we left to winter.

Seven

FOR quite a while it was Catherine's custom to date events as having occurred before or after her incarceration. "Prior," she would begin, "to the time That One made a jailbird of me." As for the rest of us, we could have divided history along similar lines; that is, in terms of before and after the tree-house. Those few autumn days were a monument and a signpost.

Except to collect his belongings, the Judge never again entered the house he'd shared with his sons and their wives, a circumstance that must have suited them, at least they made no protest when he took a room at Miss Bell's boarding house. This was a brown solemn establishment which lately has been turned into a funeral home by an undertaker who saw that to effect the correct atmosphere a minimum of renovation would be necessary. I disliked going past it, for Miss Bell's guests, ladies thorny as the blighted rosebushes littering the yard, occupied the porch in a dawn-to-dark marathon of vigilance. One of them, the twice-widowed Mamie Canfield, specialized in spotting pregnancies (some legendary fellow is supposed to have told his wife Why waste money on a doctor? just trot yourself past Miss Bell's: Mamie Canfield, she'll let the world know soon enough whether you is or ain't). Until the Judge moved there, Amos Legrand was the only man in residence at Miss Bell's. He was a godsend to the other tenants: the moments most sacred to them were when, after supper, Amos swung in the seat-swing with his little legs not touching the floor and his tongue trilling like an alarm-clock. They vied with each other in knitting him socks and sweaters, tending to his diet: at table all the best things were saved for his plate— Miss Bell had trouble keeping a cook because the ladies were forever poking around in the kitchen wanting to make a delicacy that would tempt their pet. Probably they would have done the same for the Judge, but he had no use for them, never, so they complained, stopped to pass the time of day.

The last drenching night in the tree-house had left me with a bad cold, Verena with a worse one; and we had a sneezing nurse, Dolly. Catherine wouldn't help: "Dollyheart, you can do like you please—tote That One's slopjar till you drop in your tracks. Only don't count on me to lift a finger. I've put down the load."

Rising at all hours of the night, Dolly brought the syrups that eased our throats, stoked the fires that kept us warm. Verena did not, as in other days, accept such attention simply as her due. "In the spring," she promised Dolly, "we'll make a trip together. We might go to the Grand Canyon and call on Maudie Laura. Or Florida: you've never seen the ocean." But Dolly was where she wanted to be, she had no wish to travel: "I wouldn't enjoy it, seeing the things I've known shamed by nobler sights."

Doctor Carter called regularly to see us, and one morning Dolly asked would he mind taking her temperature; she felt so flushed and weak in the legs. He put her straight to bed, and she thought it was very humorous when he told her she had walking pneumonia. "Walking pneumonia," she said to the Judge, who had come to visit her, "it must be something new, I've never heard of it. But I do feel as though I were skylarking along on a pair of stilts. Lovely," she said and fell asleep.

For three, nearly four days she never really woke up. Catherine stayed with her, dozing upright in a wicker chair and growling low whenever Verena or I tiptoed into the room. She persisted in fanning Dolly with a picture of Jesus, as though it were summertime; and it was a disgrace how she ignored Doctor Carter's instructions: "I wouldn't feed that to a hog," she'd declare, pointing to some medicine he'd sent around. Finally Doctor Carter said he wouldn't be responsible unless the patient were removed to a hospital. The nearest hospital was in Brewton, sixty miles away. Verena sent over there for an ambulance. She could have saved herself the expense, because Catherine locked Dolly's door from the inside and said

the first one to rattle the knob would need an ambulance themselves. Dolly did not know where they wanted to take her;
wherever it was, she begged not to go: "Don't wake me," she
said, "I don't want to see the ocean."

Toward the end of the week she could sit up in bed; a few
days later she was strong enough to resume correspondence
with her dropsy-cure customers. She was worried by the un-
filled orders that had piled up; but Catherine, who took the
credit for Dolly's improvement, said, "Shoot, it's no time we'll
be out there boiling a brew."

Every afternoon, promptly at four, the Judge presented himself at the garden gate and whistled for me to let him in;
by using the garden gate, rather than the front door, he lessened the chance of encountering Verena—not that she objected to his coming: indeed, she wisely supplied for his visits a
bottle of sherry and a box of cigars. Usually he brought Dolly
a gift, cakes from the Katydid Bakery or flowers, bronze bal-
loonlike chrysanthemums which Catherine swiftly confiscated
on the theory that they ate up all the nourishment in the air.
Catherine never learned he had proposed to Dolly; still, in-
tuiting a situation not quite to her liking, she sharply chap-
eroned the Judge's visits and, while swigging at the sherry that
had been put out for him, did most of the talking as well. But
I suspect that neither he nor Dolly had much to say of a
private nature; they accepted each other without excitement,
as people do who are settled in their affections. If in other
ways he was a disappointed man, it was not because of Dolly,
for I believe she became what he'd wanted, the one person in
the world—to whom, as he'd described it, everything can be
said. But when everything can be said perhaps there is nothing
more to say. He sat beside her bed, content to be there and
not expecting to be entertained. Often, drowsy with fever, she
went to sleep, and if, while she slept, she whimpered or
frowned, he wakened her, welcoming her back with a daylight
smile.

In the past Verena had not allowed us to have a radio;
cheap melodies, she contended, disordered the mind; moreover, there was the expense to consider. It was Doctor Carter
who persuaded her that Dolly should have a radio; he thought
it would help reconcile her to what he foresaw as a long
convalescence. Verena bought one, and paid a good price, I
don't doubt; but it was an ugly hood-shaped box crudely varnished. I took it out in the yard and painted it pink. Even so
Dolly wasn't certain she wanted it in her room; later on, you

couldn't have pried it away from her. That radio was always hot enough to hatch a chicken, she and Catherine played it so much. They favored broadcasts of football games. "Please don't," Dolly admonished the Judge when he attempted to explain the rules of this game. "I like a mystery. Everybody shouting, having such a fine time: it might not sound so large and happy if I knew why." Primarily the Judge was peeved because he couldn't get Dolly to root for any one team. She thought both sides should win: "They're all nice boys, I'm sure."

Because of the radio Catherine and I had words one afternoon. It was the afternoon Maude Riordan was playing in a broadcast of the state musical competition. Naturally I wanted to hear her, Catherine knew that, but she was tuned in on a Tulane-Georgia Tech game and wouldn't let me near the radio. I said, "What's come over you, Catherine? Selfish, dissatisfied, always got to have your own way, why you're worse than Verena ever was." It was as though, in lieu of prestige lost through her encounter with the law, she'd had to double her power in the Talbo house: we at least would have to respect her Indian blood, accept her tyranny. Dolly was willing; in the matter of Maude Riordan, however, she sided with me: "Let Collin find his station. It wouldn't be Christian not to listen to Maude. She's a friend of ours."

Everyone who heard Maude agreed that she should've won first prize. She placed second, which pleased her family, for it meant a half-scholarship in music at the University. Still it wasn't fair, because she performed beautifully, much better than the boy who won the larger prize. She played her father's serenade, and it seemed to me as pretty as it had that day in the woods. Since that day I'd wasted hours scribbling her name, describing in my head her charms, her hair the color of vanilla ice cream. The Judge arrived in time to hear the broadcast, and I know Dolly was glad because it was as if we were reunited again in the leaves with music like butterflies flying.

Some days afterwards I met Elizabeth Henderson on the street. She'd been at the beauty parlor, for her hair was finger-waved, her nails tinted, she did look grown-up and I complimented her. "It's for the party. I hope your costume is ready." Then I remembered: the Halloween party to which she and Maude had asked me to contribute my services as a fortuneteller. "You can't have forgotten? Oh, Collin," she said, "we've worked like dogs! Mrs. Riordan is making a *wine* punch. I shouldn't be surprised if there's drunkenness and everything. And after all it's a celebration for Maude, because she won the prize, and because," Elizabeth glanced along the street, a glum perspective of silent houses and telephone poles, "she'll be going away—to the University, you know." A loneliness fell around us, we did not want to go our separate ways: I offered to walk her home.

On our way we stopped by the Katydid where Elizabeth placed an order for a Halloween cake, and Mrs. C. C. County, her apron glittering with sugar crystals, appeared from the oven room to inquire after Dolly's condition. "Doing well as can be expected I suppose," she lamented. "Imagine it, walking pneumonia. My sister, now she had the ordinary lying-down kind. Well, we can be thankful Dolly's in her own bed; it eases my mind to know you people are home again. Ha ha, guess we can laugh about all that foolishness now. Look here, I've just pulled out a pan of doughnuts; you take them to Dolly with my blessings." Elizabeth and I ate most of those doughnuts before we reached her house. She invited me in to have a glass of milk and finish them off.

Today there is a filling station where the Henderson house used to be. It was some fifteen draughty rooms casually nailed together, a place stray animals would have claimed if Riley had not been a gifted carpenter. He had an outdoor shed, a combination of workshop and sanctuary, where he spent his mornings sawing lumber, shaving shingles. Its wall-shelves sagged with *the relics of outgrown hobbies: snakes, bees, spiders preserved in alcohol, a bat decaying in a bottle; ship models. A boyhood enthusiasm for taxidermy had resulted in a pitiful zoo of nasty-odored beasts: an eyeless rabbit with maggot-green fur and ears that drooped like a bloodhound's —objects better off buried. I'd been lately to see Riley several times; Big Eddie Stover's bullet had shattered his shoulder, and the curse of it was he had to wear an itching plaster cast which weighed, he said, a hundred pounds. Since he couldn't drive his car, or hammer a proper nail, there wasn't much for him to do except loaf around and brood.

"If you want to see Riley," said Elizabeth, "you'll find him out in the shed. I expect Maude's with him."

"Maude Riordan?" I had reason to be surprised, because on the occasions I'd visited Riley he'd made a point of our sitting in the shed; the girls wouldn't bother us there, for it was, he'd boasted, one threshold no female was permitted to cross.

"Reading to him. Poetry, plays. Maude's been absolutely adorable. And it's not as though my brother had ever treated

her with common human decency. But she's let bygones be bygones. I guess coming so near to being killed the way he was,
I guess that would change a person—make them more recep-
tive to the finer things. He lets her read to him by the hour."

The shed, shaded by fig trees, was in the back yard. Ma-
tronly Plymouth hens waddled about its doorstep picking at
the seeds of last summer's fallen sunflowers. On the door a
childhood word in faded whitewash feebly warned Beware!
It aroused a shyness in me. Beyond the door I could hear
Maude's voice—her poetry voice, a swooning chant certain
louts in school had dearly loved to mimic. Anyone who'd been
told Riley Henderson had come to this, they'd have said that
fall from the sycamore had affected his head. Stealing over to
the shed's window, I got a look at him: he was absorbed in
sorting the insides of a clock and, to judge from his face,
might have been listening to nothing more uplifting than the
hum of a fly; he jiggled a finger in his ear, as though to re-
lieve an irritation. Then, at the moment I'd decided to startle
them by rapping on the window, he put aside his clockworks
and, coming round behind Maude, reached down and shut the
book from which she was reading. With a grin he gathered in
his hand twists of her hair—she rose like a kitten lifted by the
nape of its neck. It was as though they were edged with light,
some brilliance that smarted my eyes. You could see it wasn't
the first time they'd kissed.

Not one week before, because of his experience in such
matters, I'd taken Riley into my confidence, confessed to him
my feelings for Maude: please look. I wished I were a giant so
that I could grab hold of that shed and shake it to a splinter;
knock down the door and denounce them both. Yet—of what
could I accuse Maude? Regardless of how bad she'd talked
about him I'd always known she was heartset on Riley. It
wasn't as if there had ever been an understanding between the
two of us; at the most we'd been good friends: for the last
few years, not even that. As I walked back through the yard
the pompous Plymouth hens cackled after me tauntingly.

Elizabeth said, "You didn't stay long. Or weren't they there?"

I told her it hadn't seemed right to interrupt. "They were
getting on so well with the finer things."

But sarcasm never touched Elizabeth: she was, despite the
subtleties her soulful appearance promised, too literal a person. "Wonderful, isn't it?"

"Wonderful."

"Collin—for heaven's sake: what are you sniveling about?"

"Nothing. I mean, I've got a cold."

"Well I hope it doesn't keep you away from the party. Only you must have a costume. Riley's coming as the devil."

"That's appropriate."

"Of course we want you in a skeleton suit. I know there's only a day left. . . ."

I had no intention of going to the party. As soon as I got home I sat down to write Riley a letter. Dear Riley . . . Dear Henderson. I crossed out the dear; plain Henderson would do. Henderson, your treachery has not gone unobserved. Pages were filled with recording the origins of our friendship, its honorable history; and gradually a feeling grew that there must be a mistake: such a splendid friend would not have wronged me. Until, toward the end, I found myself deliriously telling him he was my best friend, my brother. So I threw these ravings in a fireplace and five minutes later was in Dolly's room asking what were the chances of my having a skeleton suit made by the following night.

Dolly was not much of a seamstress, she had her difficulties lifting a hemline. This was also true of Catherine; it was in Catherine's makeup, however, to pretend professional status in all fields, particularly those in which she was least competent. She sent me to Verena's drygoods store for seven yards of their choicest black satin. "With seven yards there ought to be some bits left over: me and Dolly can trim our petticoats." Then she made a show of tape-measuring my lengths and widths, which was sound procedure except that she had no idea of how to apply such information to scissors and cloth. "This little piece," she said, hacking off a yard, "it'd make somebody lovely bloomers. And this here," snip, snip, ". . . . a black satin collar would dress up my old print considerable." You couldn't have covered a midget's shame with the amount of material allotted me.

"Catherine, now dear, we mustn't think of our own needs," Dolly warned her.

They worked without recess through the afternoon. The Judge, during his usual visit, was forced to thread needles, a job Catherine despised: "Makes my flesh crawl, like stuffing worms on a fishhook." At suppertime she called quits and went home to her house among the butterbean stalks.

But a desire to finish had seized Dolly, and a talkative exhilaration. Her needle soared in and out of the satin; like the seams it made, her sentences linked in a wiggling line. "Do you think," she said, "that Verena would let me give a party? Now

that I have so many friends? There's Riley, there's Charlie,
couldn't we ask Mrs. County, Maude and Elizabeth? In the
spring; a garden party—with a few fireworks. My father was
a great hand for sewing. A pity I didn't inherit it from him.
So many men sewed in the old days; there was one friend of
Papa's that won I don't know how many prizes for his scrap-
quilts. Papa said it relaxed him after the heavy rough work
around a farm. Collin. Will you promise me something? I was
against your coming here, I've never believed it was right,
raising a boy in a houseful of women. Old women and their
prejudices. But it was done; and somehow I'm not worried
about it now: you'll make your mark, you'll get on. It's this
that I want you to promise me: don't be unkind to Catherine,
try not to grow too far away from her. Some nights it keeps
me wide awake to think of her forsaken. There," she held up
my suit, "let's see if it fits."

It pinched in the crotch and in the rear drooped like an
old man's B.V.D.'s; the legs were wide as sailor pants, one
sleeve stopped above my wrist, the other shot past my finger-
tips. It wasn't, as Dolly admitted, very stylish. "But when
we've painted on the bones ..." she said. "Silver paint. Verena
bought some once to dress up a flagpole—before she took
against the government. It should be somewhere in the attic,
that little can. Look under the bed and see if you can locate my
slippers."

She was forbidden to get up, not even Catherine would
permit that. "It won't be any fun if you scold," she said and
found the slippers herself. The courthouse clock had chimed
eleven, which meant it was ten-thirty, a dark hour in a town
where respectable doors are locked at nine; it seemed later
still because in the next room Verena had closed her ledgers
and gone to bed. We took an oil lamp from the linen closet
and by its tottering light tiptoed up the ladder into the attic.
It was cold up there; we set the lamp on a barrel and lingered
near it as though it were a hearth. Sawdust heads that once
had helped sell St. Louis hats watched while we searched;
wherever we put our hands it caused a huffy scuttling of
fragile feet. Overturned, a carton of mothballs clattered on
the floor. "Oh, dear, oh, dear," cried Dolly, giggling, "if
Verena hears that she'll call the Sheriff."

We unearthed numberless brushes; the paint, discovered beneath a welter of dried holiday wreaths, proved not to be
silver but gold. "Of course that's better, isn't it? Gold, like a
king's ransom. Only do see what else I've found." It was a

shoebox secured with twine. "My valuables," she said, opening it under the lamp. A hollowed honeycomb was demonstrated against the light, a hornet's nest and a clove-stuck orange that age had robbed of its aroma. She showed me a blue perfect jaybird's egg cradled in cotton.

"I was too principled. So Catherine stole the egg for me, it was her Christmas present." She smiled; to me her face seemed a moth suspended beside the lamp's chimney, as daring, as destructible. "Charlie said that love is a chain of love. I hope you listened and understood him. Because when you can love one thing," she held the blue egg as preciously as the Judge had held a leaf, "you can love another, and that is owning, that is something to live with. You can forgive everything. Well," she sighed, "we're not getting you painted. I want to amaze Catherine; we'll tell her that while we slept the little people finished your suit. She'll have a fit."

Again the courthouse clock was floating its message, each note like a banner stirring above the chilled and sleeping town. "I know it tickles," she said, drawing a branch of ribs across my chest, "but I'll make a mess if you don't hold still." She dipped the brush and skated it along the sleeves, the trousers, designing golden bones for my arms and legs. "You must remember all the compliments: there should be many," she said as she immodestly observed her work. "Oh dear, oh dear . . ." She hugged herself, her laughter rollicked in the rafters. "Don't you see . . ."

For I was not unlike the man who painted himself into a corner. Freshly gilded front and back, I was trapped inside the suit: a fine fix for which I blamed her with a pointing finger.

"You have to whirl," she teased. "Whirling will dry you." She blissfully extended her arms and turned in slow ungainly circles across the shadows of the attic floor, her plain kimono billowing and her thin feet wobbling in their slippers. It was as though she had collided with another dancer: she stumbled, a hand on her forehead, a hand on her heart.

Far on the horizon of sound a train whistle howled, and it wakened me to the bewilderment puckering her eyes, the contractions shaking her face. With my arms around her, and the paint bleeding its pattern against her, I called Verena; somebody help me!

Dolly whispered, "Hush now, hush."

Houses at night announce catastrophe by their sudden pitiable radiance. Catherine dragged from room to room switching on lights unused for years. Shivering inside my wrecked

costume I sat in the glare of the entrance hall sharing a bench
with the Judge. He had come at once, wearing only a raincoat
slung over a flannel nightshirt. Whenever Verena approached
he brought his naked legs together primly, like a young girl.
Neighbors, summoned by our bright windows, came softly inquiring. Verena spoke to them on the porch: her sister, Miss
Dolly, she'd suffered a stroke. Doctor Carter would allow
none of us in her room, and we accepted this, even Catherine
who, when she'd set ablaze the last light, stood leaning her
head against Dolly's door.

There was in the hall a hat-tree with many antlers and a
mirror. Dolly's velvet hat hung there, and at sunrise, as breezes
trickled through the house, the mirror reflected its quivering
veil.

Then I knew as good as anything that Dolly had left us.
Some moments past she'd gone by unseen; and in my imagination I followed her. She had crossed the square, had come
to the church, now she'd reached the hill. The Indian grass
gleamed below her, she had that far to go.

It was a journey I made with Judge Cool the next September. During the intervening months we had not often encountered each other—once we met on the square and he
said to come see him any time I felt like it. I meant to, yet
whenever I passed Miss Bell's boarding house I looked the
other way.

I've read that past and future are a spiral, one coil containing the next and predicting its theme. Perhaps this is so;
but my own life has seemed to me more a series of closed
circles, rings that do not evolve with the freedom of a spiral:
for me to get from one to the other has meant a leap, not a
glide. What weakens me is the lull between, the wait before I
know where to jump. After Dolly died I was a long while
dangling.

My own idea was to have a good time.

I hung around Phil's Café winning free beers on the pin-
ball machine; it was illegal to serve me beer, but Phil had it
on his mind that someday I would inherit Verena's money
and maybe set him up in the hotel business. I slicked my hair
with brilliantine and chased off to dances in other towns,
shined flashlights and threw pebbles at girls' windows late at
night. I knew a Negro in the country who sold a brand of
gin called Yellow Devil. I courted anyone who owned a car.

Because I didn't want to spend a waking moment in the

Talbo house. It was too thick with air that didn't move. Some stranger occupied the kitchen, a pigeon-toed colored girl who sang all day, the wavery singing of a child bolstering its spirit in an ominous place. She was a sorry cook. She let the kitchen's geranium plant perish. I had approved of Verena hiring her. I thought it would bring Catherine back to work.

On the contrary, Catherine showed no interest in routing the new girl. For she'd retired to her house in the vegetable garden. She had taken the radio with her and was very comfortable. "I've put down the load, and it's down to stay. I'm after my leisure," she said. Leisure fattened her, her feet swelled, she had to cut slits in her shoes. She developed exaggerated versions of Dolly's habits, such as a craving for sweet foods; she had her suppers delivered from the drugstore, two quarts of ice cream. Candy wrappers rustled in her lap. Until she became too gross, she contrived to squeeze herself into clothes that had belonged to Dolly; it was as though, in this way, she kept her friend with her.

Our visits together were an ordeal, and I made them grudgingly, resenting it that she depended on me for company. I let a day slip by without seeing her, then three, a whole week once. When I returned after an absence I imagined the silences in which we sat, her offhand manner, were meant reproachfully; I was too conscience-ridden to realize the truth, which was that she didn't care whether or not I came. One afternoon she proved it. Simply, she removed the cotton wads that jacked up her jaws. Without the cotton her speech was as unintelligible to me as it ordinarily was to others. It happened while I was making an excuse to shorten my call. She lifted the lid of a pot-bellied stove and spit the cotton into the fire; and her cheeks caved in, she looked starved. I think now this was not a vengeful gesture: it was intended to let me know that I was under no obligation: the future was something she preferred not to share.

Occasionally Riley rode me around—but I couldn't count on him or his car; neither were much available since he'd become a man of affairs. He had a team of tractors clearing ninety acres of land he'd bought on the outskirts of town; he planned to build houses there. Several locally important persons were impressed by another scheme of his: he thought the town should put up a silkmill in which every citizen would be a stockholder; aside from the possible profits, having an industry would increase our population. There was an enthusiastic editorial in the paper about this proposal; it went on

to say that the town should be proud of having produced a
man of young Henderson's enterprise. He grew a mustache;
he rented an office and his sister Elizabeth worked as his secretary. Maude Riordan was installed at the State University,
and almost every week-end he drove his sisters over there; it
was supposed to be because the girls were so lonesome for
Maude. The engagement of Miss Maude Riordan to Mr. Riley
Henderson was announced in the *Courier* on April Fool's Day.

They were married the middle of June in a double-ring
ceremony. I acted as an usher, and the Judge was Riley's best
man. Except for the Henderson sisters, all the bridesmaids
were society girls Maude had known at the University; the
Courier called them beautiful debutantes, a chivalrous description. The bride carried a bouquet of jasmine and lilac; the
groom wore spats and stroked his mustache. They received a
sumptuous table-load of gifts. I gave them six cakes of scented
soap and an ashtray.

After the wedding I walked home with Verena under the
shade of her black umbrella. It was a blistering day, heatwaves
jiggled like a sound-graph of the celebrating Baptist bells, and
the rest of summer, a vista rigid as the noon street, lengthened before me. Summer, another autumn, winter again: not
a spiral, but a circle confined as the umbrella's shadow. If I
ever were to make the leap—with a heartskip, I made it.
"Verena, I want to go away."

We were at the garden gate; "I know. I do myself," she
said, closing her umbrella. "I'd hoped to make a trip with
Dolly. I wanted to show her the ocean." Verena had seemed
a tall woman because of her authoritative carriage; now she
stooped slightly, her head nodded. I wondered that I ever
could have been so afraid of her, for she'd grown feminine,
fearful, she spoke of prowlers, she burdened the doors with
bolts and spiked the roof with lightning rods. It had been her
custom the first of every month to stalk around collecting in
person the various rents owed her; when she stopped doing
this it caused an uneasiness in the town, people felt wrong
without their rainy day. The women said she's got no family,
she's lost without her sister; their husbands blamed Dr. Morris
Ritz: he knocked the gumption out of her, they said; and,
much as they had quarreled with Verena, held it against him.
Three years ago, when I returned to this town, my first task
was to sort the papers of the Talbo estate, and among Verena's
private possessions, her keys, her pictures of Maudie Laura
Murphy, I found a postcard. It was dated two months after

Dolly died, at Christmas, and it was from Paraguay: *As we say down here, Feliz Navidad. Do you miss me? Morris.* And I thought, reading it, of how her eyes had come permanently to have an uneven cast, an inward and agonized gaze, and I remembered how her eyes, watering in the brassy sunshine of Riley's wedding day, had straightened with momentary hope: "It could be a long trip. I've considered selling a few—a few properties. We might take a boat; you've never seen the ocean." I picked a sprig of honeysuckle from the vine flowering on the garden fence, and she watched me shred it as if I were pulling apart her vision, the voyage she saw for us. "Oh," she brushed at the mole that spotted her cheek like a tear, "well," she said in a practical voice, "what are your ambitions?"

So it was not until September that I called upon the Judge, and then it was to tell him good-bye. The suitcases were packed, Amos Legrand had cut my hair ("Honey, don't you come back here baldheaded. What I mean is, they'll try to scalp you up there, cheat you every way they can."); I had a new suit and new shoes, gray fedora ("Aren't you the cat's pajamas, Mr. Collin Fenwick?" Mrs. County exclaimed. "A lawyer you're going to be? And already dressed like one. No, child, I won't kiss you. I'd be mortified to dirty your finery with my bakery mess. You write us, hear?"): that very evening a train would rock me northward, parade me through the land to a city where in my honor pennants flurried.

At Miss Bell's they told me the Judge had gone out. I found him on the square, and it gave me a twinge to see him, a spruce sturdy figure with a Cherokee rose sprouting in his buttonhole, encamped among the old men who talk and spit and wait. He took my arm and led me away from them; and while he amiably advised me of his own days as a law student, we strolled past the church and out along the River Woods road. This road or this tree: I closed my eyes to fix their image, for I did not believe I would return, did not foresee that I would travel the road and dream the tree until they had drawn me back.

It was as though neither of us had known where we were headed. Quietly astonished, we surveyed the view from the cemetery hill, and arm in arm descended to the summer-burned, September-burnished field. A waterfall of color flowed across the dry and strumming leaves; and I wanted then for the Judge to hear what Dolly had told me: that it was a grass harp, gathering, telling, a harp of voices remembering a story. We listened.

A TREE OF NIGHT
and other stories

Master Misery

HER high heels, clacking across the marble foyer, made her think of ice cubes rattling in a glass, and the flowers, those autumn chrysanthemums in the urn at the entrance, if touched they would shatter, splinter, she was sure, into frozen dust; yet the house was warm, even somewhat overheated, but cold, and Sylvia shivered, but cold, like the snowy swollen wastes of the secretary's face: Miss Mozart, who dressed all in white, as though she were a nurse. Perhaps she really was; that, of course, could be the answer. Mr. Revercomb, you are mad, and this is your nurse; she thought about it for a moment: well, no. And now the butler brought her scarf. His beauty touched her: slender, so gentle, a Negro with freckled skin and reddish, unreflecting eyes. As he opened the door, Miss Mozart appeared, her starched uniform rustling dryly in the hall. "We hope you will return," she said, and handed Sylvia a sealed envelope. "Mrs. Revercomb was most particularly pleased."

Outside, dusk was falling like blue flakes, and Sylvia walked crosstown along the November streets until she reached the lonely upper reaches of Fifth Avenue. It occurred to her then that she might walk home through the park: an act of defiance almost, for Henry and Estelle, always insistent upon their city wisdom, had said over and again, Sylvia, you have no idea how dangerous it is, walking in the park after dark; look what happened to Myrtle Calisher. This isn't Easton, honey. That was the

101

other thing they said. And said. God, she was sick of it. Still, and aside from a few of the other typists at SnugFare, an underwear company for which she worked, who else in New York did she know? Oh, it would be all right if only she did not have to live with them, if she could afford somewhere a small room of her own; but there in that chintz-cramped apartment she sometimes felt she would choke them both. And why did she come to New York? For whatever reason, and it was indeed becoming vague, a principal cause of leaving Easton had been to rid herself of Henry and Estelle; or rather, their counterparts, though in point of fact Estelle was actually from Easton, a town north of Cincinnati. She and Sylvia had grown up together. The real trouble with Henry and Estelle was that they were so excruciatingly married. Nambypamby, bootsy-totsy, and everything had a name: the telephone was Tinkling Tillie, the sofa, Our Nelle, the bed, Big Bear; yes, and what about those His-Her towels, those He-She pillows? Enough to drive you loony. "Loony!" she said aloud, the quiet park erasing her voice. It was lovely now, and she was right to have walked here, with wind moving through the leaves, and globe lamps, freshly aglow, kindling the chalk drawings of children, pink birds, blue arrows, green hearts. But suddenly, like a pair of obscene words, there appeared on the path two boys: pimple-faced, grinning, they loomed in the dusk like menacing flames, and Sylvia, passing them, felt a burning all through her, quite as though she'd brushed fire. They turned and followed her past a deserted playground, one of them bump-bumping a stick along an iron fence, the other whistling: these sounds accumulated around her like the gathering roar of an oncoming engine, and when one of the boys, with a laugh, called, "Hey, whatsa hurry?" her mouth twisted for breath. Don't, she thought, thinking to throw down her purse and run. At that moment, a man walking a dog came up a sidepath, and she followed at his heels to the exit. Wouldn't they feel gratified, Henry and Estelle, wouldn't they we-told-you-so if she were to tell them? and, what is more, Estelle would write it home and the next thing you knew it would be all over Easton that she'd been raped in Central Park. She spent the rest of the way home despising New York: anonymity, its virtuous terror; and the squeaking drainpipe, all-night light, ceaseless footfall, subway corridor, numbered door (3C).

"Shh, honey," Estelle said, sidling out of the kitchen, "Bootsy's doing his homework." Sure enough, Henry, a law student at Columbia, was hunched over his books in the living room, and Sylvia, at Estelle's request, took off her shoes before tiptoeing through. Once inside her room, she threw herself on the bed and put her hands over her eyes. Had today really happened? Miss Mozart and Mr. Revercomb, were they really there in the tall house on Seventy-eighth Street?

"So, honey, what happened today?" Estelle had entered without knocking.

Sylvia sat up on her elbow. "Nothing. Except that I typed ninety-seven letters."

"About what, honey?" asked Estelle, using Sylvia's hairbrush.

"Oh, hell, what do you suppose? SnugFare, the shorts that safely support our leaders of Science and Industry."

"Gee, honey, don't sound so cross. I don't know what's wrong with you sometimes. You sound so cross. Ouch! Why don't you get a new brush? This one's just knotted with hair. . . ."

"Mostly yours."

"What did you say?"

"Skip it."

"Oh, I thought you said something. Anyway, like I was saying, I wish you didn't have to go to that office and come home every day feeling cross and out of sorts. Personally, and I said this to Bootsy just last night and he agreed with me one hundred percent, I said, Bootsy, I think Sylvia ought to get married: a girl high-strung like that needs her tensions relaxed. There's no earthly reason why you shouldn't. I mean maybe you're not pretty in the ordinary sense, but you have beautiful eyes, and an intelligent, really sincere look. In fact you're the sort of girl any professional man would be lucky to get. And I should think you would want to. . . Look what a different person I am since I married Henry. Doesn't it make you lonesome seeing how happy we are? I'm here to tell you, honey, that there is nothing like lying in bed at night with a man's arms around you and . . ."

"Estelle! For Christ's sake!" Sylvia sat bolt upright in bed, anger on her cheeks like rouge. But after a moment she bit her lip and lowered her eyelids. "I'm sorry," she said, "I didn't mean to shout. Only I wish you wouldn't talk like that."

"It's all right," said Estelle, smiling in a dumb, puzzled way. Then she went over and gave Sylvia a kiss. "I understand, honey. It's just that you're plain worn out. And I'll bet you haven't had anything to eat either. Come on in the kitchen and I'll scramble you some eggs."

When Estelle set the eggs before her, Sylvia felt quite ashamed; after all, Estelle was trying to be nice; and so then, as though to make it all up, she said: "Something did happen today."

Estelle sat down across from her with a cup of coffee, and Sylvia went on: "I don't know how to tell about it. It's so odd. But—well, I had lunch at the Automat today, and I had to share the table with these three men. I might as well have been invisible because they talked about the most personal things. One of the men said his girl friend was going to have a baby and he didn't know where he was going to get the money to do anything about it. So one of the other men asked him why didn't he sell something. He said he didn't have anything to sell. Whereupon the third man (he was rather delicate and didn't look as if he belonged with the others) said yes, there was something he could sell: *dreams*. Even I laughed, but the man shook his head and said very seriously: no, it was perfectly true, his wife's aunt, Miss Mozart, worked for a rich man who bought dreams, regular night-time dreams—from anybody. And he wrote down the man's name and address and gave it to his friend; but the man simply left it lying on the table. It was too crazy for him, he said."

"Me, too," Estelle put in a little righteously.

"I don't know," said Sylvia, lighting a cigarette. "But I couldn't get it out of my head. The name written on the paper was A. F. Revercomb and the address was on East Seventy-eighth Street. I only glanced at it for a moment, but it was . . . I don't know, I couldn't seem to forget it. It was beginning to give me a headache. So I left the office early . . ."

Slowly and with emphasis, Estelle put down her coffee cup. "Honey, listen, you don't mean you went to see him, this Revercomb nut?"

"I didn't mean to," she said, immediately embarrassed. To try and tell about it she now realized was a mistake. Estelle had no imagination, she would never understand. So her eyes narrowed, the way they always did when she composed a lie. "And, as a matter of fact, I didn't," she said flatly. "I started to; but then I realized how silly it was, and went for a walk instead."

"That was sensible of you," said Estelle as she began stacking dishes in the kitchen sink. "Imagine what might have happened. Buying dreams! Whoever heard! Uh uh, honey, this sure isn't Easton."

Before retiring, Sylvia took a seconal, something she seldom did; but she knew otherwise she would never rest, not with her mind so nimble and somersaulting; then, too, she felt a curious sadness, a sense of loss, as though she'd been the victim of some real or even moral theft, as though, in fact, the boys encountered in the park had snatched (abruptly she switched on the light) her purse. The envelope Miss Mozart had handed her: it was in the purse, and until now she had forgotten it. She tore it open. Inside there was a blue note folded around a bill; on the note there was written: *In payment of one dream,* $5. And now she believed it; it was true, and she had sold Mr. Revercomb a dream. Could it be really so simple as that? She laughed a little as she turned off the light again. If she were to sell a dream only twice a week, think of what she could do: a place somewhere all her own, she thought, deepening toward sleep; ease, like firelight, wavered over her, and there came the moment of twilit lantern slides, deeply deeper. His lips, his arms: telescoped, descending; and distastefully she kicked away the blanket. Were these cold man-arms the arms Estelle had spoken of? Mr. Revercomb's lips brushed her ear as he leaned far into her sleep. Tell me? he whispered.

It was a week before she saw him again, a Sunday afternoon in early December. She'd left the apartment intending to see a movie, but somehow, and as though it had happened without her knowledge, she found herself on Madison Avenue, two blocks from Mr. Revercomb's. It was a cold, silver-skied day, with winds sharp and catching as hollyhock; in store windows icicles of Christmas tinsel twinkled amid mounds of sequined snow: all to Sylvia's distress, for she hated holidays, those times when one is most alone. In one window she saw a spectacle which made her stop still. It was a life-sized, mechanical Santa Claus; slapping his stomach he rocked back and forth in a frenzy of electrical mirth. You could hear beyond the thick glass his squeaky uproarious laughter. The longer she watched the more evil he seemed, until, finally, with a shudder, she turned and made her way into the street of Mr. Revercomb's house. It was, from the outside, an ordinary town house, perhaps a trifle less polished, less imposing than some others, but relatively grand all the same. Winter-withered ivy writhed about the leaded windowpanes and trailed in octopus ropes over the door; at the sides of the door were two small stone lions with blind, chipped eyes. Sylvia took a breath, then rang the bell. Mr. Revercomb's pale and charming Negro recognized her with a courteous smile.

On the previous visit, the parlor in which she had awaited

her audience with Mr. Revercomb had been empty except for herself. This time there were others present, women of several appearances, and an excessively nervous, gnat-eyed young man. Had this group been what it resembled, namely, patients in a doctor's anteroom, he would have seemed either an expectant father or a victim of St. Vitus. Sylvia was seated next to him, and his fidgety eyes unbuttoned her rapidly: whatever he saw apparently intrigued him very little, and Sylvia was grateful when he went back to his twitchy preoccupations. Gradually, though, she became conscious of how interested in her the assemblage seemed; in the dim, doubtful light of the plant-filled room their gazes were more rigid than the chairs upon which they sat; one woman was particularly relentless. Ordinarily, her face would have had a soft commonplace sweetness, but now, watching Sylvia, it was ugly with distrust, jealousy. As though trying to tame some creature which might suddenly spring full-fanged, she sat stroking a flea-bitten neck fur, her stare continuing its assault until the earthquake footstep of Miss Mozart was heard in the hall. Immediately, and like frightened students, the group, separating into their individual identities, came to attention. "You, Mr. Pocker," accused Miss Mozart, "you're next!" and Mr. Pocker, wringing his hands, jittering his eyes, followed after her. In the duskroom the gathering settled again like sun motes.

It began then to rain; melting window reflections quivered on the walls, and Mr. Revercomb's young butler, seeping through the room, stirred a fire in the grate, set tea things upon a table. Sylvia, nearest the fire, felt drowsy with warmth and the noise of rain; her head tilted sideways, she closed her eyes, neither asleep nor really awake. For a long while only the crystal swingings of a clock scratched the polished silence of Mr. Revercomb's house. And then, abruptly, there was an enormous commotion in the hall, capsizing the room into a fury of sound: a bull-deep voice, vulgar as red, roared out: "Stop Oreilly? The ballet butler and who else?" The owner of this voice, a tub-shaped, brick-colored little man, shoved his way to the parlor threshold, where he stood drunkenly seesawing from foot to foot. "Well, well, well," he said, his gin-hoarse voice descending the scale, "and all these ladies before me? But Oreilly is a gentleman, Oreilly waits his turn."

"Not here, he doesn't," said Miss Mozart, stealing up behind him and seizing him sternly by the collar. His face went even redder and his eyes bubbled out: "You're choking me," he gasped, but Miss Mozart, whose green-pale hands were as

strong as oak roots, jerked his tie still tighter, and propelled
him toward the door, which presently slammed with shattering
effect: a tea cup tinkled, and dry dahlia leaves tumbled from
their heights. The lady with the fur slipped an aspirin into her
mouth. "Dis*gusting*," she said, and the others, all except Sylvia,
laughed delicately, admiringly, as Miss Mozart strode past
dusting her hands.

It was raining thick and darkly when Sylvia left Mr. Revercomb's. She looked around the desolate street for a taxi; there
was nothing, however, and no one; yes, someone, the drunk
man who had caused the disturbance. Like a lonely city child, he
was leaning against a parked car and bouncing a rubber ball
up and down. "Lookit, kid," he said to Sylvia, "lookit, I just
found this ball. Do you suppose that means good luck?" Sylvia
smiled at him; for all his bravado, she thought him rather
harmless, and there was a quality in his face, some grinning
sadness suggesting a clown minus make-up. Juggling his ball,
he skipped along after her as she headed toward Madison
Avenue. "I'll bet I made a fool of myself in there," he said.
"When I do things like that I just want to sit down and cry."
Standing so long in the rain seemed to have sobered him con-
siderably. "But she ought not to have choked me that way;
damn, she's too rough. I've known some rough women: my
sister Berenice could brand the wildest bull; but that other one,
she's the roughest of the lot. Mark Oreilly's word, she's going
to end up in the electric chair," he said, and smacked his lips.
"They've got no cause to treat me like that. It's every bit his
fault anyhow. I didn't have an awful lot to begin with, but then
he took it every bit, and now I've got *niente,* kid, *niente.*"

"That's too bad," said Sylvia, though she did not know what
she was being sympathetic about. "Are you a clown, Mr.
Oreilly?"

"Was," he said.

By this time they had reached the avenue, but Sylvia did
not even look for a taxi; she wanted to walk on in the rain
with the man who had been a clown. "When I was a little girl
I only liked clown dolls," she told him. "My room at home was
like a circus."

"I've been other things besides a clown. I have sold insurance, too."

"Oh?" said Sylvia, disappointed. "And what do you do now?"

Oreilly chuckled and threw his ball especially high; after the
catch his head still remained tilted upward. "I watch the sky,"
he said. "There I am with my suitcase traveling through the

blue. It's where you travel when you've got no place else to go. But what do I do on this planet? I have stolen, begged, and sold my dreams—all for purposes of whiskey. A man cannot travel in the blue without a bottle. Which brings us to a point: how'd you take it, baby, if I asked for the loan of a dollar?"

"I'd take it fine," Sylvia replied, and paused, uncertain of what she'd say next. They wandered along so slowly, the stiff rain enclosing them like an insulating pressure; it was as though she were walking with a childhood doll, one grown miraculous and capable; she reached and held his hand: dear clown traveling in the blue. "But I haven't got a dollar. All I've got is seventy cents."

"No hard feelings," said Oreilly. "But honest, is that the kind of money he's paying nowadays?"

Sylvia knew whom he meant. "No, no—as a matter of fact, I didn't sell him a dream." She made no attempt to explain; she didn't understand it herself. Confronting the graying invisibility of Mr. Revercomb (impeccable, exact as a scale, surrounded in a cologne of clinical odors; flat gray eyes planted like seed in the anonymity of his face and sealed within steel-dull lenses) she could not remember a dream, and so she told of two thieves who had chased her through the park and in and out among the swings of a playground. "Stop, he said for me to stop; there are dreams and dreams, he said, but that is not a real one, that is one you are making up. Now how do you suppose he knew that? So I told him another dream; it was about him, of how he held me in the night with balloons rising and moons falling all around. He said he was not interested in dreams concerning himself." Miss Mozart, who transcribed the dreams in shorthand, was told to call the next person. "I don't think I will go back there again," she said.

"You will," said Oreilly. "Look at me, even I go back, and he has long since finished with me, Master Misery."

"Master Misery? Why do you call him that?"

They had reached the corner where the maniacal Santa Claus rocked and bellowed. His laughter echoed in the rainy squeaking street, and a shadow of him swayed in the rainbow lights of the pavement. Oreilly, turning his back upon the Santa Claus, smiled and said: "I call him Master Misery on account of that's who he is. Master Misery. Only maybe you call him something else; anyway, he is the same fellow, and you must've known him. All mothers tell their kids about him: he lives in hollows of trees, he comes down chimneys late at night, he lurks in graveyards and you can hear his step in the attic.

The sonofabitch, he is a thief and a threat: he will take everything you have and end by leaving you nothing, not even a dream. Boo!" he shouted, and laughed louder than Santa Claus. "Now do you know who he is?"

Sylvia nodded. "I know who he is. My family called him something else. But I can't remember what. It was long ago."

"But you remember him?"

"Yes, I remember him."

"Then call him Master Misery," he said, and, bouncing his ball, walked away from her. "Master Misery," his voice trailed to a mere moth of sound, "Mas-ter Mis-er-y . . ."

It was hard to look at Estelle, for she was in front of a window, and the window was filled with windy sun, which hurt Sylvia's eyes, and the glass rattled, which hurt her head. Also, Estelle was lecturing. Her nasal voice sounded as though her throat were a depository of rusty razor blades. "I wish you could see yourself," she was saying. Or was that something she'd said a long while back? Never mind. "I don't know what's happened to you: I'll bet you don't weigh a hundred pounds, I can see every bone and vein, and your hair! You look like a poodle."

Sylvia passed a hand over her forehead. "What time is it, Estelle?"

"It's four," she said, interrupting herself long enough to look at her watch. "But where is your watch?"

"I sold it," said Sylvia, too tired to lie. It did not matter. She had sold so many things, including her beaver coat and gold mesh evening bag.

Estelle shook her head. "I give up, honey, I plain give up. And that was the watch your mother gave you for graduation. It's a shame," she said, and made an old-maid noise with her mouth, "a pity and a shame. I'll never understand why you left us. That is your business, I'm sure; only how could you have left us for this . . . this . . .?"

"Dump," supplied Sylvia, using the word advisedly. It was a furnished room in the East Sixties between Second and Third Avenues. Large enough for a daybed and a splintery old bureau with a mirror like a cataracted eye, it had one window, which looked out on a vast vacant lot (you could hear the tough afternoon voices of desperate running boys) and in the distance, like an exclamation point for the skyline, there was the black smokestack of a factory. This smokestack occurred frequently in her dreams; it never failed to arouse Miss Mozart: "Phallic,

phallic," she would mutter, glancing up from her shorthand. The floor of the room was a garbage pail of books begun but never finished, antique newspapers, even orange hulls, fruit cores, underwear, a spilled powder box.

Estelle kicked her way through this trash, and sat down on the daybed. "Honey, you don't know, but I've been worried crazy. I mean I've got pride and all that and if you don't like me, well o.k.; but you've got no right to stay away like this and not let me hear from you in over a month. So today I said to Bootsy, Bootsy I've got a feeling something terrible has happened to Sylvia. You can imagine how I felt when I called your office and they told me you hadn't worked there for the last four weeks. What happened, were you fired?"

"Yes, I was fired." Sylvia began to sit up. "Please, Estelle— I've got to get ready; I've got an appointment."

"Be still. You're not going anywhere till I know what's wrong. The landlady downstairs told me you were found sleepwalking. . . ."

"What do you mean talking to her? Why are you spying on me?"

Estelle's eyes puckered, as though she were going to cry. She put her hand over Sylvia's and petted it gently. "Tell me, honey, is it because of a man?"

"It's because of a man, yes," said Sylvia, laughter at the edge of her voice.

"You should have come to me before," Estelle sighed. "I know about men. That is nothing for you to be ashamed of. A man can have a way with a woman that kind of makes her forget everything else. If Henry wasn't the fine upstanding potential lawyer that he is, why, I would still love him, and do things for him that before I knew what it was like to be with a man would have seemed shocking and horrible. But honey, this fellow you've mixed up with, he's taking advantage of you."

"It's not that kind of relationship," said Sylvia, getting up and locating a pair of stockings in the furor of her bureau drawers. "It hasn't got anything to do with love. Forget about it. In fact, go home and forget about me altogether."

Estelle looked at her narrowly. "You scare me, Sylvia; you really scare me." Sylvia laughed and went on getting dressed. "Do you remember a long time ago when I said you ought to get married?"

"Uh huh. And now you listen." Sylvia turned around; there was a row of hairpins spaced across her mouth; she extracted them one at a time all the while she talked. "You talk about getting married as though it were the answer absolute; very well, up to a point I agree. Sure, I want to be loved; who the hell doesn't? But even if I was willing to compromise, where is the man I'm going to marry? Believe me, he must've fallen down a manhole. I mean it seriously when I say there are no men in New York—and even if there were, how do you meet them? Every man I ever met here who seemed the slightest bit attractive was either married, too poor to get married, or queer. And anyway, this is no place to fall in love; this is where you ought to come when you want to get over being in love. Sure, I suppose I could marry somebody; but I do not want that? Do I?"

Estelle shrugged. "Then what do you want?"

"More than is coming to me." She poked the last hairpin into place, and smoothed her eyebrows before the mirror. "I have an appointment, Estelle, and it is time for you to go now."

"I can't leave you like this," said Estelle, her hand waving helplessly around the room. "Sylvia, you were my childhood friend."

"That is just the point: we're not children any more; at least, I'm not. No, I want you to go home, and I don't want you to come here again. I just want you to forget about me."

Estelle fluttered at her eyes with a handkerchief, and by the time she reached the door she was weeping quite loudly. Sylvia could not afford remorse: having been mean, there was nothing to be but meaner. "Go on," she said, following Estelle into the hall, "and write home any damn nonsense about me you want to!" Letting out a wail that brought other roomers to their doors, Estelle fled down the stairs.

After this Sylvia went back into her room and sucked a piece of sugar to take the sour taste out of her mouth: it was her grandmother's remedy for bad tempers. Then she got down on her knees and pulled from under the bed a cigar box she kept hidden there. When you opened the box it played a home-made and somewhat disorganized version of "Oh How I Hate to Get up in the Morning." Her brother had made the music-box and given it to her on her fourteenth birthday. Eating the sugar, she'd thought of her grandmother, and hearing the tune she thought of her brother; the rooms of the house where they had lived rotated before her, all dark and she like a light moving among them: up the stairs, down, out and through, spring sweet and lilac shadows in the air and the creaking of a porch swing. All gone, she thought, calling their names, and now I am absolutely alone. The music stopped. But it went on in her head; she could hear it bugling above the child-cries of the vacant lot. And it interfered with her reading. She was reading a little diary-like book she kept inside the box. In this book she wrote down the essentials of her dreams; they were endless now, and it was so hard to remember. Today she would tell Mr. Revercomb about the three blind children. He would like that. The prices he paid varied, and she was sure this was at least a ten-dollar dream. The cigar-box anthem followed her down the stairs and through the streets and she longed for it to go away.

In the store where Santa Claus had been there was a new and equally unnerving exhibit. Even when she was late to Mr. Revercomb's, as now, Sylvia was compelled to pause by the window. A plaster girl with intense glass eyes sat astride a bicycle pedaling at the maddest pace; though its wheel spokes spun hypnotically, the bicycle of course never budged: all that effort and the poor girl going nowhere. It was a pitifully human situation, and one that Sylvia could so exactly identify with herself that she always felt a real pang. The music-box rewound in her head: the tune, her brother, the house, a high-school dance, the house, the tune! Couldn't Mr. Revercomb hear it? His penetrating gaze carried such dull suspicion. But he seemed pleased with her dream, and, when she left, Miss Mozart gave her an envelope containing ten dollars.

"I had a ten-dollar dream," she told Oreilly, and Oreilly, rubbing his hands together, said, "Fine! Fine! But that's just my luck, baby—you should've got here sooner 'cause I went and did a terrible thing. I walked into a liquor store up the street, snatched a quart and ran." Sylvia didn't believe him until he produced from his pinned-together overcoat a bottle of bourbon, already half gone. "You're going to get in trouble some day," she said, "and then what would happen to me? I don't know what I would do without you." Oreilly laughed and poured a shot of the whiskey into a water glass. They were sitting in an all-night cafeteria, a great glaring food depot alive with blue mirrors and raw murals. Although to Sylvia it seemed a sordid place, they met there frequently for dinner; but even if she could have afforded it she did not know where else they could go, for together they presented a curious aspect: a young girl and a doddering, drunken man. Even here people often stared at them; if they stared long enough, Oreilly would stiffen with dignity and say: "Hello, hot lips, I remember you from way back. Still working in the men's room?" But usually they were left to themselves, and sometimes they would sit talking until two and three in the morning.

"It's a good thing the rest of Master Misery's crowd don't know he gave you that ten bucks. One of them would say you stole the dream. I had that happen once. Eaten up, all of 'em, never saw such a bunch of sharks, worse than actors or clowns or businessmen. Crazy, if you think about it: you worry whether you're going to go to sleep, if you're going to have a dream, if you're going to remember the dream. Round and round. So you get a couple of bucks, so you rush to the nearest liquor store—or the nearest sleeping-pill machine. And first thing you know, you're roaming your way up outhouse alley. Why, baby, you know what it's like? It's just like life."

"No, Oreilly, that's what it isn't like. It hasn't anything to do with life. It has more to do with being dead. I feel as though everything were being taken from me, as though some thief were stealing me down to the bone. Oreilly, I tell you I haven't an ambition, and there used to be so much. I don't understand it and I don't know what to do."

He grinned. "And you say it isn't like life? Who understands life and who knows what to do?"

"Be serious," she said. "Be serious and put away that whiskey and eat your soup before it gets stone cold." She lighted a cigarette, and the smoke, smarting her eyes, intensified her frown. "If only I knew what he wanted with those dreams, all typed and filed. What does he do with them? You're right when you say he is Master Misery. . . . He can't be simply some silly quack; it can't be so meaningless as that. But why does he want dreams? Help me, Oreilly, think, think: what does it mean?"

Squinting one eye, Oreilly poured himself another drink; the clownlike twist of his mouth hardened into a line of scholarly straightness. "That is a million-dollar question, kid. Why don't you ask something easy, like how to cure the common cold? Yes, kid, what does it mean? I have thought about it a good deal. I have thought about it in the process of making love to a woman, and I have thought about it in the middle of a poker game." He tossed the drink down his throat and shuddered. "Now a sound can start a dream; the noise of one car passing in the night can drop a hundred sleepers into the deep parts of themselves. It's funny to think of that one car racing through the dark, trailing so many dreams. Sex, a sudden change of light, a pickle, these are little keys that can open up our insides, too. But most dreams begin because there are furies inside of us that blow open all the doors. I don't believe in Jesus Christ, but I do believe in people's souls; and I figure it this way, baby: dreams are the mind of the soul and the secret truth about us. Now Master Misery, maybe he hasn't got a soul, so bit by bit he borrows yours, steals it like he would steal your dolls or the chicken wing off your plate. Hundreds of souls have passed through him and gone into a filing case."

"Oreilly, be serious," she said again, annoyed because she thought he was making more jokes. "And look, your soup is . . ." She stopped abruptly, startled by Oreilly's peculiar expression. He was looking toward the entrance. Three men were there, two policemen and a civilian wearing a clerk's cloth jacket. The clerk was pointing toward their table. Oreilly's eyes circled the room with trapped despair; he sighed then, and leaned back in his seat, ostentatiously pouring himself another drink. "Good evening, gentlemen," he said, when the official party confronted him, "will you join us for a drink?"

"You can't arrest him," cried Sylvia, "you can't arrest a clown!" She threw her ten-dollar bill at them, but the policemen did not pay any attention, and she began to pound the table. All the customers in the place were staring, and the manager came running up, wringing his hands. The police said for Oreilly to get to his feet. "Certainly," Oreilly said, "though I do think it shocking you have to trouble yourselves with such petty crimes as mine when everywhere there are master thieves afoot. For instance, this pretty child," he stepped between the officers and pointed to Sylvia, "she is the recent victim of a major theft: poor baby, she has had her soul stolen."

For two days following Oreilly's arrest Sylvia did not leave her room: sun on the window, then dark. By the third day she had run out of cigarettes, so she ventured as far as the corner delicatessen. She bought a package of cupcakes, a can of sardines, a newspaper and cigarettes. In all this time she'd not eaten and it was a light, delicious, sharpening sensation; but the climb back up the stairs, the relief of closing the door, these so exhausted her she could not quite make the daybed. She slid down to the floor and did not move until it was day again. She thought afterwards that she'd been there about twenty minutes. Turning on the radio as loud as it would go, she dragged a chair up to the window and opened the newspaper on her lap: *Lana Denies, Russia Rejects, Miners Conciliate*: of all things this was saddest, that life goes on: if one leaves one's lover, life should stop for him, and if one disappears from the world, then the world should stop, too; and it never did. And that was the real reason for most people getting up in the morning: not because it would matter but because it wouldn't. But if Mr. Revercomb succeeded finally in collecting all the dreams out of every head, perhaps—the idea slipped, became entangled with radio and newspaper. *Falling Temperatures.* A snowstorm moving across Colorado, across the West, falling upon all the small towns, yellowing every light, filling every footfall, falling now and here; but how quickly it had come, the snowstorm: the roofs, the vacant lot, the distance deep in white and deepening, like sheep. She looked at the paper and she looked at the snow. But it must have been snowing all day. It could not have just started. There was no sound of traffic; in the swirling wastes of the vacant lot children circled a bonfire; a car, buried at the curb, winked its headlights: help, help! silent, like the heart's distress. She crumbled a cupcake and sprinkled it on the windowsill: northbirds would come to keep her company. And she left the window open for them; snow-wind scattered flakes that dissolved on the floor like April-fool jewels. *Presents Life Can Be Beautiful*: turn down that radio! The witch of the woods was tapping at her door: Yes, Mrs. Halloran, she said, and turned off the radio altogether. Snow-quiet, sleep-silent, only the fun-fire faraway songsinging of children; and the room was blue with cold, colder than the cold of fairytales: lie down my heart among the igloo flowers of snow. Mr. Revercomb, why do you wait upon the threshold? Ah, do come inside, it is so cold out there.

But her moment of waking was warm and held. The window was closed, and a man's arms were around her. He was singing to her, his voice gentle but jaunty: *cherryberry, moneyberry, happyberry pie, but the best old pie is a loveberry pie* . . .

"Oreilly, is it—is it really you?"

He squeezed her. "Baby's awake now. And how does she feel?"

"I had thought I was dead," she said, and happiness winged around inside her like a bird lamed but still flying. She tried to hug him and she was too weak. "I love you, Oreilly; you are my only friend and I was so frightened. I thought I would never see you again." She paused, remembering. "But why aren't you in jail?"

Oreilly's face got all tickled and pink. "I was never in jail," he said mysteriously. "But first, let's have something to eat. I brought some things up from the delicatessen this morning."

She had a sudden feeling of floating. "How long have you been here?"

"Since yesterday," he said, fussing around with bundles and paper plates. "You let me in yourself."

"That's impossible. I don't remember it at all."

"I know," he said, leaving it at that. "Here, drink your milk like a good kid and I'll tell you a real wicked story. Oh, it's wild," he promised, slapping his sides gladly and looking more than ever like a clown. "Well, like I said, I never was in jail and this bit of fortune came to me because there I was being hustled down the street by those bindlestiffs when who should I see come swinging along but the gorilla woman: you guessed it, Miss Mozart. Hi, I says to her, off to the barber shop for a shave? It's about time you were put under arrest, she says, and smiles at one of the cops. Do your duty, officer. Oh, I says to her, I'm not under arrest. Me, I'm just on my way to the station house to give them the lowdown on you, you dirty communist. You can imagine what sort of holler she set up then; she grabbed hold of me and the cops grabbed hold of her. Can't say I didn't warn them: careful, boys, I said, she's got hair on her chest. And she sure did lay about her. So I just sort of walked off down the street. Never have believed in standing around watching fist-fights the way people do in this city."

Oreilly stayed with her in the room over the weekend. It was like the most beautiful party Sylvia could remember; she'd never laughed so much, for one thing, and no one, certainly no one in her family, had ever made her feel so loved. Oreilly was a fine cook, and he fixed delicious dishes on the little electric stove; once he scooped snow off the windowsill and made sherbet flavored with strawberry syrup. By Sunday she was strong enough to dance. They turned on the radio and she danced until she fell to her knees, windless and laughing. "I'll never be afraid again," she said. "I hardly know what I was afraid of to begin with."

"The same things you'll be afraid of the next time," Oreilly told her quietly. "That is a quality of Master Misery: no one ever knows what he is—not even children, and they know mostly everything."

Sylvia went to the window; an arctic whiteness lay over the city, but the snow had stopped, and the night sky was as clear as ice: there, riding above the river, she saw the first star of evening. "I see the first star," she said, crossing her fingers.

"And what do you wish when you see the first star?"

"I wish to see another star," she said. "At least that is what I usually wish."

"But tonight?"

She sat down on the floor and leaned her head against his knee. "Tonight I wished that I could have back my dreams."

"Don't we all?" Oreilly said, stroking her hair. "But then what would you do? I mean what would you do if you could have them back?"

Sylvia was silent a moment; when she spoke her eyes were gravely distant. "I would go home," she said slowly. "And that is a terrible decision, for it would mean giving up most of my other dreams. But if Mr. Revercomb would let me have them back, then I would go home tomorrow."

Saying nothing, Oreilly went to the closet and brought back her coat. "But why?" she asked as he helped her on with it. "Never mind," he said, "just do what I tell you. We're going to pay Mr. Revercomb a call, and you're going to ask him to give you back your dreams. It's a chance."

Sylvia balked at the door. "Please, Oreilly, don't make me go. I can't, please, I'm afraid."

"I thought you said you'd never be afraid again."

But once in the street he hurried her so quickly against the wind she did not have time to be frightened. It was Sunday, stores were closed and the traffic lights seemed to wink only for them, for there were no moving cars along the snow-deep avenue. Sylvia even forgot where they were going, and chattered of trivial oddments: right here at this corner is where she'd seen Garbo, and over there, that is where the old woman was run over. Presently, however, she stopped, out of breath and overwhelmed with sudden realization. "I can't, Oreilly," she said, pulling back. "What can I say to him?"

"Make it like a business deal," said Oreilly. "Tell him straight out that you want your dreams, and if he'll give them to you you'll pay back all the money: on the installment plan, naturally. It's simple enough, kid. Why the hell couldn't he give them back? They are all right there in a filing case."

This speech was somehow convincing and, stamping her frozen feet, Sylvia went ahead with a certain courage. "That's the kid," he said. They separated on Third Avenue, Oreilly being of the opinion that Mr. Revercomb's immediate neighborhood was not for the moment precisely safe. He confined himself in a doorway, now and then lighting a match and singing aloud: *but the best old pie is a whiskeyberry pie!* Like a wolf, a long thin dog came padding over the moon-slats under the elevated, and across the street there were the misty shapes of men ganged around a bar: the idea of maybe cadging a drink in there made him groggy.

Just as he had decided on perhaps trying something of the sort, Sylvia appeared. And she was in his arms before he knew that it was really her. "It can't be so bad, sweetheart," he said softly, holding her as best he could. "Don't cry, baby; it's too cold to cry: you'll chap your face." As she strangled for words, her crying evolved into a tremulous, unnatural laugh. The air was filled with the smoke of her laughter. "Do you know what he said?" she gasped. "Do you know what he said when I asked for my dreams?" Her head fell back, and her laughter rose and carried over the street like an abandoned, wildly colored kite. Oreilly had finally to shake her by the shoulders. "He said—I couldn't have them back because—because he'd used them all up."

She was silent then, her face smoothing into an expressionless calm. She put her arm through Oreilly's, and together they moved down the street; but it was as if they were friends pacing a platform, each waiting for the other's train, and when they reached the corner he cleared his throat and said: "I guess I'd better turn off here. It's as likely a spot as any."

Sylvia held on to his sleeve. "But where will you go, Oreilly?"

"Traveling in the blue," he said, trying a smile that didn't work out very well.

She opened her purse. "A man cannot travel in the blue without a bottle," she said, and kissing him on the cheek, slipped five dollars in his pocket.

"Bless you, baby."

It did not matter that it was the last of her money, that now she would have to walk home, and alone. The pilings of snow were like the white waves of a white sea, and she rode upon them, carried by winds and tides of the moon. I do not know what I want, and perhaps I shall never know, but my only wish from every star will always be another star; and truly I am not afraid, she thought. Two boys came out of a bar and stared at her; in some park some long time ago she'd seen two boys and they might be the same. Truly I am not afraid, she thought, hearing their snowy footsteps following her; and anyway, there was nothing left to steal.

Children on Their Birthdays

(This Story is for Andrew Lyndon)

YESTERDAY afternoon the six-o'clock bus ran over Miss Bobbit. I'm not sure what there is to be said about it; after all, she was only ten years old, still I know no one of us in this town will forget her. For one thing, nothing she ever did was ordinary, not from the first time that we saw her, and that was a year ago. Miss Bobbit and her mother, they arrived on that same six-o'clock bus, the one that comes through from Mobile. It happened to be my cousin Billy Bob's birthday, and so most of the children in town were here at our house. We were sprawled on the front porch having tutti-frutti and devil cake when the bus stormed around Deadman's Curve. It was the summer that never rained; rusted dryness coated everything; sometimes when a car passed on the road, raised dust would hang in the still air an hour or more. Aunt El said if they didn't pave the highway soon she was going to move down to the seacoast; but she'd said that for such a long time. Anyway, we were sitting on the porch, tutti-frutti melting on our plates, when suddenly, just as we were wishing that something would happen, something did; for out of the red road dust appeared Miss Bobbit. A wiry little girl in a starched, lemon-colored party dress, she sassed along with a grownup mince, one hand on her hip, the other supporting a spinsterish umbrella. Her

119

mother, lugging two cardboard valises and a wind-up victrola, trailed in the background. She was a gaunt shaggy woman with silent eyes and a hungry smile.

All the children on the porch had grown so still that when a cone of wasps started humming the girls did not set up their usual holler. Their attention was too fixed upon the approach of Miss Bobbit and her mother, who had by now reached the gate. "Begging your pardon," called Miss Bobbit in a voice that was at once silky and childlike, like a pretty piece of ribbon, and immaculately exact, like a movie-star or a schoolmarm, "but might we speak with the grownup persons of the house?" This, of course, meant Aunt El; and, at least to some degree, myself. But Billy Bob and all the other boys, no one of whom was over fourteen, followed down to the gate after us. From their faces you would have thought they'd never seen a girl before. Certainly not like Miss Bobbit. As Aunt El said, whoever heard tell of a child wearing make-up? Tangee gave her lips an orange glow, her hair, rather like a costume wig, was a mass of rosy curls, and her eyes had a knowing penciled tilt; even so, she had a skinny dignity, she was a lady, and, what is more, she looked you in the eye with manlike directness. "I'm Miss Lily Jane Bobbit, Miss Bobbit from Memphis, Tennessee," she said solemnly. The boys looked down at their toes, and, on the porch, Cora McCall, who Billy Bob was courting at the time, led the girls into a fanfare of giggles. *"Country* children," said Miss Bobbit with an understanding smile, and gave her parasol a saucy whirl. "My mother," and this homely woman allowed an abrupt nod to acknowledge herself, "my mother and I have taken rooms here. Would you be so kind as to point out the house? It belongs to a Mrs. Sawyer." Why, sure, said Aunt El, that's Mrs. Sawyer's, right there across the street. The only boarding house around here, it is an old tall dark place with about two dozen lightning rods scattered on the roof: Mrs. Sawyer is scared to death in a thunderstorm.

Coloring like an apple, Billy Bob said, please, ma'am, it being such a hot day and all, wouldn't they rest a spell and have some tutti-frutti? and Aunt El said yes, by all means, but Miss Bobbit shook her head. "Very fattening, tutti-frutti; but *merci* you kindly," and they started across the road, the mother half-dragging her parcels in the dust. Then, and with an earnest expression, Miss Bobbit turned back; the sunflower yellow of her eyes darkened, and she rolled them slightly sideways, as if trying to remember a poem. "My mother has a disorder of the tongue, so it is necessary that I speak for her," she announced rapidly and heaved a sigh. "My mother is a very fine seamstress; she has made dresses for the society of many cities and towns, including Memphis and Tallahassee. No doubt you have noticed and admired the dress I am wearing. Every stitch of it was handsewn by my mother. My mother can copy any pattern, and just recently she won a twenty-five-dollar prize from the *Ladies' Home Journal.* My mother can also crochet, knit and embroider. If you want any kind of sewing done, please come to my mother. Please advise your friends and family. Thank you." And then, with a rustle and a swish, she was gone.

Cora McCall and the girls pulled their hair-ribbons nervously, suspiciously, and looked very put out and prune-faced. I'm *Miss* Bobbit, said Cora, twisting her face into an evil imitation, and I'm Princess Elizabeth, that's who I am, ha, ha, ha. Furthermore, said Cora, that dress was just as tacky as could be; personally, Cora said, all my clothes come from Atlanta; plus a pair of shoes from New York, which is not even to mention my silver turquoise ring all the way from Mexico City, Mexico. Aunt El said they ought not to behave that way about a fellow child, a stranger in the town, but the girls went on like a huddle of witches, and certain boys, the sillier ones that liked to be with the girls, joined in and said things that made Aunt El go red and declare she was going to send them all home and tell their daddies, to boot. But before she could carry forward this threat Miss Bobbit herself intervened by traipsing across the Sawyer porch, costumed in a new and startling manner.

The older boys, like Billy Bob and Preacher Star, who had sat quiet while the girls razzed Miss Bobbit, and who had watched the house into which she'd disappeared with misty, ambitious faces, they now straightened up and ambled down to the gate. Cora McCall sniffed and poked out her lower lip, but the rest of us went and sat on the steps. Miss Bobbit paid us no mind whatever. The Sawyer yard is dark with mulberry trees and it is planted with grass and sweet shrub. Sometimes after a rain you can smell the sweet shrub all the way into our house; and in the center of this yard there is a sundial which Mrs. Sawyer installed in 1912 as a memorial to her Boston bull, Sunny, who died after having lapped up a bucket of paint. Miss Bobbit pranced into the yard toting the victrola, which she put on the sundial; she wound it up, and started a record playing, and it played the Count of Luxembourg. By now it was almost nightfall, a firefly hour, blue as milkglass; and birds like arrows swooped together and swept into the folds of trees. Before storms, leaves and flowers appear to burn with a private light, color, and Miss Bobbit, got up in a little white skirt like a powder-puff and with strips of gold-glittering tinsel ribboning her hair, seemed set against the darkening all around, to contain this illuminated quality. She held her arms arched over her head, her hands lily-limp, and stood straight up on the tips of her toes. She stood that way for a good long while, and Aunt El said it was right smart of her. Then she began to waltz around and around, and around and around she went until Aunt El said, why, she was plain dizzy from the sight. She stopped only when it was time to re-wind the victrola; and when the moon came rolling down the ridge, and the last supper bell had sounded, and all the children had gone home, and the night iris was beginning to bloom, Miss Bobbit was still there in the dark turning like a top.

We did not see her again for some time. Preacher Star came every morning to our house and stayed straight through to supper. Preacher is a rail-thin boy with a butchy shock of red hair; he has eleven brothers and sisters, and even they are afraid of him, for he has a terrible temper, and is famous in these parts for his green-eyed meanness: last fourth of July he whipped Ollie Overton so bad that Ollie's family had to send him to the hospital in Pensacola, and there was another time he bit off half a mule's ear, chewed it and spit it on the ground. Before Billy Bob got his growth, Preacher played the devil with him, too. He used to drop cockleburrs down his collar, and rub pepper in his eyes, and tear up his homework. But now they are the biggest friends in town: talk alike, walk alike; and occasionally they disappear together for whole days, Lord knows where to. But during these days when Miss Bobbit did not appear they stayed close to the house. They would stand around in the yard trying to slingshot sparrows off telephone poles, or sometimes Billy Bob would play his ukulele, and they would sing so loud Uncle Billy Bob, who is Judge for this county, claimed he could hear them all the way to the courthouse: *send me a letter, send it by mail, send it in care of the Birmingham jail.* Miss Bobbit did not hear them; at least she never poked her head out the door. Then one day Mrs. Sawyer, coming over to borrow a cup of sugar, rattled on a good deal about her new boarders. You know, she said, squinting her chicken-bright eyes, the husband was a crook, uh huh, the child told me herself. Hasn't an ounce of shame, not a mite.

Said her daddy was the dearest daddy and the sweetest singing man in the whole of Tennessee. . . . And I said, honey, where is he? and just as offhand as you please she says, Oh, he's in the penitentiary and we don't hear from him no more. Say, now, does that make your blood run cold? Uh huh, and I been thinking, her mama, I been thinking she's some kinda foreigner: never says a word, and sometimes it looks like she don't understand what nobody says to her. And you know, they eat everything *raw. Raw eggs, raw turnips, carrots*—no meat whatsoever. For reasons of health, the child says, but ho! she's been straight out on the bed running a fever since last Tuesday.

That same afternoon Aunt El went out to water her roses, only to discover them gone. These were special roses, ones she'd planned to send to the flower show in Mobile, and so naturally she got a little hysterical. She rang up the Sheriff, and said, listen here, Sheriff, you come over here right fast. I mean somebody's got off with all my Lady Anne's that I've devoted myself to heart and soul since early spring. When the Sheriff's car pulled up outside our house, all the neighbors along the street came out on their porches, and Mrs. Sawyer, layers of cold cream whitening her face, trotted across the road. Oh shoot, she said, very disappointed to find no one had been murdered, oh shoot, she said, nobody's stole them roses. Your Billy Bob brought them roses over and left them for little Bobbit. Aunt El did not say one word. She just marched over to the peach tree, and cut herself a switch. Ohhh, Billy Bob, she stalked along the street calling his name, and then she found him down at Speedy's garage where he and Preacher were watching Speedy take a motor apart. She simply lifted him by the hair and, switching blueblazes, towed him home. But she couldn't make him say he was sorry and she couldn't make him cry. And when she was finished with him he ran into the backyard and climbed high into the tower of a pecan tree and swore he wasn't ever going to come down. Then his daddy came home, and it was time to have supper. His daddy stood at the window and called to him: Son, we aren't mad with you, so come down and eat your supper. But Billy Bob wouldn't budge. Aunt El went and leaned against the tree. She spoke in a voice soft as the gathering light. I'm sorry, son, she said, I didn't mean whipping you so hard like that. I've fixed a nice supper, son, potato salad and boiled ham and deviled eggs. Go away, said Billy Bob, I don't want no supper, and I hate you like all-fire. His daddy said he ought not to talk like that to his mother, and she began to cry. She stood there under the tree and cried, raising the hem of her skirt to dab at her eyes. I don't hate you, son. . . . If I don't love you I wouldn't whip you. The pecan leaves began to rattle; Billy Bob slid slowly to the ground, and Aunt El, brushing her fingers through his hair, pulled him against her. Aw, Ma, he said, Aw, Ma.

After supper Billy Bob came and flung himself on the foot of my bed. He smelled all sour and sweet, the way boys do, and I felt very sorry for him, especially because he looked so worried. His eyes were almost shut with worry. You're s'posed to send sick folks flowers, he said righteously. About this time we heard the victrola, a lilting faraway sound, and a night moth flew through the window, drifting in the air delicate as the music. But it was dark now, and we couldn't tell if Miss Bobbit was dancing. Billy Bob, as though he were in pain, doubled up on the bed like a jackknife; but his face was suddenly clear, his grubby boy-eyes twitching like candles. She's so cute, he whispered, she's the cutest dickens I ever saw, gee, to hell with it, I don't care, I'd pick all the roses in China.

Preacher would have picked all the roses in China, too. He was as crazy about her as Billy Bob. But Miss Bobbit did not notice them. The sole communication we had with her was a note to Aunt El thanking her for the flowers. Day after day she sat on her porch, always dressed to beat the band, and doing a piece of embroidery, or combing curls in her hair, or reading a Webster's dictionary—formal, but friendly enough; if you said good-day to her she said good-day to you. Even so, the boys never could seem to get up the nerve to go over and talk with her, and most of the time she simply looked through them, even when they tomcatted up and down the street trying to get her eye. They wrestled, played Tarzan, did foolheaded bicycle tricks. It was a sorry business. A great many girls in town strolled by the Sawyer house two and three times within an hour just on the chance of getting a look. Some of the girls who did this were: Cora McCall, Mary Murphy Jones, Janice Ackerman. Miss Bobbit did not show any interest in them either. Cora would not speak to Billy Bob any more. The same was true with Janice and Preacher. As a matter of fact, Janice wrote Preacher a letter in red ink on lace-trimmed paper in which she told him he was vile beyond all human beings and words, that she considered their engagement broken, that he could have back the stuffed squirrel he'd given her. Preacher, saying he wanted to act nice, stopped her the next time she passed our house, and said, well, hell, she could keep

that old squirrel if she wanted to. Afterwards, he couldn't
understand why Janice ran away bawling the way she did.

Then one day the boys were being crazier than usual; Billy
Bob was sagging around in his daddy's World War khakis, and
Preacher, stripped to the waist, had a naked woman drawn
on his chest with one of Aunt El's old lipsticks. They looked
like perfect fools, but Miss Bobbit, reclining in a swing, merely
yawned. It was noon, and there was no one passing in the
street, except a colored girl, baby-fat and sugar-plum shaped,
who hummed along carrying a pail of blackberries. But the
boys, teasing at her like gnats, joined hands and wouldn't let
her go by, not until she paid a tariff. I ain't studyin' no tariff,
she said, what kinda tariff you talkin' about, mister? A party in
the barn, said Preacher, between clenched teeth, mighty nice
party in the barn. And she, with a sulky shrug, said, huh, she
intended studyin' no barn parties. Whereupon Billy Bob cap-
sized her berry pail, and when she, with despairing, piglike
shrieks, bent down in futile gestures of rescue, Preacher, who
can be mean as the devil, gave her behind a kick which sent her
sprawling jellylike among the blackberries and the dust. Miss
Bobbit came tearing across the road, her finger wagging like a
metronome; like a schoolteacher she clapped her hands,
stamped her foot, and said: "It is a well-known fact that gentlemen are put on the face of the earth for the protection of
ladies. Do you suppose boys behave this way in towns like
Memphis, New York, London, Hollywood or Paris?" The boys
hung back, and shoved their hands in their pockets. Miss Bobbit helped the colored girl to her feet; she dusted her off, dried
her eyes, held out a handkerchief and told her to blow. "A
pretty pass," she said, "a fine situation when a lady can't walk
safely in the public daylight."

Then the two of them went back and sat on Mrs. Sawyer's
porch; and for the next year they were never far apart, Miss
Bobbit and this baby elephant, whose name was Rosalba Cat.
At first, Mrs. Sawyer raised a fuss about Rosalba being so
much at her house. She told Aunt El that it went against the
grain to have a nigger lolling smack there in plain sight on her
front porch. But Miss Bobbit had a certain magic, whatever
she did she did it with completeness, and so directly, so
solemnly, that there was nothing to do but accept it. For instance, the tradespeople in town used to snicker when they
called her *Miss* Bobbit; but by and by she was Miss Bobbit,
and they gave her stiff little bows as she whirled by spinning

her parasol. Miss Bobbit told everyone that Rosalba was her sister, which caused a good many jokes; but like most of her ideas, it gradually seemed natural, and when we would over- hear them calling each other Sister Rosalba and Sister Bobbit none of us cracked a smile. But Sister Rosalba and Sister Bob- bit did some queer things. There was the business about the dogs. Now there are a great many dogs in this town, rat- terriers, bird-dogs, bloodhounds; they trail along the forlorn noon-hot streets in sleepy herds of six to a dozen, all waiting only for dark and the moon, when straight through the lone- some hours you can hear them howling: someone is dying, someone is dead. Miss Bobbit complained to the Sheriff; she said that certain of the dogs always planted themselves under her window, and that she was a light sleeper to begin with; what is more, and as Sister Rosalba said, she did not believe they were dogs at all, but some kind of devil. Naturally the Sheriff did nothing; and so she took the matter into her own hands. One morning, after an especially loud night, she was seen stalking through the town with Rosalba at her side, Ros- alba carrying a flower basket filled with rocks; whenever they saw a dog they paused while Miss Bobbit scrutinized him. Sometimes she would shake her head, but more often she said, "Yes, that's one of them, Sister Rosalba," and Sister Rosalba, with ferocious aim, would take a rock from her basket and crack the dog between the eyes.

Another thing that happened concerns Mr. Henderson. Mr. Henderson has a back room in the Sawyer house; a tough runt of a man who formerly was a wildcat oil prospector in Oklahoma, he is about seventy years old and, like a lot of old men, obsessed by functions of the body. Also, he is a terrible drunk. One time he had been drunk for two weeks; whenever he heard Miss Bobbit and Sister Rosalba moving around the house, he would charge to the top of the stairs and bellow down to Mrs. Sawyer that there were midgets in the walls trying to get at his supply of toilet paper. They've already stolen fifteen cents' worth, he said. One evening, when the two girls were sitting under a tree in the yard, Mr. Henderson, sporting nothing more than a nightshirt, stamped out after them. Steal all my toilet paper, will you? he hollered, I'll show you midgets. . . . Somebody come help me, else these midget bitches are liable to make off with every sheet in town. It was Billy Bob and Preacher who caught Mr. Henderson and held him until some grown men arrived and began to tie him up. Miss Bobbit, who had behaved with admirable calm, told the

men they did not know how to tie a proper knot, and undertook
to do so herself. She did such a good job that all the circula-
tion stopped in Mr. Henderson's hands and feet and it was a
month before he could walk again.

It was shortly afterwards that Miss Bobbit paid us a call. She
came on Sunday and I was there alone, the family having gone
to church. "The odors of a church are so offensive," she said,
leaning forward and with her hands folded primly before her.
"I don't want you to think I'm a heathen, Mr. C.; I've had
enough experience to know that there is a God and that there
is a Devil. But the way to tame the Devil is not to go down
there to church and listen to what a sinful mean fool he is.
No, love the Devil like you do Jesus: because he is a powerful
man, and will do you a good turn if he knows you trust him.
He has frequently done me good turns, like at dancing school
in Memphis. . . . I always called in the Devil to help me get
the biggest part in our annual show. That is common sense;
you see, I knew Jesus wouldn't have any truck with dancing.
Now, as a matter of fact, I have called in the Devil just recently. He is the only one who can help me get out of this
town. Not that I live here, not exactly. I think always about
somewhere else, somewhere else where everything is dancing,
like people dancing in the streets, and everything is pretty, like
children on their birthdays. My precious papa said I live in the
sky, but if he'd lived more in the sky he'd be rich like he
wanted to be. The trouble with my papa was he did not love
the Devil, he let the Devil love him. But I am very smart in
that respect; I know the next best thing is very often the best.
It was the next best thing for us to move to this town; and
since I can't pursue my career here, the next best thing for me
is to start a little business on the side. Which is what I have
done. I am sole subscription agent in this county for an impressive list of magazines, including *Reader's Digest, Popular
Mechanics, Dime Detectiv*e and *Child's Life*. To be sure, Mr.
C., I'm not here to sell you anything. But I have a thought in
mind. I was thinking those two boys that are always hanging
around here, it occurred to me that they are men, after all.
Do you suppose they would make a pair of likely assistants?"

Billy Bob and Preacher worked hard for Miss Bobbit, and for
Sister Rosalba, too. Sister Rosalba carried a line of cosmetics
called Dewdrop, and it was part of the boys' job to deliver
purchases to her customers. Billy Bob used to be so tired in
the evening he could hardly chew his supper. Aunt El said it
was a shame and a pity, and finally one day when Billy Bob

came down with a touch of sunstroke she said, all right, that settled it, Billy Bob would just have to quit Miss Bobbit. But Billy Bob cursed her out until his daddy had to lock him in his room; whereupon he said he was going to kill himself. Some cook we'd had told him once that if you ate a mess of collards all slopped over with molasses it would kill you sure as shooting; and so that is what he did. I'm dying, he said, rolling back and forth on his bed, I'm dying and nobody cares.

Miss Bobbit came over and told him to hush up. "There's nothing wrong with you, boy," she said. "All you've got is a stomach ache." Then she did something that shocked Aunt El very much: she stripped the covers off Billy Bob and rubbed him down with alcohol from head to toe. When Aunt El told her she did not think that was a nice thing for a little girl to do, Miss Bobbit replied: "I don't know whether it's nice or not, but it's certainly very refreshing." After which Aunt El did all she could to keep Billy Bob from going back to work for her, but his daddy said to leave him alone, they would have to let the boy lead his own life.

Miss Bobbit was very honest about money. She paid Billy Bob and Preacher their exact commission and she never let them treat her, as they often tried to do, at the drugstore or to the picture-show. "You'd better save your money," she told them. "That is, if you want to go to college. Because neither one of you has got the brains to win a scholarship, not even a football scholarship." But it was over money that Billy Bob and Preacher had a big falling out; that was not the real reason, of course: the real reason was that they had grown cross-eyed jealous over Miss Bobbit. So one day, and he had the gall to do this right in front of Billy Bob, Preacher said to Miss Bobbit that she'd better check her accounts carefully because he had more than a suspicion that Billy Bob wasn't turning over to her *all* the money he collected. That's a damned lie, said Billy Bob, and with a clean left hook he knocked Preacher off the Sawyer porch and jumped after him into a bed of nasturtiums. But once Preacher got a hold on him, Billy Bob didn't stand a chance. Preacher even rubbed dirt in his eyes. During all this, Mrs. Sawyer, leaning out an upper-story window, screamed like an eagle, and Sister Rosalba, fatly cheerful, ambiguously shouted, Kill him! Kill him! Kill him! Only Miss Bobbit seemed to know what she was doing. She plugged in the lawn hose, and gave the boys a closeup, blinding bath. Gasping, Preacher staggered to his feet. Oh, honey, he said, shaking himself like a wet dog, honey, you've got to decide. "Decide *what?*" said

Miss Bobbit, right away in a huff. Oh, honey, wheezed Preacher, you don't want us boys killing each other. You got to decide who is your real true sweetheart. "Sweetheart, my eye," said Miss Bobbit. "I should've known better than to get myself involved with a lot of country children. What sort of businessman are you going to make? Now, you listen here, Preacher Star: I don't want a sweetheart, and if I did, it wouldn't be you. As a matter of fact, you don't even get up when a lady enters the room."

Preacher spit on the ground and swaggered over to Billy Bob. Come on, he said, just as though nothing had happened, she's a hard one, she is, she don't want nothing but to make trouble between two good friends. For a moment it looked as if Billy Bob was going to join him in a peaceful togetherness; but suddenly, coming to his senses, he drew back and made a gesture. The boys regarded each other a full minute, all the closeness between them turning an ugly color: you can't hate so much unless you love, too. And Preacher's face showed all of this. But there was nothing for him to do except go away. Oh, yes, Preacher, you looked so lost that day that for the first time I really liked you, so skinny and mean and lost going down the road all by yourself.

They did not make it up, Preacher and Billy Bob; and it was not because they didn't want to, it was only that there did not seem to be any straight way for their friendship to happen again. But they couldn't get rid of this friendship: each was always aware of what the other was up to; and when Preacher found himself a new buddy, Billy Bob moped around for days, picking things up, dropping them again, or doing sudden wild things, like purposely poking his finger in the electric fan. Sometimes in the evenings Preacher would pause by the gate and talk with Aunt El. It was only to torment Billy Bob, I suppose, but he stayed friendly with all of us, and at Christmas time he gave us a huge box of shelled peanuts. He left a present for Billy Bob, too. It turned out to be a book of Sherlock Holmes; and on the flyleaf there was scribbled, "Friends Like Ivy On The Wall Must Fall." That's the corniest thing I ever saw, Billy Bob said. Jesus, what a dope he is! But then, and though it was a cold winter day, he went in the backyard and climbed up into the pecan tree, crouching there all afternoon in the blue December branches.

But most of the time he was happy, because Miss Bobbit was there, and she was always sweet to him now. She and Sister Rosalba treated him like a man; that is to say, they allowed him to do everything for them. On the other hand, they let him win at three-handed bridge, they never questioned his lies, nor discouraged his ambitions. It was a happy while. However, trouble started again when school began. Miss Bobbit refused to go. "It's ridiculous," she said, when one day the principal, Mr. Copland, came around to investigate, "really ridiculous; I can read and write and there are *some* people in this town who have every reason to know that I can count money. No, Mr. Copland, consider for a moment and you will see neither of us has the time nor energy. After all, it would only be a matter of whose spirit broke first, yours or mine. And besides, what is there for you to teach me? Now, if you knew anything about dancing, that would be another matter; but under the circumstances, yes, Mr. Copland, under the circumstances, I suggest we forget the whole thing." Mr. Copland was perfectly willing to. But the rest of the town thought she ought to be whipped. Horace Deasley wrote a piece in the paper which was titled "A Tragic Situation." It was, in his opinion, a tragic situation when a small girl could defy what he, for some reason, termed the Constitution of the United States. The article ended with a question: *Can she get away with it?* She did; and so did Sister Rosalba. Only she was colored, so no one cared. Billy Bob was not as lucky. It was school for him, all right; but he might as well have stayed home for all the good it did him. On his first report card he got three F's, a record of some sort. But he is a smart boy. I guess he just couldn't live through those hours without Miss Bobbit; away from her he always seemed half-asleep. He was always in a fight, too; either his eye was black, or his lip was split, or his walk had a limp. He never talked about these fights, but Miss Bobbit was shrewd enough to guess the reason why. "You are a dear, I know, I know. And I appreciate you, Billy Bob. Only don't fight with people because of me. Of course they say mean things about me. But do you know why that is, Billy Bob? It's a compliment, kind of. Because deep down they think I'm absolutely wonderful."

And she was right: if you are not admired no one will take the trouble to disapprove. But actually we had no idea of how wonderful she was until there appeared the man known as Manny Fox. This happened late in February. The first news we had of Manny Fox was a series of jovial placards posted up in the stores around town: Manny Fox Presents the Fan Dancer Without the Fan; then, in smaller print: Also, Sensational Amateur Program Featuring Your Own Neighbors—

First Prize, A Genuine Hollywood Screen Test. All this was to take place the following Thursday. The tickets were priced at one dollar each, which around here is a lot of money; but it is not often that we get any kind of flesh entertainment, so everybody shelled out their money and made a great to-do over the whole thing. The drugstore cowboys talked dirty all week, mostly about the fan dancer without the fan, who turned out to be Mrs. Manny Fox. They stayed down the highway at the Chucklewood Tourist Camp; but they were in town all day, driving around in an old Packard which had Manny Fox's full name stenciled on all four doors. His wife was a deadpan pimento-tongued redhead with wet lips and moist eyelids; she was quite large actually, but compared to Manny Fox she seemed rather frail, for he was a fat cigar of a man.

They made the pool hall their headquarters, and every afternoon you could find them there, drinking beer and joking with the town loafs. As it developed, Manny Fox's business affairs were not restricted to theatrics. He also ran a kind of employment bureau: slowly he let it be known that for a fee of $150 he could get for any adventurous boys in the county high-class jobs working on fruit ships sailing from New Orleans to South America. The chance of a lifetime, he called it. There are not two boys around here who readily lay their hands on so much as five dollars; nevertheless, a good dozen managed to raise the money. Ada Willingham took all she'd saved to buy an angel tombstone for her husband and gave it to her son, and Acey Trump's papa sold an option on his cotton crop.

But the night of the show! That was a night when all was forgotten: mortgages, and the dishes in the kitchen sink. Aunt El said you'd think we were going to the opera, everybody so dressed up, so pink and sweet-smelling. The Odeon had not been so full since the night they gave away the matched set of sterling silver. Practically everybody had a relative in the show, so there was a lot of nervousness to contend with. Miss Bobbit was the only contestant we knew real well. Billy Bob couldn't sit still; he kept telling us over and over that we mustn't applaud for anybody but Miss Bobbit; Aunt El said that would be very rude, which sent Billy Bob off into a state again; and when his father bought us all bags of popcorn he wouldn't touch his because it would make his hands greasy, and please, another thing, we mustn't be noisy and eat ours while Miss Bobbit was performing. That she was to be a contestant had come as a last-minute surprise. It was logical enough, and there were

signs that should've told us; the fact, for instance, that she had
not set foot outside the Sawyer house in how many days? And
the victrola going half the night, her shadow whirling on the
window-shade, and the secret, stuffed look on Sister Rosalba's
face whenever asked after Sister Bobbit's health. So there was
her name on the program, listed second, in fact, though she did
not appear for a long while. First came Manny Fox, greased
and leering, who told a lot of peculiar jokes, clapping his hands,
ha, ha. Aunt El said if he told another joke like that she was
going to walk straight out: he did, and she didn't. Before Miss
Bobbit came on there were eleven contestants, including Eustacia Bernstein, who imitated movie stars so that they all
sounded like Eustacia, and there was an extraordinary Mr.
Buster Riley, a jug-eared old wool-hat from way in the back
country who played "Waltzing Matilda" on a saw. Up to that
point, he was the hit of the show; not that there was any
marked difference in the various receptions, for everybody applauded generously, everybody, that is, except Preacher Star.
He was sitting two rows ahead of us, greeting each act with a
donkey-loud boo. Aunt El said she was never going to speak to
him again. The only person he ever applauded was Miss Bobbit. No doubt the Devil was on her side, but she deserved it.
Out she came, tossing her hips, her curls, rolling her eyes.
You could tell right away it wasn't going to be one of her
classical numbers. She tapped across the stage, daintily holding
up the sides of a cloud-blue skirt. That's the cutest thing I
ever saw, said Billy Bob, smacking his thigh, and Aunt El had
to agree that Miss Bobbit looked real sweet. When she started
to twirl the whole audience broke into spontaneous applause;
so she did it all over again, hissing, "Faster, faster," at poor Miss
Adelaide, who was at the piano doing her Sunday-school best.
"I was born in China, and raised in Jay-pan . . ." We had never
heard her sing before, and she had a rowdy sandpaper voice.
". . . if you don't like my peaches, stay away from my can,
o-ho o-ho!" Aunt El gasped; she gasped again when Miss Bobbit, with a bump, up-ended her skirt to display blue-lace underwear, thereby collecting most of the whistles the boys had
been saving for the fan dancer without the fan, which was
just as well, as it later turned out, for that lady, to the tune of
"An Apple for the Teacher" and cries of gyp gyp, did her
routine attired in a bathing suit. But showing off her bottom
was not Miss Bobbit's final triumph. Miss Adelaide commenced
an ominous thundering in the darker keys, at which point
Sister Rosalba, carrying a lighted Roman candle, rushed on-

stage and handed it to Miss Bobbit, who was in the midst of a full split; she made it, too, and just as she did the Roman candle burst into fiery balls of red, white and blue, and we all had to stand up because she was singing "The Star Spangled Banner" at the top of her lungs. Aunt El said afterwards that it was one of the most gorgeous things she'd ever seen on the American stage.

Well, she surely did deserve a Hollywood screen test and, inasmuch as she won the contest, it looked as though she were going to get it. Manny Fox said she was: honey, he said, you're real star stuff. Only he skipped town the next day, leaving nothing but hearty promises. Watch the mails, my friends, you'll all be hearing from me. That is what he said to the boys whose money he'd taken, and that is what he said to Miss Bobbit. There are three deliveries daily, and this sizable group gathered at the post office for all of them, a jolly crowd growing gradually joyless. How their hands trembled when a letter slid into their mailbox. A terrible hush came over them as the days passed. They all knew what the other was thinking, but no one could bring himself to say it, not even Miss Bobbit. Postmistress Patterson said it plainly, however: the man's a crook, she said, I knew he was a crook to begin with, and if I have to look at your faces one more day I'll shoot myself.

Finally, at the end of two weeks, it was Miss Bobbit who broke the spell. Her eyes had grown more vacant than anyone had ever supposed they might, but one day, after the last mail was up, all her old sizzle came back. "O.k., boys, it's lynch law now," she said, and proceeded to herd the whole troupe home with her. This was the first meeting of the Manny Fox Hangman's Club, an organization which, in a more social form, endures to this day, though Manny Fox has long since been caught and, so to say, hung. Credit for this went quite properly to Miss Bobbit. Within a week she'd written over three hundred descriptions of Manny Fox and dispatched them to sheriffs throughout the South; she also wrote letters to papers in the larger cities, and these attracted wide attention. As a result, four of the robbed boys were offered good-paying jobs by the United Fruit Company, and late this spring, when Manny Fox was arrested in Uphigh, Arkansas, where he was pulling the same old dodge, Miss Bobbit was presented with a Good Deed Merit award from the Sunbeam Girls of America. For some reason, she made a point of letting the world know that this did not exactly thrill her. "I do not approve of the organization," she said. "All that rowdy bugle blowing. It's neither good-hearted nor truly feminine. And anyway, what is a good deed? Don't let anybody fool you, a good deed is something you do because you want something in return." It would be reassuring to report she was wrong, and that her just reward, when at last it came, was given out of kindness and love. However, this is not the case. About a week ago the boys involved in the swindle all received from Manny Fox checks covering their losses, and Miss Bobbit, with clodhopping determination, stalked into a meeting of the Hangman's Club, which is now an excuse for drinking beer and playing poker every Thursday night. "Look, boys," she said, laying it on the line, "none of you ever thought to see that money again, but now that you have, you ought to invest in something practical—like me." The proposition was that they should pool their money and finance her trip to Hollywood; in return, they would get ten percent of her life's earnings which, after she was a star, and that would not be very long, would make them all rich men. "At least," as she said, "in this part of the country." Not one of the boys wanted to do it: but when Miss Bobbit looked at you, what was there to say?

Since Monday, it has been raining buoyant summer rain shot through with sun, but dark at night and full of sound, full of dripping leaves, watery chimneys, sleepless scuttlings. Billy Bob is wide-awake, dry-eyed, though everything he does is a little frozen and his tongue is as stiff as a bell tongue. It has not been easy for him, Miss Bobbit's going. Because she'd meant more than that. Than what? Than being thirteen years old and crazy in love. She was the queer things in him, like the pecan tree and liking books and caring enough about people to let them hurt him. She was the things he was afraid to show anyone else. And in the dark the music trickled through the rain: won't there be nights when we will hear it just as though it were really there? And afternoons when the shadows will be all at once confused, and she will pass before us, unfurling across the lawn like a pretty piece of ribbon? She laughed to Billy Bob; she held his hand, she even kissed him. "I'm not going to die," she said. "You'll come out there, and we'll climb a mountain, and we'll all live there together, you and me and Sister Rosalba." But Billy Bob knew it would never happen that way, and so when the music came through the dark he would stuff the pillow over his head.

Only there was a strange smile about yesterday, and that was the day she was leaving. Around noon the sun came out, bringing with it into the air all the sweetness of wisteria. Aunt

El's yellow Lady Anne's were blooming again, and she did something wonderful, she told Billy Bob he could pick them and give them to Miss Bobbit for good-bye. All afternoon Miss Bobbit sat on the porch surrounded by people who stopped by to wish her well. She looked as though she were going to Communion, dressed in white and with a white parasol. Sister Rosalba had given her a handkerchief, but she had to borrow it back because she couldn't stop blubbering. Another little girl brought a baked chicken, presumably to be eaten on the bus; the only trouble was she'd forgotten to take out the insides before cooking it. Miss Bobbit's mother said that was all right by her, chicken was chicken, which is memorable because it is the single opinion she ever voiced. There was only one sour note. For hours Preacher Star had been hanging around down at the corner, sometimes standing at the curb tossing a coin, and sometimes hiding behind a tree, as if he didn't want anyone to see him. It made everybody nervous. About twenty minutes before bus time he sauntered up and leaned against our gate. Billy Bob was still in the garden picking roses; by now he had enough for a bonfire, and their smell was as heavy as wind. Preacher stared at him until he lifted his head. As they looked at each other the rain began again, falling fine as sea spray and colored by a rainbow. Without a word, Preacher went over and started helping Billy Bob separate the roses into two giant bouquets: together they carried them to the curb. Across the street there were bumblebees of talk, but when Miss Bobbit saw them, two boys whose flower-masked faces were like yellow moons, she rushed down the steps, her arms outstretched. You could see what was going to happen; and we called out, our voices like lightning in the rain, but Miss Bobbit, running toward those moons of roses, did not seem to hear. That is when the six o'clock bus ran over her.

Shut a Final Door

WALTER, listen to me: if everyone dislikes you, works against you, don't believe they do so arbitrarily; you create these situations for yourself."

Anna had said that, and, though his healthier side told him she intended nothing malicious (if Anna was not a friend, then who was?), he'd despised her for it, had gone around telling everybody how much he despised Anna, what a bitch she was. That woman! he said, don't trust that Anna. This plain-spoken act of hers—nothing but a cover-up for all her repressed hostility; terrible liar, too, can't believe a word she says: dangerous, my God! And naturally all he said went back to Anna, so that when he called about a play-opening they'd planned attending together she told him. "Sorry, Walter, I can't afford you any longer. I understand you very well, and I have a certain amount of sympathy. It's very compulsive, your malice, and you aren't too much to blame, but I don't want ever to see you again because I'm not so well myself that I can afford it." But why? And what had he done? Well, sure, he'd gossiped about her, but it wasn't as though he'd meant it, and after all, as he said to Jimmy Bergman (now there was a two-face if ever there was one), what was the use of having friends if you couldn't discuss them objectively?

He said you said they said we said round and round. Round and round, like the paddle-bladed ceiling-fan wheeling above; turning and turning, stirring stale air ineffectively, it made a watch-tick sound, counted seconds in the silence. Walter inched into a cooler part of the bed and closed his eyes against the dark little room. At seven that evening he'd arrived in New Orleans, at seven-thirty he'd registered in this hotel, an anonymous, sidestreet place. It was August, and it was as though bonfires burned in the red night sky, and the unnatural Southern landscape, observed so assiduously from the train, and which, trying to sublimate all else, he retraced in memory, intensified a feeling of having traveled to the end, the falling off.

But why he was here in this stifling hotel in this faraway town he could not say. There was a window in the room, but he could not seem to get it open, and he was afraid to call the bellboy (what queer eyes that kid had!), and he was afraid to leave the hotel, for what if he got lost? and if he got lost, even a little, then he would be lost altogether. He was hungry; he hadn't eaten since breakfast, so he found some peanut-butter crackers left over from a package he'd bought in Saratoga, and washed them down with a finger of Four Roses, the last. It made him sick. He vomited in the wastebasket, collapsed back on the bed, and cried until the pillow was wet. After a while he just lay there in the hot room, shivering, just lay there and watched the slow-turning fan; there was no beginning to its action, and no end; it was a circle.

An eye, the earth, the rings of a tree, everything is a circle and all circles, Walter said, have a center. It was crazy for Anna to say what had happened was his own doing. If there was anything wrong with him really, then it had been made so by circumstances beyond his control, by, say, his churchly mother, or his father, an insurance official in Hartford, or his older sister, Cecile, who'd married a man forty years her senior. "I just wanted to get out of the house." That was her excuse, and, to tell the truth, Walter had thought it reasonable enough.

But he did not know where to begin thinking about himself, did not know where to find the center. The first telephone call? No, that had been only three days ago and, properly speaking, was the end, not the beginning. Well, he could start with Irving, for Irving was the first person he'd known in New York.

Now Irving was a sweet little Jewish boy with a remarkable talent for chess and not much else: he had silky hair, and pink baby cheeks, and looked about sixteen. Actually he was twenty-three, Walter's age, and they'd met at a bar in the Village. Walter was alone and very lonesome in New York, and so when this sweet little Irving was friendly he decided maybe it would be a good idea to be friendly, too—because you never can tell. Irving knew a great many people, and everyone was very fond of him, and he introduced Walter to all his friends.

And there was Margaret. Margaret was more or less Irving's girl friend. She was only so-so looking (her eyes bulged, there was always a little lipstick on her teeth, she dressed like a child of ten), but she had a hectic brightness which Walter found attractive. He could not understand why she bothered with Irving at all. "Why do you?" he said, on one of the long walks they'd begun taking together in Central Park.

"Irving is sweet," she said, "and he loves me very purely, and who knows: I might just as well marry him."

"A damn fool thing to do," he said. "Irving could never be your husband because he's really your little brother. Irving is everyone's little brother."

Margaret was too bright not to see the truth in this. So one day when Walter asked if he might not make love to her she said, all right, she didn't mind if he did. They made love often after that.

Eventually Irving heard about it, and one Monday there was a nasty scene in, curiously enough, the same bar where they'd met. There had been that evening a party in honor of Kurt Kuhnhardt (Kuhnhardt Advertising), Margaret's boss, and she and Walter had gone together, afterwards stopping by this bar for a nightcap. Except for Irving and a couple of girls in slacks the place was empty. Irving was sitting at the bar, his cheeks quite pink, his eyes rather glazed. He looked like a little boy playing grownup, for his legs were too short to reach the stool's footrest; they dangled doll-like. The instant Margaret recognized him she tried to turn around and walk out, but Walter wouldn't let her. And anyway, Irving had seen them: never taking his eyes from them, he put down his whiskey, slowly climbed off the stool, and, with a kind of sad, ersatz toughness, strutted forward.

"Irving, dear," said Margaret, and stopped, for he'd given her a terrible look.

His chin was trembling. "You go away," he said, and it was as though he were denouncing some childhood tormentor, "I hate you." Then, almost in slow motion, he swung out and, as if he clutched a knife, struck Walter's chest. It was not much of a blow, and when Walter did nothing but smile, Irving slumped against a jukebox, screaming: "Fight me, you damned coward; come on, and I'll kill you, I swear before God I will." So that was how they left him.

Walking home, Margaret began to cry in a soft tired way. "He'll never be sweet again," she said.

And Walter said, "I don't know what you mean."

"Oh, yes, you do," she told him, her voice a whisper. "Yes, you do; the two of us, we've taught him how to hate. Somehow I don't think he ever knew before."

Walter had been in New York now four months. His original capital of five hundred dollars had fallen to fifteen, and Margaret lent him money to pay his January rent at the Brevoort. Why, she wanted to know, didn't he move to some place cheaper? Well, he told her, it was better to have a good address. And what about a job? When was he going to start working? Or was he? Sure, he said, sure, as a matter of fact he thought about it a good deal. But he didn't intend fooling around with just any little jerkwater thing that came along. He wanted something good, something with a future, something in, say, advertising. All right, said Margaret, maybe she could help him; at any rate, she'd speak with her boss, Mr. Kuhnhardt.

2

The K.K.A., so called, was a middle-sized agency, but, as such things go, very good, the best. Kurt Kuhnhardt, who'd founded it in 1925, was a curious man with a curious reputation: a lean, fastidious German, a bachelor, he lived in an elegant black house on Sutton Place, a house interestingly furnished with, among other things, three Picassos, a superb musicbox, South Sea Island masks, and a burly Danish youngster, the houseboy. He invited occasionally some one of his staff in to dinner, whoever was favorite at the moment, for he was continually selecting proteges. It was a dangerous position, these alliances being, as they were, whimsical and uncertain: the protégé found himself checking the want ads when, just the evening previous, he'd dined most enjoyably with his benefactor. During his second week at the K.K.A., Walter, who had been hired as Margaret's assistant, received a memorandum from Mr. Kuhnhardt asking him to lunch, and this, of course, excited him unspeakably.

"Kill-joy?" said Margaret, straightening his tie, plucking lint off his lapel. "Nothing of the sort. It's just that—well, Kuhnhardt's wonderful to work for so long as you don't get too involved—or you're likely not to be working—period."

Walter knew what she was up to; she didn't fool him a minute; he felt like telling her so, too, but restrained himself; it wasn't time yet. One of these days, though, he was going to have to get rid of her, and soon. It was degrading, his working for Margaret. And besides, the tendency from now on would be to keep him down. But nobody could do that, he thought, looking into Mr. Kuhnhardt's sea-blue eyes, nobody could keep Walter down.

"You're an idiot," Margaret told him. "My God, I've seen these little friendships of K. K.'s a dozen times, and they don't mean a damn. He used to palsy-walsy around with the switchboard operator. All K. K. wants is someone to play the fool. Take my word, Walter, there aren't any short cuts: what matters is how you do your job."

He said: "And have you complaints on that score? I'm doing as well as could be expected."

"It depends on what you mean by expected," she said.

One Saturday not long afterwards he made a date to meet her in Grand Central. They were going up to Hartford to spend the afternoon with his family, and for this she'd bought a new dress, new hat, and shoes. But he did not show up. Instead, he drove out on Long Island with Mr. Kuhnhardt, and was the most awed of three hundred guests at Rosa Cooper's debut ball. Rosa Cooper (nee Kuppermann) was heiress to the Cooper Dairy Products: a dark, plump, pleasant child with an unnatural British accent, the result of four years at Miss Jewett's. She wrote a letter to a friend named Anna Stimson, who subsequently showed it to Walter: "Met the divinest man. Danced with him six times, a divine dancer. He is an Advertising Executive, and is terribly divinely good-looking. We have a date—dinner and the theater!"

Margaret did not mention the episode, nor did Walter. It was as though nothing had happened, except that now, unless there was office business to discuss, they never spoke, never saw each other. One afternoon, knowing she would not be at home, he went to her apartment and used a passkey given him long ago; there were things he'd left here, clothes, some books, his pipe; rummaging around collecting all this he discovered a photograph of himself scrawled red with lipstick: it gave him for an instant the sensation of falling in a dream. He also came across the only gift he'd ever made her, a bottle of L'Heure Bleue, still unopened. He sat down on the bed, and, smoking a cigarette, stroked his hand over the cool pillow, remembering the way her head had laid there, remembering, too, how they used to lie here Sunday mornings reading the funnies aloud, Barney Google and Dick Tracy and Joe Palooka.

He looked at the radio, a little green box; they'd always made love to music, any kind, jazz, symphonies, choir programs: it had been their signal, for whenever she'd wanted him, she'd said, "Shall we listen to the radio, darling?" Anyway, it was finished, and he hated her, and that was what he needed to remember. He found the bottle of perfume again, and put it in his pocket: Rosa might like a surprise.

In the office the next day he stopped by the water cooler and Margaret was standing there. She smiled at him fixedly, and said: "Well, I didn't know you were a thief." It was the first overt disclosure of the hostility between them. And suddenly it occurred to Walter he hadn't in all the office a single ally. Kuhnhardt? He could never count on him. And everyone else was an enemy: Jackson, Einstein, Fischer, Porter, Capehart, Ritter, Villa, Byrd. Oh, sure, they were all smart enough not to tell him point-blank, not so long as K. K.'s enthusiasm continued.

Well, dislike was at least positive, and the one thing he could not tolerate was vague relations, possibly because his own feelings were so indecisive, ambiguous. He was never certain whether he liked X or not. He needed X's love, but was incapable of loving. He could never be sincere with X, never tell him more than fifty percent of the truth. On the other hand, it was impossible for him to permit X these same imperfections: somewhere along the line Walter was sure he'd be betrayed. He was afraid of X, terrified. Once in high school he'd plagiarized a poem, and printed it in the school magazine; he could not forget its final line, *All our acts are acts of fear.* And when his teacher caught him, had anything ever seemed to him more unjust?

3

He spent most of the early summer week ends at Rosa Cooper's Long Island place. The house was, as a rule, well staffed with hearty Yale and Princeton undergraduates, which was irritating, for they were the sort of boys who, around Hartford, made green birds fly in his stomach, and seldom allowed him to meet them on their own ground. As for Rosa herself, she was a darling; everyone said so, even Walter.

But darlings are rarely serious, and Rosa was not serious about Walter. He didn't mind too much. He was able on these week ends to make a good many contacts: Taylor Ovington, Joyce Randolph (the starlet), E. L. McEvoy, a dozen or so people whose names cast considerable glare in his address book. One evening he went with Anna Stimson to see a film featuring the Randolph girl, and before they were scarcely seated everyone for aisles around knew she was a Friend of his, knew she drank too much, was immoral, and not nearly so pretty as Hollywood made her out to be. Anna told him he was an adolescent female. "You're a man in only one respect, sweetie," she said.

It was through Rosa that he'd met Anna Stimson. An editor on a fashion magazine, she was almost six feet tall, wore black suits, affected a monocle, a walking cane, and pounds of jingling Mexican silver. She'd been married twice, once to Buck Strong, the horse-opera idol, and she had a child, a fourteen-year-old son who'd had to be put away in what she called a "corrective academy."

"He was a nasty child," she said. "He liked to take potshots out the window with a .22, and throw things, and steal from Woolworth's: awful brat, just like you."

Anna was good to him, though, and in her less depressed, less malevolent moments listened kindly while he groaned out his problems, while he explained why he was the way he was. All his life some cheat had been dealing him the wrong cards. Attributing to Anna every vice but stupidity, he liked to use her as a kind of confessor: there was nothing he could tell her of which she might legitimately disapprove. He would say: "I've told Kuhnhardt a lot of lies about Margaret; I suppose that's pretty rotten, but she would do the same for me; and anyway my idea is not for him to fire her, but maybe transfer her to the Chicago office."

Or, "I was in a bookshop, and a man was standing there and we began talking: a middle-aged man, rather nice, very intelligent. When I went outside he followed, a little ways behind: I crossed the street, he crossed the street, I walked fast, he walked fast. This kept up six or seven blocks, and when I finally figured out what was going on I felt tickled, I felt like kidding him on. So I stopped at the corner and hailed a cab; then I turned around and gave this guy a long, long look, and he came rushing up, all smiles. And I jumped in the cab, and slammed the door and leaned out the window and laughed out loud: the look on his face, it was awful, it was like Christ. I can't forget it. And tell me, Anna, why did I do this crazy thing? It was like paying back all the people who've ever hurt me, but it was something else, too." He would tell Anna these stories, go home and go to sleep. His dreams were clear blue.

Now the problem of love concerned him, mainly because he did not consider it a problem. Nevertheless, he was conscious of being unloved. This knowledge was like an extra heart beating inside him. But there was no one. Anna, perhaps. Did Anna love him? "Oh," said Anna, "when was anything ever what it seemed to be? Now it's a tadpole, now it's a frog. It looks like gold but you put it on your finger and it leaves a green ring. Take my second husband: he looked like a nice guy, and turned out to be just another heel. Look around this very room: why, you couldn't burn incense in that fireplace, and those mirrors, they give space, they tell a lie. Nothing, Walter, is ever what it seems to be. Christmas trees are cellophane, and snow is only soap chips. Flying around inside us is something called the Soul, and when you die you're never dead; yes, and when we're alive we're never alive. And so you want to know if I love you? Don't be dumb, Walter, we're not even friends. . . ."

4

Listen, the fan: turning wheels of whisper: he said you said they said we said round and round fast and slow while time recalled itself in endless chatter. Old broken fan breaking silence: August the third the third the third.

August the third, a Friday, and it was there, right in Winchell's column, his own name: "Big shot Ad exec Walter Ranney and dairy heiress Rosa Cooper are telling intimates to start buying rice." Walter himself had given the item to a friend of a friend of Winchell's. He showed it to the counter boy at the Whelan's where he ate breakfast. "That's me," he said, "I'm the guy," and the look on the boy's face was good for his digestion.

It was late when he reached the office that morning, and as he walked down the aisle of desks a small gratifying flurry among the typists preceded him. No one said anything, however. Around eleven, after a pleasant hour of doing nothing but feel exhilarated, he went to the drugstore downstairs for a cup of coffee. Three men from the office, Jackson, Ritter and Byrd, were there, and when Walter came in Jackson poked Byrd, and Byrd poked Ritter, and all of them turned around.

"Whatcha say, big shot?" said Jackson, a pink man prematurely bald, and the other two laughed. Acting as if he hadn't heard, Walter stepped quickly into a phone booth. "Bastards," he said, pretending to dial a number. And finally, after waiting a long while for them to leave, he made a real call. "Rosa, hello, did I wake you up?"

"No."

"Say, did you see Winchell?"

"Yes."

Walter laughed. "Where do you suppose he gets that stuff?" Silence.

"What's the matter? You sound kind of funny."

"Do I?"

"Are you mad or something?"

"Just disappointed."

"About what?"

Silence. And then: "It was a cheap thing to do, Walter, pretty cheap."

"I don't know what you mean."

"Good-bye, Walter."

On the way out he paid the cashier for a cup of coffee he'd forgotten to have. There was a barbershop in the building. He said he wanted a shave; no—make it a haircut; no—a manicure; and suddenly, seeing himself in the mirror, where his face reflected as pale almost as the barber's bib, he knew he did not know what he wanted. Rosa had been right, he was cheap. He'd always been willing to confess his faults, for, by admitting them, it was as if he made them no longer to exist. He went back upstairs, and sat at his desk, and felt as though he were bleeding inside, and wished very much to believe in God. A pigeon strutted on the ledge outside his window. For some time he watched the shimmering sunlit feathers, the wobbly sedateness of its movements; then, before realizing it, he'd picked up and thrown a glass paperweight: the pigeon climbed calmly upward, the paperweight careened like a giant raindrop: suppose, he thought, listening for a faraway scream, suppose it hits someone, kills them? But there was nothing. Only the ticking fingers of typists, a knocking at the door! "Hey, Ranney, K. K. wants to see you."

"I'm sorry," said Mr. Kuhnhardt, doodling with a gold pen. "And I'll write a letter for you, Walter. Any time."

Now in the elevator the enemy, all submerging with him, crushed Walter between them; Margaret was there wearing a blue hair-ribbon. She looked at him, and her face was different from other faces, not vacant as theirs were, and sterile: here still was compassion. But as she looked at him, she looked through him, too. This is my dream: he must not allow himself to believe otherwise; and yet under his own arm he carried the dream's contradiction, a manila envelope stuffed with all the personals saved from his desk. When the elevator emptied into the lobby, he knew he must speak with Margaret, ask her to forgive him, beg her protection, but she was slipping swiftly toward an exit, losing herself among the enemy. I love you, he said, running after her, I love you, he said, saying nothing.

"Margaret! Margaret!"

She turned around. The blue hair-ribbon matched her eyes, and her eyes, gazing up at him, softened, became rather friendly. Or pitying.

"Please," he said, "I thought we could have a drink together, go over to Benny's, maybe. We used to like Benny's, remember?"

She shook her head. "I've got a date, and I'm late already."

"Oh."

"Yes—well, I'm late" she said, and began to run. He stood watching as she raced down the street, her ribbon streaming, shining in the darkening summer light. And then she was gone.

His apartment, a one-room walk-up near Gramercy Park, needed an airing, a cleaning, but Walter, after pouring a drink, said to hell with it and stretched out on the couch. What was the use? No matter what you did or how hard you tried, it all came finally to zero; everyday everywhere everyone was being cheated, and who was there to blame? It was strange, though; lying here sipping whiskey in the dusk-graying room he felt calmer than he had for God knows how long. It was like the time he'd failed algebra and felt so relieved, so free: failure was definite, a certainty, and there is always peace in certainties. Now he would leave New York, take a vacation trip; he had a few hundred dollars, enough to last until fall.

And, wondering where he should go, he all at once saw, as if a film had commenced running in his head, silk caps, cherry-colored and lemon, and little, wise-faced men wearing exquisite polka-dot shirts. Closing his eyes, he was suddenly five years old, and it was delicious remembering the cheers, the hot dogs, his father's big pair of binoculars. Saratoga! Shadows masked his face in the sinking light. He turned on a lamp, fixed another drink, put a rumba record on the phonograph, and began to dance, the soles of his shoes whispering on the carpet: he'd often thought that with a little training he could've been a professional.

Just as the music ended, the telephone rang. He simply stood there, afraid somehow to answer, and the lamplight, the furniture, everything in the room went quite dead. When at last he thought it had stopped, it commenced again; louder, it seemed, and more insistent. He tripped over a footstool, picked up the receiver, dropped and recovered it, said: "Yes?"

Long-distance: a call from some town in Pennsylvania, the name of which he didn't catch. Following a series of spasmic rattlings, a voice, dry and sexless and altogether unlike any he'd ever heard before, came through: "Hello, Walter."

"Who is this?"

No answer from the other end, only a sound of strong orderly breathing; the connection was so good it seemed as though whoever it was was standing beside him with lips pressed against his ear. "I don't like jokes. Who is this?"

"Oh, you know me, Walter. You've known me a long time." A click, and nothing.

5

It was night and raining when the train reached Saratoga. He'd slept most of the trip, sweating in the hot dampness of the car, and dreamed of an old castle where only old turkeys lived, and dreamed a dream involving his father, Kurt Kuhnhardt, someone no-faced, Margaret and Rosa, Anna Stimson, and a queer fat lady with diamond eyes. He was standing on a long, deserted street; except for an approaching procession of slow, black, funeral-like cars there was no sign of life. Still, he knew, eyes unseen observed his nakedness from every window, and he hailed frantically the first of the limousines; it stopped and a man, his father, invitingly held open the door. Daddy, he yelled, running forward, and the door slammed shut, mashing off his fingers, and his father, with a great belly-laugh, leaned out of the window to toss an enormous wreath of roses. In the second car was Margaret, in the third the lady with the diamond eyes (wasn't this Miss Casey, his old algebra teacher?), in the fourth Mr. Kuhnhardt and a new protégé, the no-faced creature. Each door opened, each closed, all laughed, all threw roses. The procession rolled smoothly away down the silent street. And with a terrible scream Walter fell among the mountain of roses: thorns tore wounds, and a sudden rain, a gray cloudburst, shattered the blooms, and washed pale blood bleeding over the leaves.

By the fixed stare of a woman sitting opposite, he realized at once he'd yelled aloud in his sleep. He smiled at her sheepishly, and she looked away with, he imagined, some embarrassment. She was a cripple; on her left foot she wore a giant shoe. Later, in the Saratoga station, he helped with her luggage, and they shared a taxi; there was no conversation: each sat in his corner looking at the rain, the blurred lights. In New York a few hours before he'd withdrawn from the bank all his savings, locked the door of his apartment, and left no messages; furthermore, there was in this town not a soul who knew him. It was a good feeling.

The hotel was filled: not to mention the racing crowd, there was, the desk clerk told him, a medical convention. No, sorry, he didn't know of a room anywhere. Maybe tomorrow.

So Walter found the bar. As long as he was going to stay up all night he might as well do it drunk. The bar, very large, very hot and noisy, was brilliant with summer-season grotesques: sagging silver-fox ladies, and little stunted jockeys, and pale loud-voiced men wearing cheap fantastic checks. After a couple of drinks, though, the noise seemed faraway. Then, glancing around, he saw the cripple. She was alone at a table where she sat primly sipping crème de menthe. They exchanged a smile. Rising, Walter went to join her. "It's not like we were strangers," she said, as he sat down. "Here for the races, I suppose?"

"No," he said, "just a rest. And you?"

She pursed her lips. "Maybe you noticed I've got a clubfoot. Oh, sure now, don't look surprised: you noticed, everybody does. Well, see," she said, twisting the straw in her glass, "see, my doctor's going to give a talk at this convention, going to talk about me and my foot on account of I'm pretty special. Gee, I'm scared. I mean I'm going to have to show off my foot."

Walter said he was sorry, and she said, oh, there was nothing to be sorry about; after all, she was getting a little vacation out of it, wasn't she? "And I haven't been out of the city in six years. It was six years ago I spent a week at the Bear Mountain Inn." Her cheeks were red, rather mottled, and her eyes, set too closely together, were lavender-colored, intense: they seemed never to blink. She wore a gold band on her wedding finger; play-acting, to be sure: it would not have fooled anybody.

"I'm a domestic," she said, answering a question. "And there's nothing wrong with that. It's honest and I like it. The

people I work for have the cutest kid, Ronnie. I'm better to
him than his mother, and he loves me more; he's told me so.
That one, she stays drunk all the time."

It was depressing to listen to, but Walter, afraid suddenly to
be alone, stayed and drank and talked in the way he'd once
talked to Anna Stimson. Shh! she said at one point, for his
voice had risen too high, and a good many people were staring.
Walter said the hell with them, he didn't care; it was as if his
brain were made of glass, and all the whiskey he'd drunk had
turned into a hammer; he could feel the shattered pieces
rattling in his head, distorting focus, falsifying shape; the cripple, for instance, seemed not one person, but several: Irving,
his mother, a man named Bonaparte, Margaret, all those and
others: more and more he came to understand experience is a
circle of which no moment can be isolated, forgotten.

6

The bar was closing. They went Dutch on the check and,
while waiting for change, neither spoke. Watching him with
her unblinking lavender eyes, she seemed quite controlled, but
there was going on inside, he could tell, some subtle agitation.
When the waiter returned they divided the change, and she
said: "If you want to, you can come to my room." A rash-
like blush covered her face. "I mean, you said you didn't have
any place to sleep . . ." Walter reached out and took her
hand: the smile she gave him was touchingly shy.

Reeking with dime-store perfume, she came out of the bathroom wearing only a sleazy flesh-colored kimono, and the mon-
strous black shoe. It was then that he realized he could never
go through with it. And he'd never felt so sorry for himself:
not even Anna Stimson would ever have forgiven him this.
"Don't look," she said, and there was a trembling in her voice,
"I'm funny about anybody seeing my foot."

He turned to the window, where pressing elm leaves rustled
in the rain, and lightning, too far off for sound, winked whitely.
"All right," she said. Walter did not move.

"All right," she repeated anxiously. "Shall I put out the
light? I mean, maybe you like to get ready—in the dark."

He came to the edge of the bed, and, bending down, kissed
her cheek. "I think you're so very sweet, but . . ."

The telephone interrupted. She looked at him dumbly.
"Jesus God," she said, and covered the mouthpiece with her
hand, "it's long-distance! I'll bet it's about Ronnie! I'll bet he's

sick, or—hello—what?—Ranney? Gee, no. You've got the wrong . . ."

"Wait," said Walter, taking the receiver. "This is me, this is Walter Ranney."

"Hello, Walter."

The voice, dull and sexless and remote, went straight to the pit of his stomach. The room seemed to seesaw, to buckle. A mustache of sweat sprouted on his upper lip. "Who is this?" he said so slowly the words did not connect coherently.

"Oh, you know me, Walter. You've known me a long time." Then silence: whoever it was had hung up.

"Gee," said the woman, "now how do you suppose they knew you were in my room? I mean—say, was it bad news? You look kind of . . ."

Walter fell across her, clutching her to him, pressing his wet cheek against hers. "Hold me," he said, discovering he could still cry. "Hold me, please."

"Poor little boy," she said, patting his back. "My poor little boy: we're awfully alone in this world, aren't we?" And presently he went to sleep in her arms.

But he had not slept since, nor could he now, not even listening to the lazy lull of the fan; in its turning he could hear train wheels: Saratoga to New York, New York to New Orleans. And New Orleans he'd chosen for no special reason, except that it was a town of strangers, and a long way off. Four spinning fan blades, wheels and voices, round and round; and after all, as he saw it now, there was to this network of malice no ending, none whatever.

Water flushed down wall pipes, steps passed overhead, keys jangled in the hall, a news commentator rumbled somewhere beyond, next door a little girl said, why? Why? WHY? Yet in the room there was a sense of silence. His feet shining in the transom-light looked like amputated stone: the gleaming toe-nails were ten small mirrors, all reflecting greenly. Sitting up, he rubbed sweat off with a towel; now more than anything the heat frightened him, for it made him know tangibly his own helplessness. He threw the towel across the room, where, landing on a lampshade, it swung back and forth. At this moment the telephone rang. And rang. And it was ringing so loud he was sure all the hotel could hear. An army would be pounding at his door. So he pushed his face into the pillow, covered his ears with his hands, and thought: think of nothing things, think of wind.

Jug of Silver

AFTER school I used to work in the Valhalla drugstore. It was owned by my uncle, Mr. Ed Marshall. I call him Mr. Marshall because everybody, including his wife, called him Mr. Marshall. Nevertheless he was a nice man.

This drugstore was maybe old-fashioned, but it was large and dark and cool: during summer months there was no pleasanter place in town. At the left, as you entered, was a tobacco-magazine counter behind which, as a rule, sat Mr. Marshall: a squat, square-faced, pinkfleshed man with looping, manly, white mustaches. Beyond this counter stood the beautiful soda fountain. It was very antique and made of fine, yellowed marble, smooth to the touch but without a trace of cheap glaze. Mr. Marshall bought it at an auction in New Orleans in 1910 and was plainly proud of it. When you sat on the high, delicate stools and looked across the fountain you could see yourself reflected softly, as though by candlelight, in a row of ancient, mahogany-framed mirrors. All general merchandise was displayed in glass-doored, curio-like cabinets that were locked with brass keys. There was always in the air the smell of syrup and nutmeg and other delicacies.

The Valhalla was the gathering place of Wachata County till a certain Rufus McPherson came to town and opened a second drugstore directly across the courthouse square. This old Rufus McPherson was a villain; that is, he took away my uncle's trade. He installed fancy equipment such as electric fans and colored lights; he provided curb service and made grilled-cheese sandwiches to order. Naturally, though some remained devoted to Mr. Marshall, most folks couldn't resist Rufus McPherson.

For a while, Mr. Marshall chose to ignore him: if you were to mention McPherson's name he would sort of snort, finger his mustaches and look the other way. But you could tell he was mad. And getting madder. Then one day toward the middle of October I strolled into the Valhalla to find him sitting at the fountain playing dominoes and drinking wine with Hamurabi.

Hamurabi was an Egyptian and some kind of dentist, though he didn't do much business as the people here-abouts have unusually strong teeth, due to an element in the water. He spent a great deal of his time loafing around the Valhalla and was my uncle's chief buddy. He was a handsome figure of a man, this Hamurabi, being dark-skinned and nearly seven feet tall; the matrons of the town kept their daughters under lock and key and gave him the eye themselves. He had no foreign accent whatsoever, and it was always my opinion that he wasn't any more Egyptian than the man in the moon.

Anyway, there they were swigging red Italian wine from a gallon jug. It was a troubling sight, for Mr. Marshall was a renowned teetotaler. So naturally, I thought: Oh, golly, Rufus McPherson has finally got his goat. That was not the case, however.

"Here, son," said Mr. Marshall, "come have a glass of wine."

"Sure," said Hamurabi, "help us finish it up. It's storebought, so we can't waste it."

Much later, when the jug was dry, Mr. Marshall picked it up and said, "Now we shall see!" And with that disappeared out into the afternoon.

"Where's he off to?" I asked.

"Ah," was all Hamurabi would say. He liked to devil me.

A half-hour passed before my uncle returned. He was stooped and grunting under the load he carried. He set the jug atop the fountain and stepped back, smiling and rubbing his hands together. "Well, what do you think?"

"Ah," purred Hamurabi.

"Gee . . ." I said.

It was the same wine jug, God knows, but there was a

wonderful difference; for now it was crammed to the brim
with nickels and dimes that shone dully through the thick glass.

"Pretty, eh?" said my uncle. "Had it done over at the First
National. Couldn't get in anything bigger-sized than a nickel.
Still, there's lotsa money in there, let me tell you."

"But what's the point, Mr. Marshall?" I said. "I mean, what's
the idea?"

Mr. Marshall's smile deepened to a grin. "This here's a jug
of silver, you might say. . . ."

"The pot at the end of the rainbow," interrupted Hamurabi.

". . . and the idea, as you call it, is for folks to guess how
much money is in there. For instance, say you buy a quarter's
worth of stuff—well, then you get to take a chance. The more
you buy, the more chances you get. And I'll keep all guesses
in a ledger till Christmas Eve, at which time whoever comes
closest to the right amount will get the whole shebang."

Hamurabi nodded solemnly. "He's playing Santa Claus—a
mighty crafty Santa Claus," he said. "I'm going home and
write a book: *The Skillful Murder of Rufus McPherson.*" To
tell the truth, he sometimes did write stories and send them
out to the magazines. They always came back.

It was surprising, really like a miracle, how Wachata County
took to the jug. Why, the Valhalla hadn't done so much business since Station Master Tully, poor soul, went stark raving
mad and claimed to have discovered oil back of the depot,
causing the town to be overrun with wildcat prospectors. Even
the poolhall bums who never spent a cent on anything not
connected with whiskey or women took to investing their
spare cash in milk shakes. A few elderly ladies publicly dis-
approved of Mr. Marshall's enterprise as a kind of gambling,
but they didn't start any trouble and some even found occasion to visit us and hazard a guess. The school kids were
crazy about the whole thing, and I was very popular because
they figured I knew the answer.

"I'll tell you why all this is," said Hamurabi, lighting one of
the Egyptian cigarettes he bought by mail from a concern in
New York City. "It's not for the reason you may imagine;
not, in other words, avidity. No. It's the mystery that's enchanting. Now you look at those nickels and dimes and what
do you think: ah, so much! No, no. You think: ah, *how* much?
And that's a profound question, indeed. It can mean different
things to different people. Understand?"

And oh, was Rufus McPherson wild! When you're in trade,

you count on Christmas to make up a large share of your yearly profit, and he was hard pressed to find a customer. So he tried to imitate the jug; but being such a stingy man he filled his with pennies. He also wrote a letter to the editor of *The Banner*, our weekly paper, in which he said that Mr. Marshall ought to be "tarred and feathered and strung up for turning innocent little children into confirmed gamblers and sending them down the path to Hell!" You can imagine what kind of laughing stock he was. Nobody had anything for McPherson but scorn. And so by the middle of November he just stood on the sidewalk outside his store and gazed bitterly at the festivities across the square.

At about this time Appleseed and sister made their first appearance.

He was a stranger in town. At least no one could recall ever having seen him before. He said he lived on a farm a mile past Indian Branches; told us his mother weighed only seventy-four pounds and that he had an older brother who would play the fiddle at anybody's wedding for fifty cents. He claimed that Appleseed was the only name he had and that he was twelve years old. But his sister, Middy, said he was eight. His hair was straight and dark yellow. He had a tight, weather-tanned little face with anxious green eyes that had a very wise and knowing look. He was small and puny and high-strung; and he wore always the same outfit: a red sweater, blue denim britches and a pair of man-sized boots that went clop-clop with every step.

It was raining that first time he came into the Valhalla; his hair was plastered round his head like a cap and his boots were caked with red mud from the country roads. Middy trailed behind as he swaggered like a cowboy up to the fountain where I was wiping some glasses.

"I hear you folks got a bottle fulla money you fixin' to give 'way," he said, looking me square in the eye. "Seein' as you-all are givin' it away, we'd be obliged iffen you'd give it to us. Name's Appleseed, and this here's my sister, Middy."

Middy was a sad, sad-looking kid. She was a good bit taller and older-looking than her brother: a regular bean pole. She had tow-colored hair that was chopped short, and a pale pitiful little face. She wore a faded cotton dress that came way up above her bony knees. There was something wrong with her teeth, and she tried to conceal this by keeping her lips primly pursed like an old lady.

"Sorry," I said, "but you'll have to talk with Mr. Marshall."

So sure enough he did. I could hear my uncle explaining what he would have to do to win the jug. Appleseed listened attentively, nodding now and then. Presently he came back and stood in front of the jug and, touching it lightly with his hand, said, "Ain't it a pretty thing, Middy?"

Middy said, "Is they gonna give it to us?"

"Naw. What you gotta do, you gotta guess how much money's inside there. And you gotta buy two bits' worth so's even to get a chance."

"Huh, we ain't got no two bits. Where you 'spec we gonna get us two bits?"

Appleseed frowned and rubbed his chin. "That'll be the easy part, just leave it to me. The only worrisome thing is: I can't just take a chance and guess. . . . I gotta *know*."

Well, a few days later they showed up again. Appleseed perched on a stool at the fountain and boldly asked for two glasses of water, one for him and one for Middy. It was on this occasion that he gave out the information about his family: ". . . then there's Papa Daddy, that's my mama's papa, who's a Cajun, an' on accounta that he don't speak English good. My brother, the one what plays the fiddle, he's been in jail three times. . . . It's on accounta him we had to pick up and leave Louisiana. He cut a fella bad in a razor fight over a woman ten years older'n him. She had yellow hair."

Middy, lingering in the background, said nervously, "You oughtn't to be tellin' our personal private fam'ly business thataway, Appleseed."

"Hush now, Middy," he said, and she hushed. "She's a good little gal," he added, turning to pat her head, "but you can't let her get away with much. You go look at the picture books, honey, and stop frettin' with your teeth. Appleseed here's got some figurin' to do."

This figuring meant staring hard at the jug, as if his eyes were trying to eat it up. With his chin cupped in his hand, he studied it for a long period, not batting his eyelids once. "A lady in Louisiana told me I could see things other folks couldn't see 'cause I was born with a caul on my head."

"It's a cinch you aren't going to see how much there is," I told him. "Why don't you just let a number pop into your head, and maybe that'll be the right one."

"Uh, uh," he said, "too darn risky. Me, I can't take no sucha chance. Now, the way I got it figured, there ain't but one sure-fire thing and that's to count every nickel and dime."

"Count!"

"Count what?" asked Hamurabi, who had just moseyed inside and was settling himself at the fountain.

"This kid says he's going to count how much is in the jug," I explained.

Hamurabi looked at Appleseed with interest. "How do you plan to do that, son?"

"Oh, by countin'," said Appleseed matter-of-factly.

Hamurabi laughed. "You better have X-ray eyes, son, that's all I can say."

"Oh, no. All you gotta do is be born with a caul on your head. A lady in Louisiana told me so. She was a witch; she loved me and when my ma wouldn't give me to her she put a hex on her and now my ma don't weigh but seventy-four pounds."

"Ve-ry in-ter-esting," was Hamurabi's comment as he gave Appleseed a queer glance.

Middy sauntered up, clutching a copy of *Screen Secrets*. She pointed out a certain photo to Appleseed and said: "Ain't she the nicest-lookin' lady? Now you see, Appleseed, you see how pretty her teeth are? Not a one outa joint."

"Well, don't you fret none," he said.

After they left Hamurabi ordered a bottle of orange Nehi and drank it slowly, while smoking a cigarette. "Do you think maybe that kid's o.k. upstairs?" he asked presently in a puzzled voice.

Small towns are best for spending Christmas, I think. They catch the mood quicker and change and come alive under its spell. By the first week in December house doors were decorated with wreaths, and store windows were flashy with red paper bells and snowflakes of glittering isinglass. The kids hiked out into the woods and came back dragging spicy evergreen trees. Already the women were busy baking fruit cakes, unsealing jars of mincemeat and opening bottles of blackberry and scuppernong wine. In the courthouse square a huge tree was trimmed with silver tinsel and colored electric bulbs that were lighted up at sunset. Late of an afternoon you could hear the choir in the Presbyterian church practicing carols for their annual pageant. All over town the japonicas were in full bloom.

The only person who appeared not the least touched by this heartwarming atmosphere was Appleseed. He went about his declared business of counting the jug-money with great, persistent care. Every day now he came to the Valhalla and concentrated on the jug, scowling and mumbling to himself. At first we were all fascinated, but after a while, it got tiresome and nobody paid him any mind whatsoever. He never bought anything, apparently having never been able to raise the two bits. Sometimes he'd talk to Hamurabi, who had taken a tender interest in him and occasionally stood treat to a jawbreaker or a penny's worth of licorice.

"Do you still think he's nuts?" I asked.

"I'm not so sure," said Hamurabi. "But I'll let you know. He doesn't eat enough. I'm going to take him over to the Rainbow Café and buy him a plate of barbecue."

"He'd appreciate it more if you'd give him a quarter."

"No. A dish of barbecue is what he needs. Besides, it would be better if he never was to make a guess. A high-strung kid like that, so unusual, I wouldn't want to be the one responsible if he lost. Say, it would be pitiful."

I'll admit that at the time Appleseed struck me as being just funny. Mr. Marshall felt sorry for him, and the kids tried to tease him, but had to give it up when he refused to respond. There you could see him plain as day sitting at the fountain with his forehead puckered and his eyes fixed forever on that jug. Yet he was so withdrawn you sometimes had this awful creepy feeling that, well, maybe he didn't exist. And when you were pretty much convinced of this he'd wake up and say something like, "You know, I hope a 1913 buffalo nickel's in there. A fella was tellin' me he saw where a 1913 buffalo nickel's worth fifty dollars." Or, "Middy's gonna be a big lady in the picture shows. They make lotsa money, the ladies in the picture shows do, and then we ain't gonna never eat another collard green as long as we live. Only Middy says she can't be in the picture shows 'less her teeth look good."

Middy didn't always tag along with her brother. On those occasions when she didn't come, Appleseed wasn't himself; he acted shy and left soon.

Hamurabi kept his promise and stood treat to a dish of barbecue at the café. "Mr. Hamurabi's nice, all right," said Appleseed afterward, "but he's got peculiar notions: has a notion that if he lived in this place named Egypt he'd be a king or somethin'."

And Hamurabi said, "That kid has the most touching faith. It's a beautiful thing to see. But I'm beginning to despise the whole business." He gestured toward the jug. "Hope of this kind is a cruel thing to give anybody, and I'm damned sorry I was ever a party to it."

Around the Valhalla the most popular pastime was deciding what you would buy if you won the jug. Among those who participated were: Solomon Katz, Phoebe Jones, Carl Kuhnhardt, Puly Simmons, Addie Foxcroft, Marvin Finkle, Trudy Edwards and a colored man named Erskine Washington. And these were some of their answers: a trip to and a permanent wave in Birmingham, a second-hand piano, a Shetland pony, a gold bracelet, a set of *Rover Boys* books and a life insurance policy.

Once Mr. Marshall asked Appleseed what he would get. "It's a secret," was the reply, and no amount of prying could make him tell. We took it for granted that whatever it was, he wanted it real bad.

Honest winter, as a rule, doesn't settle on our part of the country till late January, and then is mild, lasting only a short time. But in the year of which I write we were blessed with a singular cold spell the week before Christmas. Some still talk of it, for it was so terrible: water pipes froze solid; many folks had to spend the days in bed snuggled under their quilts, having neglected to lay in enough kindling for the fireplace; the sky turned that strange dull gray as it does just before a storm, and the sun was pale as a waning moon. There was a sharp wind: the old dried-up leaves of last fall fell on the icy ground, and the evergreen tree in the courthouse square was twice stripped of its Christmas finery. When you breathed, your breath made smoky clouds. Down by the silk mill where the very poor people lived, the families huddled together in the dark at night and told tales to keep their minds off the cold. Out in the country the farmers covered their delicate plants with gunny sacks and prayed; some took advantage of the weather to slaughter their hogs and bring the fresh sausage to town. Mr. R. C. Judkins, our town drunk, outfitted himself in a red cheesecloth suit and played Santa Claus at the five 'n' dime. Mr. R. C. Judkins was the father of a big family, so everybody was happy to see him sober enough to earn a dollar. There were several church socials, at one of which Mr. Marshall came face to face with Rufus McPherson: bitter words were passed but not a blow was struck.

Now, as has been mentioned, Appleseed lived on a farm a mile below Indian Branches; this would be approximately three miles from town; a mighty long and lonesome walk. Still, despite the cold, he came every day to the Valhalla and stayed till closing time which, as the days had grown short, was after nightfall. Once in a while he'd catch a ride partway home with the foreman from the silk mill, but not often. He looked tired, and there were worry lines about his mouth. He was always cold and shivered a lot. I don't think he wore any warm drawers underneath his red sweater and blue britches.

It was three days before Christmas when out of the clear sky, he announced: "Well, I'm finished. I mean I know how much is in the bottle." He claimed this with such grave, solemn sureness it was hard to doubt him.

"Why, say now, son, hold on," said Hamurabi, who was present. "You can't know anything of the sort. It's wrong to think so: you're just heading to get yourself hurt."

"You don't need to preach to me, Mr. Hamurabi. I know what I'm up to. A lady in Louisiana, she told me . . ."

"Yes yes yes—but you got to forget that. If it were me, I'd go home and stay put and forget about this god-damned jug."

"My brother's gonna play the fiddle at a wedding over in Cherokee City tonight and he's gonna give me the two bits," said Appleseed stubbornly. "Tomorrow I'll take my chance."

So the next day I felt kind of excited when Appleseed and Middy arrived. Sure enough, he had his quarter: it was tied for safekeeping in the corner of a red bandanna.

The two of them wandered hand in hand among the showcases, holding a whispery consultation as to what to purchase. They decided finally on a thimble-sized bottle of gardenia cologne which Middy promptly opened and partly emptied on her hair. "I smells like . . . Oh, darlin' Mary, I ain't never smelled nothin' as sweet. Here, Appleseed, honey, let me douse some on your hair." But he wouldn't let her.

Mr. Marshall got out the ledger in which he kept his records, while Appleseed strolled over to the fountain and cupped the jug between his hands, stroking it gently. His eyes were bright and his cheeks flushed from excitement. Several persons who were in the drugstore at that moment crowded close. Middy stood in the background quietly scratching her leg and smelling the cologne. Hamurabi wasn't there.

Mr. Marshall licked the point of his pencil and smiled. "Okay, son, what do you say?"

Appleseed took a deep breath. "Seventy-seven dollars and thirty-five cents," he blurted.

In picking such an uneven sum he showed originality, for the run-of-the-mill guess was a plain round figure. Mr. Marshall repeated the amount solemnly as he copied it down.

"When'll I know if I won?"

"Christmas Eve," someone said.

"That's tomorrow, huh?"

"Why, so it is," said Mr. Marshall, not surprised. "Come at four o'clock."

During the night the thermometer dropped even lower, and toward dawn there was one of those swift, summerlike rainstorms, so that the following day was bright and frozen. The town was like a picture postcard of a Northern scene, what with icicles sparkling whitely on the trees and frost flowers coating all windowpanes. Mr. R. C. Judkins rose early and, for no clear reason, tramped the streets ringing a supper bell, stopping now and then to take a swig of whiskey from a pint which he kept in his hip pocket. As the day was windless, smoke climbed lazily from various chimneys straightway to the still, frozen sky. By mid-morning the Presbyterian choir was in full swing; and the town kids (wearing horror masks, as at Hallowe'en) were chasing one another round and round the square, kicking up an awful fuss.

Hamurabi dropped by at noon to help us fix up the Valhalla. He brought along a fat sack of Satsumas, and together we ate every last one, tossing the hulls into a newly installed potbellied stove (a present from Mr. Marshall to himself) which stood in the middle of the room. Then my uncle took the jug off the fountain, polished and placed it on a prominently situated table. He was no help after that whatsoever, for he squatted in a chair and spent his time tying and retying a tacky green ribbon around the jug. So Hamurabi and I had the rest to do alone: we swept the floor and washed the mirrors and dusted the cabinets and strung streamers of red and green crepe paper from wall to wall. When we were finished it looked very fine and elegant.

But Hamurabi gazed sadly at our work, and said: "Well, I think I better be getting along now."

"Aren't you going to stay?" asked Mr. Marshall, shocked.

"No, oh, no," said Hamurabi, shaking his head slowly. "I don't want to see that kid's face. This is Christmas and I mean to have a rip-roaring time. And I couldn't, not with something like that on my conscience. Hell, I wouldn't sleep."

"Suit yourself," said Mr. Marshall. And he shrugged, but you could see he was really hurt. "Life's like that—and besides, who knows, he might win."

Hamurabi sighed gloomily. "What's his guess?"

"Seventy-seven dollars and thirty-five cents," I said.

"Now I ask you, isn't that fantastic?" said Hamurabi. He slumped in a chair next to Mr. Marshall and crossed his legs and lit a cigarette. "If you got any Baby Ruths I think I'd like one; my mouth tastes sour."

As the afternoon wore on, the three of us sat around the table feeling terribly blue. No one said hardly a word and, as the kids had deserted the square, the only sound was the clock tolling the hour in the courthouse steeple. The Valhalla was closed to business, but people kept passing by and peeking in the window. At three o'clock Mr. Marshall told me to unlock the door.

Within twenty minutes the place was jam full; everyone was wearing his Sunday best, and the air smelled sweet, for most of the little silk-mill girls had scented themselves with vanilla flavoring. They scrunched up against the walls, perched on the fountain, squeezed in wherever they could; soon the crowd had spread to the sidewalk and stretched into the road. The square was lined with team-drawn wagons and Model T Fords that had carted farmers and their families into town. There was much laughter and shouting and joking—several outraged ladies complained of the cursing and the rough, shoving ways of the younger men, but nobody left. At the side entrance a gang of colored folks had formed and were having the most fun of all. Everybody was making the best of a good thing. It's usually so quiet around here: nothing much ever happens. It's safe to say that nearly all of Wachata County was present, but invalids and Rufus McPherson. I looked around for Appleseed but didn't see him anywhere.

Mr. Marshall harumphed, and clapped for attention. When things quieted down and the atmosphere was properly tense, he raised his voice like an auctioneer, and called: "Now listen, everybody, in this here envelope you see in my hand"—he held a manila envelope above his head—" well, in it's the *answer*—which nobody but God and the First National Bank knows up to now, ha, ha. And in this book"—he held up the ledger with his free hand—"I've got written down what you folks guessed. Are there any questions?" All was silence. "Fine. Now, if we could have a volunteer . . ."

Not a living soul budged an inch: it was as if an awful shyness had overcome the crowd, and even those who were ordinarily natural-born show-offs shuffled their feet, ashamed. Then a voice, Appleseed's, hollered, "Lemme by . . . Outa the way, please, ma'am." Trotting along behind as he pushed forward were Middy and a lanky, sleepy-eyed fellow who was evidently the fiddling brother. Appleseed was dressed the same as usual, but his face was scrubbed rosy clean, his boots polished and his hair slicked back skin tight with Stacomb. "Did we get here in time?" he panted.

But Mr. Marshall said, "So you want to be our volunteer?"

Appleseed looked bewildered, then nodded vigorously.

"Does anybody have an objection to this young man?"

Still there was dead quiet. Mr. Marshall handed the envelope to Appleseed who accepted it calmly. He chewed his under lip while studying it a moment before ripping the flap.

In all that congregation there was no sound except an occasional cough and the soft tinkling of Mr. R. C. Judkins' supper bell. Hamurabi was leaning against the fountain, staring up at the ceiling; Middy was gazing blankly over her brother's shoulder, and when he started to tear open the envelope she let out a pained little gasp.

Appleseed withdrew a slip of pink paper and, holding it as though it was very fragile, muttered to himself whatever was written there. Suddenly his face paled and tears glistened in his eyes.

"Hey, speak up, boy," someone hollered.

Hamurabi stepped forward and all but snatched the slip away. He cleared his throat and commenced to read when his expression changed most comically. "Well, Mother o' God . . ." he said.

"Louder! Louder!" an angry chorus demanded.

"Buncha crooks!" yelled Mr. R. C. Judkins, who had a snootful by this time. "I smell a rat and he smells to high heaven!" Whereupon a cyclone of catcalls and whistling rent the air.

Appleseed's brother whirled round and shook his fist. "Shuddup, shuddup 'fore I bust every one of your goddamn heads together so's you got knots the size a musk melons, hear me?"

"Citizens," cried Mayor Mawes, "citizens—I say, this is Christmas . . . I say . . ."

And Mr. Marshall hopped up on a chair and clapped and stamped till a minimum of order was restored. It might as well be noted here that we later found out Rufus McPherson had paid Mr. R. C. Judkins to start the rumpus. Anyway, when the outbreak was quelled, who should be in possession of the slip but me . . . don't ask how.

Without thinking, I shouted, "Seventy-seven dollars and

thirty-five cents." Naturally, due to the excitement, I didn't at first catch the meaning; it was just a number. Then Appleseed's brother let forth with his whooping yell, and so I understood. The name of the winner spread quickly, and the awed, murmuring whispers were like a rainstorm.

Oh, Appleseed himself was a sorry sight. He was crying as though he was mortally wounded, but when Hamurabi lifted him onto his shoulders so the crowd could get a gander, he dried his eyes with the cuffs of his sweater and began grinning. Mr. R. C. Judkins yelled, "Gyp! Lousy gyp!" but was drowned out by a deafening round of applause.

Middy grabbed my arm. "My teeth," she squealed. "Now I'm gonna get my teeth."

"Teeth?" said I, kind of dazed.

"The false kind," says she. "That's what we're gonna get us with the money—a lovely set of white false teeth."

But at that moment my sole interest was in how Appleseed had known. "Hey, tell me," I said desperately, "tell me, how in God's name did he know there was just exactly seventy-seven dollars and thirty-five cents?"

Middy gave me this *look*. "Why, I thought he told you," she said, real serious. "He counted."

"Yes, but how—how?"

"Gee, don't you even know how to count?"

"But is that all he did?"

"Well," she said, following a thoughtful pause, "he did do a little praying, too." She started to dart off, then turned back and called, "Besides, he was born with a caul on his head."

And that's the nearest anybody ever came to solving the mystery. Thereafter, if you were to ask Appleseed "How come?" he would smile strangely and change the subject. Many years later he and his family moved to somewhere in Florida and were never heard from again.

But in our town his legend flourishes still; and, till his death a year ago last April, Mr. Marshall was invited each Christmas Day to tell the story of Appleseed to the Baptist Bible class. Hamurabi once typed up an account and mailed it around to various magazines. It was never printed. One editor wrote back and said that "If the little girl really turned out to be a movie star, then there might be something to your story." But that's not what happened, so why should you lie?

Miriam

For several years, Mrs. H. T. Miller had lived alone in a pleasant apartment (two rooms with kitchenette) in a remodeled brownstone near the East River. She was a widow: Mr. H. T. Miller had left a reasonable amount of insurance. Her interests were narrow, she had no friends to speak of, and she rarely journeyed farther than the corner grocery. The other people in the house never seemed to notice her: her clothes were matter-of-fact, her hair iron-gray, clipped and casually waved; she did not use cosmetics, her features were plain and inconspicuous, and on her last birthday she was sixty-one. Her activities were seldom spontaneous: she kept the two rooms immaculate, smoked an occasional cigarette, prepared her own meals and tended a canary.

Then she met Miriam. It was snowing that night. Mrs. Miller had finished drying the supper dishes and was thumbing through an afternoon paper when she saw an advertisement of a picture playing at a neighborhood theater. The title sounded good, so she struggled into her beaver coat, laced her galoshes and left the apartment, leaving one light burning in the foyer: she found nothing more disturbing than a sensation of darkness.

The snow was fine, falling gently, not yet making an impression on the pavement. The wind from the river cut only at street crossings. Mrs. Miller hurried, her head bowed, oblivious as a mole burrowing a blind path. She stopped at a drugstore and bought a package of peppermints.

A long line stretched in front of the box office; she took her place at the end. There would be (a tired voice groaned) a short wait for all seats. Mrs. Miller rummaged in her leather handbag till she collected exactly the correct change for admission. The line seemed to be taking its own time and, looking around for some distraction, she suddenly became conscious of a little girl standing under the edge of the marquee.

Her hair was the longest and strangest Mrs. Miller had ever seen: absolutely silver-white, like an albino's. It flowed waist-length in smooth, loose lines. She was thin and fragilely constructed. There was a simple, special elegance in the way she stood with her thumbs in the pockets of a tailored plum-velvet coat.

Mrs. Miller felt oddly excited, and when the little girl glanced toward her, she smiled warmly. The little girl walked over and said, "Would you care to do me a favor?"

"I'd be glad to, if I can," said Mrs. Miller.

"Oh, it's quite easy. I merely want you to buy a ticket for me; they won't let me in otherwise. Here, I have the money." And gracefully she handed Mrs. Miller two dimes and a nickel.

They went into the theater together. An usherette directed them to a lounge; in twenty minutes the picture would be over.

"I feel just like a genuine criminal," said Mrs. Miller gaily, as she sat down. "I mean that sort of thing's against the law, isn't it? I do hope I haven't done the wrong thing. Your mother knows where you are, dear? I mean she does, doesn't she?"

The little girl said nothing. She unbuttoned her coat and folded it across her lap. Her dress underneath was prim and dark blue. A gold chain dangled about her neck, and her fingers, sensitive and musical-looking, toyed with it. Examining her more attentively, Mrs. Miller decided the truly distinctive feature was not her hair, but her eyes; they were hazel, steady, lacking any childlike quality whatsoever and, because of their size, seemed to consume her small face.

Mrs. Miller offered a peppermint. "What's your name, dear?"

"Miriam," she said, as though, in some curious way, it were information already familiar.

"Why, isn't that funny—my name's Miriam, too. And it's not

a terribly common name either. Now, don't tell me your last name's Miller!"

"Just Miriam."

"But isn't that funny?"

"Moderately," said Miriam, and rolled the peppermint on her tongue.

Mrs. Miller flushed and shifted uncomfortably. "You have such a large vocabulary for such a little girl."

"Do I?"

"Well, yes," said Mrs. Miller, hastily changing the topic to: "Do you like the movies?"

"I really wouldn't know," said Miriam. "I've never been before."

Women began filling the lounge; the rumble of the newsreel bombs exploded in the distance. Mrs. Miller rose, tucking her purse under her arm. "I guess I'd better be running now if I want to get a seat," she said. "It was nice to have met you."

Miriam nodded ever so slightly.

It snowed all week. Wheels and footsteps moved soundlessly on the street, as if the business of living continued secretly behind a pale but impenetrable curtain. In the falling quiet there was no sky or earth, only snow lifting in the wind, frosting the window glass, chilling the rooms, deadening and hushing the city. At all hours it was necessary to keep a lamp lighted, and Mrs. Miller lost track of the days: Friday was no different from Saturday and on Sunday she went to the grocery: closed, of course.

That evening she scrambled eggs and fixed a bowl of tomato soup. Then, after putting on a flannel robe and coldcreaming her face, she propped herself up in bed with a hotwater bottle under her feet. She was reading the *Times* when the doorbell rang. At first she thought it must be a mistake and whoever it was would go away. But it rang and rang and settled to a persistent buzz. She looked at the clock: a little after eleven; it did not seem possible, she was always asleep by ten.

Climbing out of bed, she trotted barefoot across the living room. "I'm coming, please be patient." The latch was caught; she turned it this way and that way and the bell never paused an instant. "Stop it," she cried. The bolt gave way and she opened the door an inch. "What in heaven's name?"

"Hello," said Miriam.

"Oh . . . why, hello," said Mrs. Miller, stepping hesitantly into the hall. "You're that little girl."

"I thought you'd never answer, but I kept my finger on the button; I knew you were home. Aren't you glad to see me?"

Mrs. Miller did not know what to say. Miriam, she saw, wore the same plum-velvet coat and now she had also a beret to match; her white hair was braided in two shining plaits and looped at the ends with enormous white ribbons.

"Since I've waited so long, you could at least let me in," she said.

"It's awfully late. . . ."

Miriam regarded her blankly. "What difference does that make? Let me in. It's cold out here and I have on a silk dress." Then, with a gentle gesture, she urged Mrs. Miller aside and passed into the apartment.

She dropped her coat and beret on a chair. She was indeed wearing a silk dress. White silk. White silk in February. The skirt was beautifully pleated and the sleeves long; it made a faint rustle as she strolled about the room. "I like your place," she said. "I like the rug, blue's my favorite color." She touched a paper rose in a vase on the coffee table. "Imitation," she commented wanly. "How sad. Aren't imitations sad?" She seated herself on the sofa, daintily spreading her skirt.

"What do you want?" asked Mrs. Miller.

"Sit down," said Miriam. "It makes me nervous to see people stand."

Mrs. Miller sank to a hassock. "What do you want?" she repeated.

"You know, I don't think you're glad I came."

For a second time Mrs. Miller was without an answer; her hand motioned vaguely. Miriam giggled and pressed back on a mound of chintz pillows. Mrs. Miller observed that the girl was less pale than she remembered; her cheeks were flushed.

"How did you know where I lived?"

Miriam frowned. "That's no question at all. What's your name? What's mine?"

"But I'm not listed in the phone book."

"Oh, let's talk about something else."

Mrs. Miller said, "Your mother must be insane to let a child like you wander around at all hours of the night—and in such ridiculous clothes. She must be out of her mind."

Miriam got up and moved to a corner where a covered

bird cage hung from a ceiling chain. She peeked beneath the cover. "It's a canary," she said. "Would you mind if I woke him? I'd like to hear him sing."

"Leave Tommy alone," said Mrs. Miller, anxiously. "Don't you dare wake him."

"Certainly," said Miriam. "But I don't see why I can't hear him sing." And then, "Have you anything to eat? I'm starving! Even milk and a jam sandwich would be fine."

"Look," said Mrs. Miller, rising from the hassock, "look— if I make some nice sandwiches will you be a good child and run along home? It's past midnight, I'm sure."

"It's snowing," reproached Miriam. "And cold and dark."

"Well, you shouldn't have come here to begin with," said Mrs. Miller, struggling to control her voice. "I can't help the weather. If you want anything to eat you'll have to promise to leave."

Miriam brushed a braid against her cheek. Her eyes were thoughtful, as if weighing the proposition. She turned toward the bird cage. "Very well," she said, "I promise."

How old is she? Ten? Eleven? Mrs. Miller, in the kitchen, unsealed a jar of strawberry preserves and cut four slices of bread. She poured a glass of milk and paused to light a cigarette. *And why has she come?* Her hand shook as she held the match, fascinated, till it burned her finger. The canary was singing; singing as he did in the morning and at no other time. "Miriam," she called, "Miriam, I told you not to disturb Tommy." There was no answer. She called again; all she heard was the canary. She inhaled the cigarette and discovered she had lighted the cork-tip end and—oh, really, she mustn't lose her temper.

She carried the food in on a tray and set it on the coffee table. She saw first that the bird cage still wore its night cover. And Tommy was singing. It gave her a queer sensation. And no one was in the room. Mrs. Miller went through an alcove leading to her bedroom; at the door she caught her breath.

"What are you doing?" she asked.

Miriam glanced up and in her eyes there was a look that was not ordinary. She was standing by the bureau, a jewel case opened before her. For a minute she studied Mrs. Miller, forcing their eyes to meet, and she smiled. "There's nothing good here," she said. "But I like this." Her hand held a cameo brooch. "It's charming."

"Suppose—perhaps you'd better put it back," said Mrs.

Miller, feeling suddenly the need of some support. She leaned
against the door frame; her head was unbearably heavy; a
pressure weighted the rhythm of her heartbeat. The light
seemed to flutter defectively. "Please, child—a gift from my
husband . . ."

"But it's beautiful and I want it," said Miriam. *"Give it to
me."*

As she stood, striving to shape a sentence which would somehow save the brooch, it came to Mrs. Miller there was no one
to whom she might turn; she was alone; a fact that had not
been among her thoughts for a long time. Its sheer emphasis
was stunning. But here in her own room in the hushed snow-
city were evidences she could not ignore or, she knew with
startling clarity, resist.

Miriam ate ravenously, and when the sandwiches and milk
were gone, her fingers made cobweb movements over the
plate, gathering crumbs. The cameo gleamed on her blouse, the
blonde profile like a trick reflection of its wearer. "That was
very nice," she sighed, "though now an almond cake or a
cherry would be ideal. Sweets are lovely, don't you think?"

Mrs. Miller was perched precariously on the hassock, smoking a cigarette. Her hair net had slipped lopsided and loose
strands straggled down her face. Her eyes were stupidly concentrated on nothing and her cheeks were mottled in red
patches, as though a fierce slap had left permanent marks.

"Is there a candy—a cake?"

Mrs. Miller tapped ash on the rug. Her head swayed slightly
as she tried to focus her eyes. "You promised to leave if I
made the sandwiches," she said.

"Dear me, did I?"

"It was a promise and I'm tired and I don't feel well at all."

"Mustn't fret," said Miriam. "I'm only teasing."

She picked up her coat, slung it over her arm, and arranged
her beret in front of a mirror. Presently she bent close to Mrs.
Miller and whispered, "Kiss me good night."

"Please—I'd rather not," said Mrs. Miller.

Miriam lifted a shoulder, arched an eyebrow. "As you like,"
she said, and went directly to the coffee table, seized the vase
containing the paper roses, carried it to where the hard surface
of the floor lay bare, and hurled it downward. Glass sprayed
in all directions and she stamped her foot on the bouquet.

Then slowly she walked to the door, but before closing it she looked back at Mrs. Miller with a slyly innocent curiosity.

Mrs. Miller spent the next day in bed, rising once to feed the canary and drink a cup of tea; she took her temperature and had none, yet her dreams were feverishly agitated; their unbalanced mood lingered even as she lay staring wide-eyed at the ceiling. One dream threaded through the others like an elusively mysterious theme in a complicated symphony, and the scenes it depicted were sharply outlined, as though sketched by a hand of gifted intensity: a small girl, wearing a bridal gown and a wreath of leaves, led a gray procession down a mountain path, and among them there was unusual silence till a woman at the rear asked, "Where is she taking us?" "No one knows," said an old man marching in front. "But isn't she pretty?" volunteered a third voice. "Isn't she like a frost flower . . . so shining and white?"

Tuesday morning she woke up feeling better; harsh slats of sunlight, slanting through Venetian blinds, shed a disrupting light on her unwholesome fancies. She opened the window to discover a thawed, mild-as-spring day; a sweep of clean new clouds crumpled against a vastly blue, out-of-season sky; and across the low line of roof-tops she could see the river and smoke curving from tug-boat stacks in a warm wind. A great silver truck plowed the snow-banked street, its machine sound humming in the air.

After straightening the apartment, she went to the grocer's, cashed a check and continued to Schrafft's where she ate breakfast and chatted happily with the waitress. Oh, it was a wonderful day—more like a holiday—and it would be so foolish to go home.

She boarded a Lexington Avenue bus and rode up to Eighty-sixth Street; it was here that she had decided to do a little shopping.

She had no idea what she wanted or needed, but she idled along, intent only upon the passers-by, brisk and preoccupied, who gave her a disturbing sense of separateness.

It was while waiting at the corner of Third Avenue that she saw the man: an old man, bowlegged and stooped under an armload of bulging packages; he wore a shabby brown coat and a checkered cap. Suddenly she realized they were exchanging a smile: there was nothing friendly about this smile, it was merely two cold flickers of recognition. But she was certain she had never seen him before.

He was standing next to an El pillar, and as she crossed the street he turned and followed. He kept quite close; from the corner of her eye she watched his reflection wavering on the shopwindows.

Then in the middle of the block she stopped and faced him. He stopped also and cocked his head, grinning. But what could she say? Do? Here, in broad daylight, on Eighty-sixth Street? It was useless and, despising her own helplessness, she quickened her steps.

Now Second Avenue is a dismal street, made from scraps and ends; part cobblestone, part asphalt, part cement; and its atmosphere of desertion is permanent. Mrs. Miller walked five blocks without meeting anyone, and all the while the steady crunch of his footfalls in the snow stayed near. And when she came to a florist's shop, the sound was still with her. She hurried inside and watched through the glass door as the old man passed; he kept his eyes straight ahead and didn't slow his pace, but he did one strange, telling thing: he tipped his cap.

"Six white ones, did you say?" asked the florist. "Yes," she told him, "white roses." From there she went to a glassware store and selected a vase, presumably a replacement for the one Miriam had broken, though the price was intolerable and the vase itself (she thought) grotesquely vulgar. But a series of unaccountable purchases had begun, as if by prearranged plan: a plan of which she had not the least knowledge or control.

She bought a bag of glazed cherries, and at a place called the Knickerbocker Bakery she paid forty cents for six almond cakes.

Within the last hour the weather had turned cold again; like blurred lenses, winter clouds cast a shade over the sun, and the skeleton of an early dusk colored the sky; a damp mist mixed with the wind and the voices of a few children who romped high on mountains of gutter snow seemed lonely and cheerless. Soon the first flake fell, and when Mrs. Miller reached the brownstone house, snow was falling in a swift screen and foot tracks vanished as they were printed.

The white roses were arranged decoratively in the vase. The glazed cherries shone on a ceramic plate. The almond cakes, dusted with sugar, awaited a hand. The canary fluttered on its swing and picked at a bar of seed.

At precisely five the doorbell rang. Mrs. Miller *knew* who it was. The hem of her housecoat trailed as she crossed the floor. "Is that you?" she called.

"Naturally," said Miriam, the word resounding shrilly from the hall. "Open this door."

"Go away," said Mrs. Miller.

"Please hurry . . . I have a heavy package."

"Go away," said Mrs. Miller. She returned to the living room, lighted a cigarette, sat down and calmly listened to the buzzer; on and on and on. "You might as well leave. I have no intention of letting you in."

Shortly the bell stopped. For possibly ten minutes Mrs. Miller did not move. Then, hearing no sound, she concluded Miriam had gone. She tiptoed to the door and opened it a sliver; Miriam was half-reclining atop a cardboard box with a beautiful French doll cradled in her arms.

"Really, I thought you were never coming," she said peevishly. "Here, help me get this in, it's awfully heavy."

It was not spell-like compulsion that Mrs. Miller felt, but rather a curious passivity; she brought in the box, Miriam the doll. Miriam curled up on the sofa, not troubling to remove her coat or beret, and watched disinterestedly as Mrs. Miller dropped the box and stood trembling, trying to catch her breath.

"Thank you," she said. In the daylight she looked pinched and drawn, her hair less luminous. The French doll she was loving wore an exquisite powdered wig and its idiot glass eyes sought solace in Miriam's. "I have a surprise," she continued. "Look into my box."

Kneeling, Mrs. Miller parted the flaps and lifted out another doll; then a blue dress which she recalled as the one Miriam had worn that first night at the theater; and of the remainder she said, "It's all clothes. Why?"

"Because I've come to live with you," said Miriam, twisting a cherry stem. "Wasn't it nice of you to buy me the cherries . . .?"

"But you can't! For God's sake go away—go away and leave me alone!"

". . . and the roses and the almond cakes? How really wonderfully generous. You know, these cherries are delicious. The last place I lived was with an old man; he was terribly poor and we never had good things to eat. But I think I'll be happy here." She paused to snuggle her doll closer. "Now, if you'll just show me where to put my things . . ."

Mrs. Miller's face dissolved into a mask of ugly red lines; she began to cry, and it was an unnatural, tearless sort of weeping, as though, not having wept for a long time, she had forgotten how. Carefully she edged backward till she touched the door.

She fumbled through the hall and down the stairs to a landing below. She pounded frantically on the door of the first apartment she came to; a short, red-headed man answered and she pushed past him. "Say, what the hell is this?" he said. "Anything wrong, lover?" asked a young woman who appeared from the kitchen, drying her hands. And it was to her that Mrs. Miller turned.

"Listen," she cried, "I'm ashamed behaving this way but—well, I'm Mrs. H. T. Miller and I live upstairs and . . ." She pressed her hands over her face. "It sounds so absurd. . . ."

The woman guided her to a chair, while the man excitedly rattled pocket change. "Yeah?"

"I live upstairs and there's a little girl visiting me, and I suppose that I'm afraid of her. She won't leave and I can't make her and—she's going to do something terrible. She's already stolen my cameo, but she's about to do something worse—something terrible!"

The man asked, "Is she a relative, huh?"

Mrs. Miller shook her head. "I don't know who she is. Her name's Miriam, but I don't know for certain who she is."

"You gotta calm down, honey," said the woman, stroking Mrs. Miller's arm. "Harry here'll tend to this kid. Go on, lover." And Mrs. Miller said, "The door's open—5A."

After the man left, the woman brought a towel and bathed Mrs. Miller's face. "You're very kind," Mrs. Miller said. "I'm sorry to act like such a fool, only this wicked child . . ."

"Sure, honey," consoled the woman. "Now, you better take it easy."

Mrs. Miller rested her head in the crook of her arm; she was quiet enough to be asleep. The woman turned a radio dial; a piano and a husky voice filled the silence and the woman, tapping her foot, kept excellent time. "Maybe we oughta go up too," she said.

"I don't want to see her again. I don't want to be anywhere near her."

"Uh huh, but what you shoulda done, you shoulda called a cop."

Presently they heard the man on the stairs. He strode into the room frowning and scratching the back of his neck. "Nobody there," he said, honestly embarrassed. "She musta beat it."

"Harry, you're a jerk," announced the woman. "We been sitting here the whole time and we woulda seen . . ." she stopped abruptly, for the man's glance was sharp.

"I looked all over," he said, "and there just ain't nobody there. Nobody, understand?"

"Tell me," said Mrs. Miller, rising, "tell me, did you see a large box? Or a doll?"

"No, ma'am, I didn't."

And the woman, as if delivering a verdict, said, "Well, for cryin out loud. . . ."

Mrs. Miller entered her apartment softly; she walked to the center of the room and stood quite still. No, in a sense it had not changed: the roses, the cakes, and the cherries were in place. But this was an empty room, emptier than if the furnishings and familiars were not present, lifeless and petrified as a funeral parlor. The sofa loomed before her with a new strangeness: its vacancy had a meaning that would have been less penetrating and terrible had Miriam been curled on it. She gazed fixedly at the space where she remembered setting the box and, for a moment, the hassock spun desperately. And she looked through the window; surely the river was real, surely snow was falling—but then, one could not be certain witness to anything: Miriam, so vividly *there*—and yet, where was she? Where, where?

As though moving in a dream, she sank to a chair. The room was losing shape; it was dark and getting darker and there was nothing to be done about it; she could not lift her hand to light a lamp.

Suddenly, closing her eyes, she felt an upward surge, like a diver emerging from some deeper, greener depth. In times of terror or immense distress, there are moments when the mind waits, as though for a revelation, while a skein of calm is woven over thought; it is like a sleep, or a supernatural trance; and during this lull one is aware of a force of quiet reasoning: well, what if she had never really known a girl named Miriam? that she had been foolishly frightened on the street? In the end, like everything else, it was of no importance. For the only thing she had lost to Miriam was her identity, but now she knew she had found again the person who lived in this room, who cooked her own meals, who owned a canary, who was someone she could trust and believe in: Mrs. H. T. Miller.

Listening in contentment, she became aware of a double sound: a bureau drawer opening and closing; she seemed to hear it long after completion—opening and closing. Then gradually, the harshness of it was replaced by the murmur of a silk dress and this, delicately faint, was moving nearer and swelling in intensity till the walls trembled with the vibration and the room was caving under a wave of whispers. Mrs. Miller stiffened and opened her eyes to a dull, direct stare.

"Hello," said Miriam.

The Headless Hawk

THEY are of those that rebel against the light; they know not the ways thereof, nor abide in the paths thereof. In the dark they dig through houses, which they had marked for themselves in the daytime: they know not the light. For the morning is to them as the shadow of death: if one know them, they are in the terrors of the shadow of death. —JOB 24: 13, 16, 17

VINCENT switched off the lights in the gallery. Outside, after locking the door, he smoothed the brim of an elegant Panama, and started toward Third Avenue, his umbrella-cane tap-tap-tapping along the pavement. A promise of rain had darkened the day since dawn, and a sky of bloated clouds blurred the five o'clock sun; it was hot, though, humid as tropical mist, and voices, sounding along the gray July street, sounding muffled and strange, carried a fretful undertone. Vincent felt as though he moved below the sea. Buses, cruising crosstown through Fifty-seventh Street, seemed like green-bellied fish, and faces loomed and rocked like wave-riding masks. He studied each passer-by, hunting one, and presently he saw her, a girl in a green raincoat. She was standing on the downtown corner of Fifty-seventh and Third, just standing there smoking a ciga-

rette, and giving somehow the impression she hummed a tune.
The raincoat was transparent. She wore dark slacks, no socks,
a pair of huaraches, a man's white shirt. Her hair was fawn-
colored, and cut like a boy's. When she noticed Vincent
crossing toward her, she dropped the cigarette and hurried
down the block to the doorway of an antique store.

Vincent slowed his step. He pulled out a handkerchief and
dabbed his forehead; if only he could get away, go up to the
Cape, lie in the sun. He bought an afternoon paper, and fumbled
his change. It rolled in the gutter, dropped silently out of sight
down a sewer grating. "Ain't but a nickel, bub," said the news-
dealer, for Vincent, though actually unaware of his loss,
looked heartbroken. And it was like that often now, never
quite in contact, never sure whether a step would take him
backward or forward, up or down. Very casually, with the
handle of the umbrella hooked over an arm, and his eyes concentrated on the paper's headlines—but what did the damn
thing say?—he continued downtown. A swarthy woman carrying a shopping bag jostled him, glared, muttered in coarsely
vehement Italian. The ragged cut of her voice seemed to come
through layers of wool. As he approached the antique store
where the girl in the green raincoat waited, he walked slower
still, counting one, two, three, four, five, six—at six he halted
before the window.

The window was like a corner of an attic; a lifetime's dis-
cardings rose in a pyramid of no particular worth: vacant picture frames, a lavender wig, Gothic shaving mugs, beaded
lamps. There was an oriental mask suspended on a ceiling cord,
and wind from an electric fan whirling inside the shop revolved
it slowly round and round. Vincent, by degrees, lifted his gaze,
and looked at the girl directly. She was hovering in the doorway so that he saw her greenness distorted wavy through
double glass; the elevated pounded overhead and the window
trembled. Her image spread like a reflection on silverware,
then gradually hardened again: she was watching him.

He hung an Old Gold between his lips, rummaged for a
match and, finding none, sighed. The girl stepped from the
doorway. She held out a cheap little lighter; as the flame pulsed
up, her eyes, pale, shallow, cat-green, fixed him with alarming
intensity. Her eyes had an astonished, a shocked look, as
though, having at one time witnessed a terrible incident, they'd
locked wide open. Carefree bangs fringed her forehead; this
boy haircut emphasized the childish and rather poetic quality of her narrow, hollow-cheeked face. It was the kind of

face one sometimes sees in paintings of medieval youths.

Letting the smoke pour out his nose, Vincent, knowing it was useless to ask, wondered, as always, what she was living on, and where. He flipped away the cigarette, for he had not wanted it to begin with, and then, pivoting, crossed rapidly under the El; as he approached the curb he heard a crash of brakes, and suddenly, as if cotton plugs had been blasted from his ears, city noises crowded in. A cab driver hollered: "Fa crissake, sistuh, get the lead outa yuh pants!" but the girl did not even bother turning her head; trance-eyed, undisturbed as a sleepwalker, and staring straight at Vincent, who watched dumbly, she moved across the street. A colored boy wearing a jazzy purple suit took her elbow. "You sick, Miss?" he said, guiding her forward, and she did not answer. "You look mighty funny, Miss. If you sick, I . . ." then, following the direction of her eyes, he released his hold. There was something here which made him all still inside. "Uh—yeah," he muttered, backing off with a grinning display of tartar-coated teeth.

So Vincent began walking in earnest, and his umbrella tapped code-like block after block. His shirt was soaked through with itchy sweat, and the noises, now so harsh, banged in his head: a trick car horn hooting "My Country, 'Tis of Thee," electric spray of sparks crackling bluely off thundering rails, whiskey laughter hiccuping through gaunt doors of beer-stale bars where orchid juke machines manufactured U.S.A. music—"I got spurs that jingle jangle jingle. . . ." Occasionally he caught a glimpse of her, once mirrored in the window of Paul's Seafood Palace where scarlet lobsters basked on a beach of flaked ice. She followed close with her hands shoved into the pockets of her raincoat. The brassy lights of a movie marquee blinked, and he remembered how she loved movies: murder films, spy chillers, Wild West shows. He turned into a side street leading toward the East River; it was quiet here, hushed like Sunday: a sailor-stroller munching an Eskimo pie, energetic twins skipping rope, an old velvety lady with gardenia-white hair lifting aside lace curtains and peering listlessly into rain-dark space—a city landscape in July. And behind him the soft insistent slap of sandals. Traffic lights on Second Avenue turned red; at the corner a bearded midget, Ruby the Popcorn Man, wailed, "Hot buttered popcorn, big bag, yah?" Vincent shook his head, and the midget looked very put out, then: "Yuh see?" he jeered, pushing a shovel inside of the candlelit cage where bursting kernels bounced like crazy moths. "Yuh see, de girlie knows popcorn's nourishin'."

She bought a dime's worth, and it was in a green sack matching her raincoat, matching her eyes.

This is my neighborhood, my street, the house with the gateway is where I live. To remind himself of this was necessary, inasmuch as he'd substituted for a sense of reality a knowledge of time, and place. He glanced gratefully at sourfaced, faded ladies, at the pipe-puffing males squatting on the surrounding steps of brownstone stoops. Nine pale little girls shrieked round a corner flower cart begging daisies to pin in their hair, but the peddler said, "Shoo!" and, fleeing like beads of a broken bracelet, they circled in the street, the wild ones leaping with laughter, and the shy ones, silent and isolated, lifting summer-wilted faces skyward: the rain, would it never come?

Vincent, who lived in a basement apartment, descended several steps and took out his keycase; then, pausing behind the hallway door, he looked back through a peephole in the paneling. The girl was waiting on the sidewalk above; she leaned against a brownstone banister, and her arms fell limp—and popcorn spilled snowlike round her feet. A grimy little boy crept slyly up to pick among it like a squirrel.

2

For Vincent it was a holiday. No one had come by the gallery all morning, which, considering the arctic weather, was not unusual. He sat at his desk devouring tangerines, and enjoying immensely a Thurber story in an old *New Yorker*. Laughing loudly, he did not hear the girl enter, see her cross the dark carpet, notice her at all, in fact, until the telephone rang. "Garland Gallery, hello." She was odd, most certainly, that indecent haircut, those depthless eyes—"Oh, Paul. *Comme ci, comme ça*, and you?"—and dressed like a freak: no coat, just a lumberjack's shirt, navy-blue slacks and—was it a joke?—pink ankle socks, a pair of huaraches. "The ballet? Who's dancing? Oh, her!" Under an arm she carried a flat parcel wrapped in sheets of funny-paper—"Look, Paul, what say I call back? There's someone here . . ." and, anchoring the receiver, assuming a commercial smile, he stood up. "Yes?"

Her lips, crusty with chap, trembled with unrealized words as though she had possibly a defect of speech, and her eyes rolled in their sockets like loose marbles. It was the kind of disturbed shyness one associates with children. "I've a picture," she said. "You buy pictures?"

At this, Vincent's smile became fixed. "We exhibit."

"I painted it myself," she said, and her voice, hoarse and

slurred, was Southern. "My picture—I painted it. A lady told me there were places around here that bought pictures."

Vincent said, "Yes, of course, but the truth is"—and he made a helpless gesture—"the truth is I've no authority whatever. Mr. Garland—this is his gallery, you know—is out of town." Standing there on the expanse of fine carpet, her body sagging sideways with the weight of her package, she looked like a sad rag doll. "Maybe," he began, "maybe Henry Krueger up the street at Sixty-five . . ." but she was not listening.

"I did it myself," she insisted softly. "Tuesdays and Thursdays were our painting days, and a whole year I worked. The others, they kept messing it up, and Mr. Destronelli . . ." Suddenly, as though aware of an indiscretion, she stopped and bit her lip. Her eyes narrowed. "He's not a friend of yours?"

"Who?" said Vincent, confused.

"Mr. Destronelli."

He shook his head, and wondered why it was that eccentricity always excited in him such curious admiration. It was the feeling he'd had as a child toward carnival freaks. And it was true that about those whom he'd loved there was always a little something wrong, broken. Strange, though, that this quality, having stimulated an attraction, should, in his case, regularly end it by destroying it. "Of course I haven't any authority," he repeated, sweeping tangerine hulls into a wastebasket, "but, if you like, I suppose I could look at your work."

A pause; then, kneeling on the floor, she commenced stripping off the funny-paper wrapping. It originally had been, Vincent noticed, part of the New Orleans *Times-Picayune.* "From the South, aren't you?" he said. She did not look up, but he saw her shoulders stiffen. "No," she said. Smiling, he considered a moment, decided it would be tactless to challenge so transparent a lie. Or could she have misunderstood? And all at once he felt an intense longing to touch her head, finger her boyish hair. He shoved his hands in his pockets and glanced at the window. It was spangled with February frost, and some passer-by had scratched on the glass an obscenity.

"There," she said.

A headless figure in a monklike robe reclined complacently on top a tacky vaudeville trunk; in one hand she held a fuming blue candle, in the other a miniature gold cage, and her severed head lay bleeding at her feet: it was the girl's, this head, but here her hair was long, very long, and a snowball kitten with crystal spitfire eyes playfully pawed, as it would a spool of yarn, the sprawling ends. The wings of a hawk, headless, scarlet-breasted, copper-clawed, curtained the background like a nightfall sky. It was a crude painting, the hard pure colors molded with male brutality, and, while there was not technical merit evident, it had that power often seen in something deeply felt, though primitively conveyed. Vincent reacted as he did when occasionally a phrase of music surprised a note of inward recognition, or a cluster of words in a poem revealed to him a secret concerning himself: he felt a powerful chill of pleasure run down his spine. "Mr. Garland is in Florida," he said cautiously, "but I think he should see it; you couldn't leave it for, say, a week?"

"I had a ring and I sold it," she said, and he had the feeling she was talking in a trance. "It was a nice ring, a wedding ring—not mine—with writing on it. I had an overcoat, too." She twisted one of her shirt buttons, pulled till it popped off and rolled on the carpet like a pearl eye. "I don't want much —fifty dollars; is that unfair?"

"Too much," said Vincent, more curtly than he intended. Now he wanted her painting, not for the gallery, but for himself. There are certain works of art which excite more interest in their creators than in what they have created, usually because in this kind of work one is able to identify something which has until that instant seemed a private inexpressible perception, and you wonder: who is this that knows me, and how? "I'll give thirty."

For a moment she gaped at him stupidly, and then, sucking her breath, held out her hand, palm up. This directness, too innocent to be offensive, caught him off guard. Somewhat embarrassed, he said, "I'm most awfully afraid I'll have to mail a check. Could you . . .?" The telephone interrupted, and, as he went to answer, she followed, her hand outstretched, a frantic look pinching her face. "Oh, Paul, may I call back? Oh, I see. Well, hold on a sec." Cupping the mouthpiece against his shoulder, he pushed a pad and pencil across the desk. "Here, write your name and address."

But she shook her head, the dazed, anxious expression deepening.

"*Check,*" said Vincent, "I have to mail a check. Please, your name and address." He grinned encouragingly when at last she began to write.

"Sorry, Paul . . . Whose party? Why, the little bitch, she didn't invite . . . Hey!" he called, for the girl was moving toward the door. "Please, hey!" Cold air chilled the gallery, and the door slammed with a glassy rattle. Hellohellohello. Vincent did not answer; he stood puzzling over the curious information she'd left printed on his pad: D. J.—Y.W.C.A. Hellohellohello.

It hung above his mantel, the painting, and on those nights when he could not sleep he would pour a glass of whiskey and talk to the headless hawk, tell it the stuff of his life: he was, he said, a poet who had never written poetry, a painter who had never painted, a lover who had never loved (absolutely)—someone, in short, without direction, and quite headless. Oh, it wasn't that he hadn't tried—good beginnings, always, bad endings, always. Vincent, white, male, age 36, college graduate: a man in the sea, fifty miles from shore; a victim, born to be murdered, either by himself or another; an actor unemployed. It was there, all of it, in the painting, everything disconnected and cockeyed, and who was she that she should know so much? Inquiries, those he'd made, had led nowhere, not another dealer knew of her, and to search for a D. J. living in, presumably, a Y.W.C.A. seemed absurd. Then, too, he'd quite expected she would reappear, but February passed, and March. One evening, crossing the square which fronts the Plaza, he had a queer thing happen. The archaic hansom drivers who line that location were lighting their carriage lamps, for it was dusk, and lamplight traced through moving leaves. A hansom pulled from the curb and rolled past in the twilight. There was a single occupant, and this passenger, whose face he could not see, was a girl with chopped fawn-colored hair. So he settled on a bench, and whiled away time talking with a soldier, and a fairy colored boy who quoted poetry, and a man out airing a dachshund: night characters with whom he waited—but the carriage, with the one for whom he waited, never came back. Again he saw her (or supposed he did) descending subway stairs, and this time lost her in the tiled tunnels of painted arrows and Spearmint machines. It was as if her face were imposèd upon his mind; he could no more dispossess it than could, for example, a dead man rid his legendary eyes of the last image seen. Around the middle of April he went up to Connecticut to spend a weekend with his married sister; keyed-up, caustic, he wasn't, as she complained, at all like himself. "What is it, Vinny, darling—if you need money . . ." "Oh, shut up!" he said. "Must be love," teased his brother-in-law. "Come on, Vinny, 'fess up; what's she like?" And all this so annoyed him he caught the next train home. From a booth in Grand Central he called to apologize, but a sick nervousness hummed inside him, and he hung up while the operator was still trying to make a connection. He wanted a drink. At the Commodore Bar he spent an hour or so drowning four daiquiris—it was Saturday, it was nine, there was nothing to do unless he did it alone, he was feeling sad for himself. Now in the park behind the Public Library sweethearts moved whisperingly under trees, and drinking-fountain water bubbled softly, like their voices, but for all the white April evening meant to him, Vincent, drunk a little and wandering, might as well have been old, like the old bench-sitters rasping phlegm.

In the country, spring is a time of small happenings happening quietly, hyacinth shoots thrusting in a garden, willows burning with a sudden frosty fire of green, lengthening afternoons of long flowing dusk, and midnight rain opening lilac; but in the city there is the fanfare of organ-grinders, and odors, undiluted by winter wind, clog the air; windows long closed go up, and conversation, drifting beyond a room, collides with the jangle of a peddler's bell. It is the crazy season of toy balloons and roller skates, of courtyard baritones and men of freakish enterprise, like the one who jumped up now like a jack-in-the-box. He was old, he had a telescope and a sign: 25c See the Moon! See the Stars! 25c! No stars could penetrate a city's glare, but Vincent saw the moon, a round, shadowed whiteness, and then a blaze of electric bulbs: Four Roses, Bing Cro——he was moving through caramel-scented staleness, swimming through oceans of cheese-pale faces, neon, and darkness. Above the blasting of a jukebox, bulletfire boomed, a cardboard duck fell plop, and somebody screeched: "Yay Iggy!" It was a Broadway funhouse, a penny arcade, and jammed from wall to wall with Saturday splurgers. He watched a penny movie (*What The Bootblack Saw*), and had his fortune told by a wax witch leering behind glass: "Yours is an affectionate nature" . . . but he read no further, for up near the jukebox there was an attractive commotion. A crowd of kids, clapping in time to jazz music, had formed a circle around two dancers. These dancers were both colored, both girls. They swayed together slow and easy, like lovers, rocked and stamped and rolled serious savage eyes, their muscles rythmically attuned to the ripple of a clarinet, the rising harangue of a drum. Vincent's gaze traveled round the audience, and when he saw her a bright shiver went through him, for something of the dance's violence was reflected in her face. Standing there beside a tall ugly boy, it was as if she were the sleeper and the Negroes a dream. Trumpet-drum-piano, bawling on behind a black girl's froggy voice, wailed toward a rocking finale. The clapping ended, the dancers parted. She was alone now; though Vincent's instinct was to leave before she noticed, he advanced, and, as one would gently waken a sleeper, lightly touched her shoulder. "Hello," he said, his voice too loud. Turning, she stared at him, and her eyes were clear-blank. First terror, then puzzlement replaced the dead lost look. She took a step backward, and, just as the jukebox commenced hollering again, he seized her wrist: "You remember me," he prompted, "the gallery? Your painting?" She blinked, let the lids sink sleepily over those eyes, and he could feel the slow relaxing of tension in her arm. She was thinner than he recalled, prettier, too, and her hair, grown out somewhat, hung in casual disorder. A little silver Christmas ribbon dangled sadly from a stray lock. He started to say, "Can I buy you a drink?" but she leaned against him, her head resting on his chest like a child's, and he said: "Will you come home with me?" She lifted her face; the answer, when it came, was a breath, a whisper: "Please," she said.

Vincent stripped off his clothes, arranged them neatly in the closet, and admired his nakedness before a mirrored door. He was not so handsome as he supposed, but handsome all the same. For his moderate height he was excellently proportioned; his hair was dark yellow, and his delicate, rather snub-nosed face had a fine, ruddy coloring. The rumble of running water broke the quiet; she was in the bathroom preparing to bathe. He dressed in loose-fitting flannel pajamas, lit a cigarette, said, "Everything all right?" The water went off, a long silence, then: "Yes, thank you." On the way home in a cab he'd made an attempt at conversation, but she had said nothing, not even when they entered the apartment—and this last offended him, for, taking rather female pride in his quarters, he'd expected a complimentary remark. It was one enormously high-ceilinged room, a bath and kitchenette, a backyard garden. In the furnishings he'd combined modern with antique and produced a distinguished result. Decorating the walls were a trio of Toulouse-Lautrec prints, a framed circus poster, D. J.'s painting, photographs of Rilke, Nijinsky and Duse. A candelabra of lean blue candles burned on a desk; the room, washed in their delirious light, wavered. French doors led into the yard. He never used it much, for it was a place impossible to keep clean. There were a few dead tulip stalks dark in the moonshine, a puny heaven tree, and an old weather-worn chair left by the last tenant. He paced back and forth over the cold

flagstones, hoping that in the cool air the drugged drunk sensation he felt would wear off. Nearby a piano was being badly
mauled, and in a window above there was a child's face. He
was thumbing a blade of grass when her shadow fell long
across the yard. She was in the doorway. "You mustn't come
out," he said, moving toward her. "It's turned a little cold."

There was about her now an appealing softness; she seemed
somehow less angular, less out of tune with the average, and
Vincent, offering a glass of sherry, was delighted at the delicacy
with which she touched it to her lips. She was wearing his
terry-cloth robe; it was by yards too large. Her foot were bare,
and she tucked them up beside her on the couch. "It's like
Glass Hill, the candlelight," she said, and smiled. "My Granny
lived at Glass Hill. We had lovely times, sometimes; do you
know what she used to say? She used to say, 'Candles are magic
wands; light one and the world is a story book.' "

"What a dreary old lady she must've been," said Vincent,
quite drunk. "We should probably have hated each other."

"Granny would've loved you," she said. "She loved any kind
of man, every man she ever met, even Mr. Destronelli."

"Destronelli?" It was a name he'd heard before.

Her eyes slid slyly sideways, and this look seemed to say:
There must be no subterfuge between us, we who understand
each other have no need of it. "Oh, you know," she said with a
conviction that, under more commonplace circumstances,
would have been surprising. It was, however, as if he'd abandoned temporarily the faculty of surprise. "Everybody knows
him."

He curved an arm around her, and brought her nearer.
"Not me, I don't," he said, kissing her mouth, neck; she was
not responsive especially, but he said—and his voice had gone
adolescently shaky—"Never met Mr. Whoozits." He slipped a
hand inside her robe, loosening it away from her shoulders.
Above one breast she had a birthmark, small and star-shaped.
He glanced at the mirrored door where uncertain light rippled
their reflections, made them pale and incomplete. She was
smiling. "Mr. Whoozits," he said, "what does he look like?"
The suggestion of a smile faded, a small monkeylike frown
flickered on her face. She looked above the mantel at her
painting, and he realized that this was the first notice she'd
shown it; she appeared to study in the picture a particular
object, but whether hawk or head he could not say. "Well,"
she said quietly, pressing closer to him, "he looks like you, like
me, like most anybody."

It was raining; in the wet noon light two nubs of candle still burned, and at an open window gray curtains tossed forlornly. Vincent extricated his arm; it was numb from the weight of her body. Careful not to make a noise, he eased out of bed, blew out the candles, tiptoed into the bathroom, and doused his face with cold water. On the way to the kitchenette he flexed his arms, feeling, as he hadn't for a long time, an intensely male pleasure in his strength, a healthy wholeness of person. He made and put on a tray orange juice, raisin-bread toast, a pot of tea; then, so inexpertly that everything on the tray rattled, he brought the breakfast in and placed it on a table beside the bed.

She had not moved; her ruffled hair spread fanwise across the pillow, and one hand rested in the hollow where his head had lain. He leaned over and kissed her lips, and her eyelids, blue with sleep, trembled. "Yes, yes, I'm awake," she murmured, and rain, lifting in the wind, sprayed against the window like surf. He somehow knew that with her there would be none of the usual artifice: no avoidance of eyes, no shamefaced, accusing pause. She raised herself on her elbow; she looked at him, Vincent thought, as if he were her husband, and, handing her the orange juice, he smiled his gratitude.

"What is today?"

"Sunday," he told her, bundling under the quilt, and settling the tray across his legs.

"But there are no church bells," she said. "And it's raining."

Vincent divided a piece of toast. "You don't mind that, do you? Rain—such a peaceful sound." He poured tea. "Sugar? Cream?"

She disregarded this, and said, "Today is Sunday what? What month, I mean?"

"Where have you been living, in the subway?" he said, grinning. And it puzzled him to think she was serious. "Oh, April . . . April something-or-other."

"April," she repeated. "Have I been here long?"

"Only since last night."

"Oh."

Vincent stirred his tea, the spoon tinkling in the cup like a bell. Toast crumbs spilled among the sheets, and he thought of the *Tribune* and the *Times* waiting outside the door, but they, this morning, held no charms; it was best lying here beside her in the warm bed, sipping tea, listening to the rain. Odd, when you stopped to consider, certainly very odd. She did not know his name, nor he hers. And so he said, "I still owe you thirty dollars, do you realize that? Your own fault, of course—leaving such a damn fool address. And D.J., what is that supposed to mean?"

"I don't think I'd better tell you my name," she said. "I could make up one easy enough: Dorothy Jordan, Delilah Johnson; see? There are all kinds of names I could make up, and if it wasn't for him I'd tell you right."

Vincent lowered the tray to the floor. He rolled over on his side, and, facing her, his heartbeat quickened. "Who's him?" Though her expression was calm, anger muddied her voice when she said, "If you don't know him, then tell me, why am I here?"

Silence, and outside the rain seemed suddenly suspended. A ship's horn moaned in the river. Holding her close, he combed his fingers through her hair, and, wanting so much to be believed, said, "Because I love you."

She closed her eyes. "What became of them?"

"Who?"

"The others you've said that to."

It commenced again, the rain spattering grayly at the window, falling on hushed Sunday streets; listening, Vincent remembered. He remembered his cousin, Lucille, poor, beautiful, stupid Lucille who sat all day embroidering silk flowers on scraps of linen. And Allen T. Baker—there was the winter they'd spent in Havana, the house they'd lived in, crumbling rooms of rose-colored rock; poor Allen, he'd thought it was to be forever. Gordon, too. Gordon, with the kinky yellow hair, and a head full of old Elizabethan ballads. Was it true he'd shot himself? And Connie Silver, the deaf girl, the one who had wanted to be an actress—what had become of her? Or Helen, Louise, Laura? "There was just one," he said, and to his own ears, this had a truthful ring. "Only one, and she's dead."

Tenderly, as if in sympathy, she touched his cheek. "I suppose he killed her," she said, her eyes so close he could see the outline of his face imprisoned in their greenness. "He killed Miss Hall, you know. The dearest woman in the world, Miss Hall, and so pretty your breath went away. I had piano lessons with her, and when she played the piano, when she said hello and when she said good-bye—it was like my heart would stop." Her voice had taken on an impersonal tone, as though she were talking of matters belonging to another age, and in which she was not concerned directly. "It was the end of summer when she married him—September, I think. She went to Atlanta, and they were married there, and she never came back. It was just that sudden." She snapped her fingers. "Just like that. I saw a picture of him in the paper. Sometimes I think if she'd known how much I loved her—why are there some you can't ever tell?—I think maybe she wouldn't have married; maybe it would've all been different, like I wanted it." She turned her face into the pillow, and if she cried there was no sound.

On May twentieth she was eighteen; it seemed incredible—Vincent had thought her many years older. He wanted to introduce her at a surprise party, but had finally to admit that this was an unsuitable plan. First off, though the subject was always there on the tip of his tongue, not once had he ever mentioned D. J. to any of his friends; secondly, he could visualize discouragingly well the entertainment provided them at meeting a girl about whom, while they openly shared an apartment, he knew nothing, not even her name. Still the birthday called for some kind of treat. Dinner and the theater were hopeless. She hadn't, through no fault of his, a dress of any sort. He'd given her forty-odd dollars to buy clothes, and here is what she spent it on: a leather windbreaker, a set of military brushes, a raincoat, a cigarette lighter. Also, her suitcase, which she'd brought to the apartment, had contained nothing but hotel soap, a pair of scissors she used for pruning her hair, two Bibles, and an appalling color-tinted photograph. The photograph showed a simpering middle-aged woman with dumpy features. There was an inscription: Best Wishes and Good Luck from Martha Lovejoy Hall.

Because she could not cook they had their meals out; his salary and the limitations of her wardrobe confined them mostly to the Automat—her favorite: the macaroni was so delicious!—or one of the bar-grills along Third. And so the birthday dinner was eaten in an Automat. She'd scrubbed her face until the skin shone red, trimmed and shampooed her hair, and with the messy skill of a six-year-old playing grownup, varnished her nails. She wore the leather windbreaker, and on it pinned a sheaf of violets he'd given her; it must have looked amusing, for two rowdy girls sharing their table giggled frantically. Vincent said if they didn't shut up . . .

"Oh, yeah, who do you think you are?"

"Superman. Jerk things he's superman."

It was too much, and Vincent lost his temper. He shoved back from the table, upsetting a ketchup jar. "Let's get the hell out of here," he said, but D. J., who had paid the fracas no attention whatever, went right on spooning blackberry cobbler; furious as he was, he waited quietly until she finished, for he respected her remoteness, and yet wondered in what period of time she lived. It was futile, he'd discovered, to question her past; still, she seemed only now and then aware of the present, and it was likely the future didn't mean much to her. Her mind was like a mirror reflecting blue space in a barren room.

"What would you like now?" he said, as they came into the street. "We could ride in a cab through the park."

She wiped off with her jacket-cuff flecks of blackberry staining the corners of her mouth, and said, "I want to go to a picture show."

The movies. Again. In the last month he'd seen so many films, snatches of Hollywood dialogue rumbled in his dreams. One Saturday at her insistence they'd bought tickets to three different theaters, cheap places where smells of latrine disinfectant poisoned the air. And each morning before leaving for work he left on the mantel fifty cents—rain or shine, she went to a picture show. But Vincent was sensitive enough to see why: there had been in his own life a certain time of limbo when he'd gone to movies every day, often sitting through several repeats of the same film; it was in its way like religion, for there, watching the shifting patterns of black and white, he knew a release of conscience similar to the kind a man must find confessing to his father.

"Handcuffs," she said, referring to an incident in *The Thirty-Nine Steps,* which they'd seen at the Beverly in a program of Hitchcock revivals. "That blonde woman and the man handcuffed together—well, it made me think of something else." She stepped into a pair of his pajamas, pinned the corsage of violets to the edge of her pillow, and folded up on the bed. "People getting caught like that, locked together."

Vincent yawned. "Uh huh," he said, and turned off the lights. "Again, happy birthday darling, it was a happy birthday?"

She said, "Once I was in this place, and there were two girls dancing; they were so free—there was just them and nobody else, and it was beautiful like a sunset." She was silent a long while; then, her slow Southern voice dragging over the words: "It was mighty nice of you to bring me violets."

"Glad—like them," he answered sleepily.

"It's a shame they have to die."

"Yes, well, good night."

"Good night."

Close-up. Oh, but John, it isn't for my sake after all we've the children to consider a divorce would ruin their lives! Fadeout. The screen trembles; rattle of drums, flourish of trumpets: R.K.O. PRESENTS . . .

Here is a hall without exit, a tunnel without end. Overhead, chandeliers sparkle, and wind-bent candles float on currents of air. Before him is an old man rocking in a rocking chair, an old man with yellow-dyed hair, powdered cheeks, kewpie-doll lips: Vincent recognizes Vincent. Go away, screams Vincent, the young and handsome, but Vincent, the old and horrid, creeps forward on all fours, and climbs spiderlike onto his back. Threats, pleas, blows, nothing will dislodge him. And so he races with his shadow, his rider jogging up and down. A serpent of lightning blazes, and all at once the tunnel seethes with men wearing white tie and tails, women costumed in brocaded gowns. He is humiliated; how gauche they must think him appearing at so elegant a gathering carrying on his back, like Sinbad, a sordid old man. The guests stand about in petrified pairs, and there is no conversation. He notices then that many are also saddled with malevolent semblances of themselves, outward embodiments of inner decay. Just beside him a lizard-like man rides an albino-eyed Negro. A man is coming toward him, the host; short, florid, bald, he steps lightly, precisely in glacé shoes; one arm, held stiffly crooked, supports a massive headless hawk whose talons, latched to the wrist, draw blood. The hawk's wings unfurl as its master struts by. On a pedestal there is perched an old-time phonograph. Winding the handle, the host supplies a record: a tinny worn-out waltz vibrates the morning-glory horn. He lifts a hand, and in a soprano voice announces: "Attention! The dancing will commence." The host with his hawk weaves in and out as round and round they dip, they turn. The walls widen, the ceiling grows tall. A girl glides into Vincent's arms, and a cracked, cruel imitation of his voice says: "Lucille, how divine; that exquisite scent, is it violet?" This is Cousin Lucille, and then, as they circle the room, her face changes. Now he waltzes with another. "Why, Connie, Connie Silver! How marvelous to see you," shrieks the voice, for Connie is quite deaf. Suddenly a gentleman with a bullet-bashed head cuts in: "Gordon, forgive me, I never meant . . ." but they are gone, Gordon and Connie, dancing together. Again, a new partner. It is D. J., and she too has a figure barnacled to her back, an enchanting auburn-haired child; like an emblem of innocence, the child cuddles to her chest a snowball kitten. "I am heavier than I look," says the child, and the terrible voice retorts, "But I am heaviest of all." The instant their hands meet he begins to feel the weight upon him diminish; the old Vincent is fading. His feet lift off the floor, he floats upward from her embrace. The victrola grinds away loud as ever, but he is rising high, and the white receding faces gleam below like mushrooms on a dark meadow.

The host releases his hawk, sends it soaring. Vincent thinks, no matter, it is a blind thing, and the wicked are safe among the blind. But the hawk wheels above him, swoops down, claws foremost; at last he knows there is to be no freedom.

And the blackness of the room filled his eyes. One arm lolled over the bed's edge, his pillow had fallen to the floor. Instinctively he reached out, asking mother-comfort of the girl beside him. Sheets smooth and cold; emptiness, and the tawdry fragrance of drying violets. He snapped up straight: "You, where are you?"

The French doors were open. An ashy trace of moon swayed on the threshold, for it was not yet light, and in the kitchen the refrigerator purred like a giant cat. A stack of papers rustled on the desk. Vincent called again, softly this time, as if he wished himself unheard. Rising, he stumbled forward on dizzy legs, and looked into the yard. She was there, leaning, half-kneeling, against the heaven tree. "What?" and she whirled around. He could not see her well, only a dark substantial shape. She came closer. A finger pressed her lips.

"What is it?" he whispered.

She rose on tiptoe, and her breath tingled in his ear. "I warn you, go inside."

"Stop this foolishness," he said in a normal voice. "Out here barefooted, you'll catch . . ." but she clamped a hand over his mouth.

"I saw him," she whispered. "He's here."

Vincent knocked her hand away. It was hard not to slap her. "Him! Him! Him! What's the matter with you? Are you——" he tried too late to prevent the word—"crazy?" There, the acknowledgment of something he'd known, but had not allowed his conscious mind to crystallize. And he thought: Why should this make a difference? A man cannot be held to account for those he loves. Untrue. Feeble-witted Lucille weaving mosaics on silk, embroidering his name on scarves; Connie, in her hushed deaf world, listening for his footstep, a sound she would surely hear; Allen T. Baker thumbing his photograph, still needing love, but old now, and lost—all betrayed.

And he'd betrayed himself with talents unexploited, voyages never taken, promises unfulfilled. There had seemed nothing left him until—oh, why in his lovers must he always find the broken image of himself? Now, as he looked at her in the aging dawn, his heart was cold with the death of love.

She moved away, and under the tree. "Leave me here," she said, her eyes scanning tenement windows. "Only a moment."

Vincent waited, waited. On all sides windows looked down like the doors of dreams, and overhead, four flights up, a family's laundry whipped a washline. The setting moon was like the early moon of dusk, a vaporish cartwheel, and the sky, draining of dark, was washed with gray. Sunrise wind shook the leaves of the heaven tree, and in the paling light the yard assumed a pattern, objects a position, and from the roofs came the throaty morning rumble of pigeons. A light went on. Another.

And at last she lowered her head; whatever she was looking for, she had not found it. Or, he wondered as she turned to him with tilted lips, had she?

"Well, you're home kinda early, aren't you, Mr. Waters?" It was Mrs. Brennan, the super's bowlegged wife. "And, well, Mr. Waters—lovely weather, ain't it?—you and me got sumpin' to talk about."

"Mrs. Brennan—" how hard it was to breathe, to speak; the words grated his hurting throat, sounded loud as thunderclaps—"I'm rather ill, so if you don't mind . . ." and he tried to brush past her.

"Say, that's a pity. Ptomaine, must be ptomaine. Yessir, I tell you a person can't be too careful. It's them Jews, you know. They run all them delicatessens. Uh uh, none of that Jew food for me." She stepped before the gate, blocking his path, and pointed an admonishing finger: "Trouble with you, Mr. Waters, is that you don't lead no kinda *normal* life."

A knot of pain was set like a malignant jewel in the core of his head; each aching motion made jeweled pinpoints of color flare out. The super's wife blabbed on, but there were blank moments when, fortunately, he could not hear at all. It was like a radio—the volume turned low, then full blast. "Now I know she's a decent Christian lady, Mr. Waters, or else what would a gentleman like you be doing with—hm. Still, the fact is, Mr. Cooper don't tell lies, and he's a real calm man, besides. Been gas meter man for this district I don't know how long." A truck rolled down the street spraying water, and her voice, submerged below its roar, came up again like a shark.

"Mr. Cooper had every reason to believe she meant to kill him—well, you can imagine, her standin' there with them scissors, and shoutin'. She called him an Eyetalian name. Now all you got to do is look at Mr. Cooper to know he ain't no Eyetalian. Well, you can see, Mr. Waters, such carryings-on are bound to give the house a bad . . ."

Brittle sunshine plundering the depths of his eyes made tears, and the super's wife, wagging her finger, seemed to break into separate pieces: a nose, a chin, a red, red eye. "Mr. Destronelli," he said. "Excuse me, Mrs. Brennan, I mean excuse me." She thinks I'm drunk, and I'm sick, and can't she see I'm sick? "My guest is leaving. She's leaving today, and she won't be back."

"Well, now, you don't say," said Mrs. Brennan, clucking her tongue. "Looks like she needs a rest, poor little thing. So pale, sorta. Course I don't want no more to do with them Eyetalians than the next one, but imagine thinking Mr. Cooper was an Eyetalian. Why, he's white as you or me." She tapped his shoulder solicitously. "Sorry you feel so sick, Mr. Waters; ptomaine, I tell you. A person can't be too care . . ."

The hall smelled of cooking and incinerator ashes. There was a stairway which he never used, his apartment being on the first floor, straight ahead. A match snapped fire, and Vincent, groping his way, saw a small boy—he was not more than three or four—squatting under the stairwell; he was playing with a big box of kitchen matches, and Vincent's presence appeared not to interest him. He simply struck another match. Vincent could not make his mind work well enough to phrase a reprimand, and as he waited there, tongue-tied, a door, his door, opened.

Hide. For if she saw him she would know something was wrong, suspect something. And if she spoke, if their eyes met, then he would never be able to go through with it. So he pressed into a dark corner behind the little boy, and the little boy said, "Whatcha doin', Mister?" She was coming—he heard the slap of her sandals, the green whisper of her raincoat. "Whatcha doin', Mister?" Quickly, his heart banging in his chest, Vincent stooped and, squeezing the child against him, pressed his hand over its mouth so it could not make a sound. He did not see her pass; it was later, after the front door clicked, that he realized she was gone. The little boy sank back on the floor. "Whatcha doin', Mister?"

Four aspirins, one right after the other, and he came back

into the room; the bed had not been tidied for a week, a spilt
ash tray messed the floor, odds and ends of clothing decorated
improbable places, lampshades and such. But tomorrow, if he
felt better, there would be a general cleaning; perhaps he'd
have the walls repainted, maybe fix up the yard. Tomorrow he
could begin thinking about his friends again, accept invita-
tions, entertain. And yet this prospect, tasted in advance, was
without flavor: all he'd known before seemed to him now sterile
and spurious. Footsteps in the hall; could she return this soon,
the movie over, the afternoon gone? Fever can make time pass
so queerly, and for an instant he felt as though his bones
were floating loose inside him. Clopclop, a child's sloppy shoe-
fall, the footsteps passed up the stairs, and Vincent moved,
floated toward the mirrored closet. He longed to hurry, knowing he must, but the air seemed thick with gummy fluid. He
brought her suitcase from the closet, and put it on the bed, a
sad cheap suitcase with rusty locks and a warped hide. He
eyed it with guilt. Where would she go? How would she live?
When he'd broken with Connie, Gordon, all the others, there
had been about it at least a certain dignity. Really, though—
and he'd thought it out—there was no other way. So he
gathered her belongings. Miss Martha Lovejoy Hall peeked
out from under the leather windbreaker, her music-teacher's
face smiling an oblique reproach. Vincent turned her over,
face down, and tucked in the frame an envelope containing
twenty dollars. That would buy a ticket back to Glass Hill, or
wherever it was she came from. Now he tried to close the
case, and, too weak with fever, collapsed on the bed. Quick
yellow wings glided through the window. A butterfly. He'd
never seen a butterfly in this city, and it was like a floating
mysterious flower, like a sign of some sort, and he watched
with a kind of horror as it waltzed in the air. Outside, somewhere, the razzle-dazzle of a beggar's grind-organ started up;
it sounded like a broken-down pianola, and it played *La Mar-
seillaise*. The butterfly lighted on her painting, crept across
crystal eyes, and flattened its wings like a ribbon bow over
the loose head. He fished about in the suitcase until he found
her scissors. He first purposed to slash the butterfly's wings,
but it spiraled to the ceiling and hung there like a star. The
scissors stabbed the hawk's heart, ate through canvas like a
ravening steel mouth, scraps of picture flaking the floor like
cuttings of stiff hair. He went on his knees, pushed the pieces
into a pile, put them in the suitcase, and slammed the lid shut.
He was crying. And through the tears the butterfly magnified

on the ceiling, huge as a bird, and there was more: a flock of lilting, winking yellow; whispering lonesomely, like surf sucking a shore. The wind from their wings blew the room into space. He heaved forward, the suitcase banging his leg, and threw open the door. A match flared. The little boy said: "Whatcha doin', Mister?" And Vincent, setting the suitcase in the hall, grinned sheepishly. He closed the door like a thief, bolted the safety lock and, pulling up a chair, tilted it under the knob. In the still room there was only the subtlety of shifting sunlight and a crawling butterfly; it drifted downward like a tricky scrap of crayon paper, and landed on a candlestick. *Sometimes he is not a man at all*—she'd told him that, huddling here on the bed, talking swiftly in the minutes before dawn—*sometimes he is something very different: a hawk, a child, a butterfly.* And then she'd said: *At the place where they took me there were hundreds of old ladies, and young men, and one of the young men said he was a pirate, and one of the old ladies—she was near ninety—used to make me feel her stomach. "Feel," she'd say, "feel how strong he kicks?" This old lady took painting class, too, and her paintings looked like crazy quilts. And naturally he was in this place. Mr. Destronelli. Only he called himself Gum. Doctor Gum. Oh, he didn't fool me, even though he wore a gray wig, and made himself up to look real old and kind, I knew. And then one day I left, ran clear away, and hid under a lilac bush, and a man came along in a little red car, and he had a little mouse-haired mustache, and little cruel eyes. But it was him. And when I told him who he was he made me get out of his car. And then another man, that was in Philadelphia, picked me up in a café and took me into an alley. He talked Italian, and had tattoo pictures all over. But it was him. And the next man, he was the one who painted his toenails, sat down beside me in a movie because he thought I was a boy, and when he found out I wasn't he didn't get mad but let me live in his room, and cooked pretty things for me to eat. But he wore a silver locket and one day I looked inside and there was a picture of Miss Hall. So I knew it was him, so I had this feeling she was dead, so I knew he was going to murder me. And he will. He will."* Dusk, and nightfall, and the fibers of sound called silence wove a shiny blue mask. Waking, he peered through eyeslits, heard the frenzied pulse-beat of his watch, the scratch of a key in a lock. Somewhere in this dusk a murderer separates himself from shadow and with a rope follows the flash of silk legs up doomed stairs. And here the dreamer staring through his mask dreams of deceit. Without investigating he knows the suitcase is missing, that she has come, that she has gone; why, then, does he feel so little the pleasure of safety, and only cheated, and small—small as the night when he searched the moon through an old man's telescope?

3

Like fragments of an old letter, scattered popcorn lay trampled flat, and she, leaning back in a watchman's attitude, allowed her gaze to hunt among it, as if deciphering here and there a word, an answer. Her eyes shifted discreetly to the man mounting the steps, Vincent. There was about him the freshness of a shower, shave, cologne, but dreary blue circled his eyes, and the crisp seersucker into which he'd changed had been made for a heavier man: a long month of pneumonia, and wakeful burning nights had lightened his weight a dozen pounds, and more. Each morning, evening, meeting her here at his gate, or near the gallery, or outside the restaurant where he lunched, a nameless disorder took hold, a paralysis of time and identity. The wordless pantomime of her pursuit contracted his heart, and there were coma-like days when she seemed not one, but all, a multiple person, and her shadow in the street every shadow, following and followed. And once they'd been alone together in an automatic elevator, and he'd screamed: "I am not him! Only me, only me!" But she smiled as she'd smiled telling of the man with painted toenails, because, after all, she knew.

It was suppertime, and, not knowing where to eat, he paused under a street lamp that, blooming abruptly, fanned complex light over stone; while he waited there came a clap of thunder, and all along the street every face but two, his and the girl's, tilted upward. A blast of river breeze tossed the children's laughter as they, linking arms, pranced like carousel ponies, and carried the mama's voice who, leaning from a window, howled: rain, Rachel, rain—gonna rain gonna rain! And the gladiola, ivy-filled flower cart jerked crazily as the peddler, one eye slanted skyward, raced for shelter. A potted geranium fell off, and the little girls gathered the blooms and tucked them behind their ears. The blending spatter of running feet and raindrops tinkled on the xylophone sidewalks—the slamming of doors, the lowering of windows, then nothing but silence, and rain. Presently, with slow scraping steps, she came below the lamp to stand beside him, and it was as if the sky were a thunder-cracked mirror, for the rain fell between them like a curtain of splintered glass.

My Side of the Matter

I KNOW what is being said about me and you can take my side or theirs, that's your own business. It's my word against Eunice's and Olivia-Ann's, and it should be plain enough to anyone with two good eyes which one of us has their wits about them. I just want the citizens of the U.S.A. to know the facts, that's all.

The facts: On Sunday, August 12, this year of our Lord, Eunice tried to kill me with her papa's Civil War sword and Olivia-Ann cut up all over the place with a fourteen-inch hog knife. This is not even to mention lots of other things.

It began six months ago when I married Marge. That was the first thing I did wrong. We were married in Mobile after an acquaintance of only four days. We were both sixteen and she was visiting my cousin Georgia. Now that I've had plenty of time to think it over, I can't for the life of me figure how I fell for the likes of her. She has no looks, no body, and no brains whatsoever. But Marge is a natural blonde and maybe that's the answer. Well, we were married going on three months when Marge ups and gets pregnant; the second thing I did wrong. Then she starts hollering that she's got to go home to Mama—only she hasn't got no mama, just these two aunts. Eunice and Olivia-Ann. So she makes me quit my perfectly

swell position clerking at the Cash'n' Carry and move here to
Admiral's Mill which is nothing but a damn gap in the road
any way you care to consider it.

The day Marge and I got off the train at the L&N depot it
was raining cats and dogs and do you think anyone came to
meet us? I'd shelled out forty-one cents for a telegram, too!
Here my wife's pregnant and we have to tramp seven miles in
a downpour. It was bad on Marge as I couldn't carry hardly
any of our stuff on account of I have terrible trouble with my
back. When I first caught sight of this house I must say I was
impressed. It's big and yellow and has real columns out in
front and japonica trees, both red and white, lining the yard.

Eunice and Olivia-Ann had seen us coming and were
waiting in the hall. I swear I wish you could get a look at
these two. Honest, you'd die! Eunice is this big old fat thing
with a behind that must weight a tenth of a ton. She troops
around the house, rain or shine, in this real old-fashioned
nighty, calls it a kimono, but it isn't anything in this world but
a dirty flannel nighty. Furthermore she chews tobacco and
tries to pretend so ladylike, spitting on the sly. She keeps gab-
bing about what a fine education she had, which is her way of
attempting to make me feel bad, although, personally, it never
bothers me so much as one whit as I know for a fact she
can't even read the funnies without she spells out every single,
solitary word. You've got to hand her one thing, though—she
can add and subtract money so fast that there's no doubt but
what she could be up in Washington, D.C., working where
they make the stuff. Not that she hasn't got plenty of money!
Naturally she says she hasn't but I know she has because one
day, accidentally, I happened to find close to a thousand
dollars hidden in a flower pot on the side porch. I didn't touch
one cent, only Eunice says I stole a hundred-dollar bill which
is a venomous lie from start to finish. Of course anything
Eunice says is an order from headquarters as not a breathing
soul in Admiral's Mill can stand up and say he doesn't owe her
money and if she said Charlie Carson (a blind, ninety-year-old
invalid who hasn't taken a step since 1896) threw her on her
back and raped her everybody in this county would swear the
same on a stack of Bibles.

Now Olivia-Ann is worse, and that's the truth! Only she's
not so bad on the nerves as Eunice, for she is a natural-born
half-wit and ought really to be kept in somebody's attic. She's
real pale and skinny and has a mustache. She squats around
most of the time whittling on a stick with her fourteen-inch

hog knife, otherwise she's up to some devilment, like what she did to Mrs. Harry Steller Smith. I swore not ever to tell anyone that, but when a vicious attempt has been made on a person's life, I say the hell with promises.

Mrs. Harry Steller Smith was Eunice's canary named after a woman from Pensacola who makes home-make cure-all that Eunice takes for the gout. One day I heard this terrible racket in the parlor and upon investigating, what did I find but Olivia-Ann shooing Mrs. Harry Steller Smith out an open window with a broom and the door to the bird cage wide. If I hadn't walked in at exactly that moment she might never have been caught. She got scared that I would tell Eunice and blurted out the whole thing, said it wasn't fair to keep one of God's creatures locked up that way, besides which she couldn't stand Mrs. Harry Steller Smith's singing. Well, I felt kind of sorry for her and she gave me two dollars, so I helped her cook up a story for Eunice. Of course I wouldn't have taken the money except I thought it would ease her conscience.

The very *first* words Eunice said when I stepped inside this house were, "So this is what you ran off behind our back and married, Marge?"

Marge says, "Isn't he the best-looking thing, Aunt Eunice?"

Eunice eyes me u-p and d-o-w-n and says, "Tell him to turn around."

While my back is turned, Eunice says, "You sure must've picked the runt of the litter. Why, this isn't any sort of man at all."

I've never been so taken back in my life! True, I'm slightly stocky, but then I haven't got my full growth yet.

"He is too," says Marge.

Olivia-Ann, who's been standing there with her mouth so wide the flies could buzz in and out, says, "You heard what Sister said. He's not any sort of a man whatsoever. The very idea of this little runt running around claiming to be a man! Why, he isn't even of the male sex!"

Marge says, "You seem to forget, Aunt Olivia-Ann, that this is my husband, the father of my unborn child."

Eunice made a nasty sound like only she can and said, "Well, all I can say is I most certainly wouldn't be bragging about it."

Isn't that a nice welcome? And after I gave up my perfectly swell position clerking at the Cash 'n' Carry.

But it's not a drop in the bucket to what came later that same evening. After Bluebell cleared away the supper dishes,

Marge asked, just as nice as she could, if we could borrow the car and drive over to the picture show at Phoenix City.

"You must be clear out of your head," says Eunice, and, honest, you'd think we'd asked for the kimono off her back.

"You must be clear out of your head," says Olivia-Ann.

"It's six o'clock," says Eunice, "and if you think I'd let that runt drive my just-as-good-as-brand-new 1934 Chevrolet as far as the privy and back you must've gone clear out of your head."

Naturally such language makes Marge cry.

"Never you mind, honey," I said, "I've driven pulenty of Cadillacs in my time."

"Humf," says Eunice.

"Yeah," says I.

Eunice says, "If he's ever so much as driven a plow I'll eat a dozen gophers fried in turpentine."

"I won't have you refer to my husband in any such manner," says Marge. "You're acting simply outlandish! Why, you'd think I'd picked up some absolutely strange man in some absolutely strange place."

"If the shoe fits, wear it!" says Eunice.

"Don't think you can pull the sheep over our eyes," says Olivia-Ann in that braying voice of hers so much like the mating call of a jackass you can't rightly tell the difference.

"We weren't born just around the corner, you know," says Eunice.

Marge says, "I'll give you to understand that I'm legally wed till death do us part to this man by a certified justice of the peace as of three and one-half months ago. Ask anybody. Furthermore, Aunt Eunice, he is free, white and sixteen. Furthermore, George Far Sylvester does not appreciate hearing his father referred to in any such manner."

George Far Sylvester is the name we've planned for the baby. Has a strong sound, don't you think? Only the way things stand I have positively no feelings in the matter now whatsoever.

"How can a girl have a baby with a girl?" says Olivia-Ann, which was a calculated attack on my manhood. "I do declare there's something new every day."

"Oh, shush up," says Eunice. "Let us hear no more about the picture show in Phoenix City."

Marge sobs, "Oh-h-h, but it's Judy Garland."

"Never mind, honey," I said, "I most likely saw the show in Mobile ten years ago."

"That's a deliberate falsehood," shouts Olivia-Ann. "Oh, you are a scoundrel, you are. Judy hasn't been in the pictures ten years." Olivia-Ann's never seen not even one picture show in her entire fifty-two years (she won't tell anybody how old she is but I dropped a card to the capitol in Montgomery and they were very nice about answering), but she subscribes to eight movie books. According to Postmistress Delancey, it's the only mail she ever gets outside of the Sears & Roebuck. She has this positively morbid crush on Gary Cooper and has one trunk and two suitcases full of his photos.

So we got up from the table and Eunice lumbers over to the window and looks out to the chinaberry tree and says, "Birds settling in their roost—time we went to bed. You have your old room, Marge, and I've fixed a cot for this gentleman on the back porch."

It took a solid minute for that to sink in.

I said, "And what, if I'm not too bold to ask, is the objection to my sleeping with my lawful wife?"

Then they both started yelling at me.

So Marge threw a conniption fit right then and there. "Stop it, stop it, stop it! I can't sand any more. Go on, babydoll—gon on and sleep wherever they say. Tomorrow we'll see. . . ."

Eunice says, "I swanee if the child hasn't got a grain of sense, after all."

"Poor dear," says Olivia-Ann, wrapping her arm around Marge's waist and herding her off, "poor dear, so young, so innocent. Let's us just go and have a good cry on Olivia-Ann's shoulder."

May, June, and July and the best part of August I've squatted and sweltered on that damn back porch without an ounce of screening. And Marge—she hasn't opened her mouth in protest, not once! This part of Alabama is swampy, with mosquitoes that could murder a buffalo, given half a chance, not to mention dangerous flying roaches and a posse of local rats big enough to haul a wagon train from here to Timbuctoo. Oh, if it wasn't for that little unborn George I would've been making dust tracks on the road, way before now. I mean to say I haven't had five seconds alone with Marge since that first night. One or the other is always chaperoning and last week they like to have blown their tops when Marge locked herself in her room and they couldn't find me nowhere. The truth is I'd been down watching the niggers bale cotton but just for spite I let on to Eunice like Marge and I'd been up to no good. After that they added Bluebell to the shift.

And all this time I haven't even had cigarette change.

Eunice has hounded me day in and day out about getting a job. "Why don't the little heathen go out and get some honest work?" says she. As you've probably noticed, she never speaks to me directly, though more often than not I am the only one in her royal presence. "If he was any sort of man you could call a man he'd be trying to put a crust of bread in that girl's mouth instead of stuffing his own off my vittles." I think you should know that I've been living almost exclusively on cold yams and leftover grits for three months and thirteen days and I've been down to consult Dr. A. N. Carter twice. He's not exactly sure whether I have the scurvy or not.

And as for my not working, I'd like to know what a man of my abilities, a man who held a perfectly swell position with the Cash'n' Carry would find to do in a flea-bag like Admiral's Mill? There is all of one store here and Mr. Tubberville, the proprietor, is actually so lazy its painful for him have to sell anything. Then we have the Morning Star Baptist Church but they already have a preacher, an awful old turd named Shell whom Eunice drug over one day to see about the salvation of my soul. I heard him with my own ears tell her I was too far gone.

But it's what Eunice has done to Marge that really takes the cake. She has turned that girl against me in the most villainous fashion that words could not describe. Why, she even reached the point when she was sassing me back, but I provided her with a couple of good slaps and put a stop to that. No wife of mine is ever going to be disrespectful to me, not on your life!

The enemy lines are stretched tight: Bluebell, Olivia-Ann, Eunice, Marge, and the whole rest of Admiral's Mill (pop. 342). Allies: none. Such was the situation as of Sunday, August 12, when the attempt was made upon my very life.

Yesterday was quiet and hot enough to melt rock. The trouble began at exactly two o'clock. I know because Eunice has one of those fool cuckoo contraptions and it scares the daylights out of me. I was minding my own personal business in the parlor, composing a song on the upright piano which Eunice bought for Olivia-Ann and hired her a teacher to come all the way from Columbus, Georgia, once a week. Postmistress Delancey, who was my friend till she decided that it was maybe not so wise, says that the fancy teacher tore out of this house one afternoon like old Adolf Hitler was on his tail and leaped in his Ford coupé, never to be heard from again. Like I say, I'm trying to keep cool in the parlor not bothering a living soul when Olivia-Ann trots in with her hair all twisted

up in curlers and shrieks, "Cease that infernal racket this very
instant! Can't you give a body a minute's rest? And get off my
piano right smart. It's not your piano, it's my piano and if
you don't get off it right smart I'll have you in court like a
shot the first Monday in September."

She's not anything in this world but jealous on account of
I'm a natural-born musician and the songs I make up out of
my own head are absolutely marvelous.

"And just look what you've done to my genuine ivory keys,
Mr. Sylvester," says she, trotting over to the piano, "torn
nearly every one of them off right at the roots for purentee
meanness, that's what you've done."

She knows good and well that the piano was ready for the
junk heap the moment I entered this house.

I said, "Seeing as you're such a know-it-all, Miss Olivia-
Ann, maybe it would interest you to know that I'm in the
possession of a few interesting tales myself. A few things that
maybe other people would be very grateful to know. Like what
happened to Mrs. Harry Steller Smith, as for instance."

Remember Mrs. Harry Steller Smith?

She paused and looked at the empty bird cage. "You gave
me your oath," says she and turned the most terrifying shade
of purple.

"Maybe I did and again maybe I didn't," says I. "You did an
evil thing when you betrayed Eunice that way but if some
people will leave other people alone then maybe I can overlook
it."

Well, sir, she walked out of there just as *nice* and *quiet* as
you please. So I went and stretched out on the sofa which is
the most horrible piece of furniture I've ever seen and is part
of a matched set Eunice bought in Atlanta in 1912 and paid
two thousand dollars for, cash—or so she claims. This set is
black and olive plush and smells like wet chicken feathers on
a damp day. There is a big table in one corner of the parlor
which supports two pictures of Miss E and O-A's mama and
papa. Papa is kind of handsome but just between you and me
I'm convinced he has black blood in him from somewhere. He
was a captain in the Civil War and that is one thing I'll never
forget on account of his sword which is displayed over the
mantel and figures prominently in the action yet to come.
Mama has that hang-dog, half-wit look like Olivia-Ann, though
I must say Mama carries it better.

So I had just dozed off when I heard Eunice bellowing,
"Where is he? Where is he?" And the next thing I know she's

framed in the doorway with her hands planted plumb on those hippo hips and the whole pack scrunched up behind her: Bluebell, Olivia-Ann and Marge.

Several seconds passed with Eunice tapping her big old bare foot just as fast and furious as she could and fanning her fat face with this cardboard picture of Niagara Falls.

"Where is it?" says she. "Where's my hundred dollars that he made away with while my trusting back was turned?"

"*This* is the straw that broke the camel's back," says I, but I was too hot and tired to get up.

"That's not the only back that's going to be broke," says she, her bug eyes about to pop clear out of their sockets. "That was my funeral money and I want it back. Wouldn't you know he'd steal from the dead?"

"Maybe he didn't take it," says Marge.

"You keep your mouth out of this, missy," says Olivia-Ann.

"He stole my money sure as shooting," says Eunice. "Why, look at his eyes—black with guilt!"

I yawned and said, "Like they say in the courts—if the party of the first part falsely accuses the party of the second part then the party of the first part can be locked away in jail even if the State Home is where they rightfully belong for the protection of all concerned."

"God will punish him," says Eunice.

"Oh, Sister," says Olivia-Ann, "let us not wait for God."

Whereupon Eunice advances on me with this most peculiar look, her dirty flannel nighty jerking along the floor. And Olivia-Ann leeches after her and Bluebell lets forth this moan that must have been heard clear to Eufala and back while Marge stands there wringing her hands and whimpering.

"Oh-h-h," sobs Marge, "please give her back that money, babydoll."

I said, "et tu Brute?" which is from William Shakespeare.

"Look at the likes of him," says Eunice, "lying around all day not doing so much as licking a postage stamp."

"Pitiful," clucks Olivia-Ann.

"You'd think he was having a baby instead of that poor child." Eunice speaking.

Bluebell tosses in her two cents, "Ain't it the truth?"

"Well, if it isn't the old pots calling the kettle black," says I.

"After loafing here for three months does this runt have the audacity to cast aspersions in my direction?" says Eunice.

I merely flicked a bit of ash from my sleeve and not the least bit fazed said, "Dr. A. N. Carter has informed me that

I am in a dangerous scurvy condition and can't stand the least excitement whatsoever—otherwise I'm liable to foam at the mouth and bite somebody."

Then Bluebell says, "Why don't he go back to that trash in Mobile, Miss Eunice? I'se sick and tired of carryin' his ol' slop jar."

Naturally that coal-black nigger made me so mad I couldn't see straight.

So just as calm as a cucumber I arose and picked up this umbrella off the hat tree and rapped her across the head with it until it cracked smack in two.

"My real Japanese silk parasol!" shrieks Olivia-Ann.

Marge cries, "You've killed Bluebell, you've killed poor old Bluebell!"

Eunice shoves Olivia-Ann and says, "He's gone clear out of his head, Sister! Run! Run and get Mr. Tubberville!"

"I don't like Mr. Tubberville," says Olivia-Ann staunchly. "I'll go get my hog knife." And she makes a dash for the door but seeing as I care nothing for death I brought her down with a sort of tackle. It wrenched my back something terrible.

"He's going to kill her!" hollers Eunice loud enough to bring the house down. "He's going to murder us all! I warned you, Marge. Quick, child, get Papa's sword!"

So Marge gets Papa's sword and hands it to Eunice. Talk about wifely devotion! And, if that's not bad enough, Olivia-Ann gives me this terrific knee punch and I had to let go. The next thing you know we hear her out in the yard bellowing hymns.

> *Mine eyes have seen the glory of the*
> *coming of the Lord;*
> *He is trampling out the vintage where*
> *the grapes of wrath are stored. . . .*

Meanwhile Eunice is sashaying all over the place wildly thrashing Papa's sword and somehow I've managed to clamber atop the piano. Then Eunice climbs up on the piano stool and how that rickety contraption survived a monster like her I'll never be the one to tell.

"Come down from there, you yellow coward, before I run you through," says she and takes a whack and I've got a half-inch cut to prove it.

By this time Bluebell has recovered and skittered away to join Olivia-Ann holding services in the front yard. I guess they were expecting my body and God knows it would've been theirs if Marge hadn't passed out cold.

That's the only good thing I've got to say for Marge.

What happened after that I can't rightly remember except for Olivia-Ann reappearing with her fourteen-inch hog knife and a bunch of the neighbors. But suddenly Marge was the star attraction and I suppose they carried her to her room. Anyway, as soon as they left I barricaded the parlor door.

I've got all those black and olive plush chairs pushed against it and that big mahogany table that must weight a couple of tons and the hat tree and lots of other stuff. I've locked the windows and pulled down the shades. Also I've found a five-pound box of Sweet Love candy and this very minute I'm munching a juicy, creamy, chocolate cherry. Sometimes they come to the door and knock and yell and plead. Oh, yes, they've started singing a song of a very different color. But as for me—I give them a tune on the piano every now and then just to let them know I'm cheerful.

A Tree of Night

Iᴛ wᴀs winter. A string of naked light bulbs, from which it seemed all warmth had been drained, illuminated the little depot's cold, windy platform. Earlier in the evening it had rained, and now icicles hung along the station-house eaves like some crystal monster's vicious teeth. Except for a girl, young and rather tall, the platform was deserted. The girl wore a gray flannel suit, a raincoat, and a plaid scarf. Her hair, parted in the middle and rolled up neatly on the sides, was rich blondish-brown; and, while her face tended to be too thin and narrow, she was, though not extraordinarily so, attractive. In addition to an assortment of magazines and a gray suede purse on which elaborate brass letters spelled Kay, she carried conspicuously a green Western guitar.

When the train, spouting steam and glaring with light, came out of the darkness and rumbled to a halt, Kay assembled her paraphernalia and climbed up into the last coach.

The coach was a relic with a decaying interior of ancient red-plush seats, bald in spots, and peeling iodine-colored woodwork. An old-time copper lamp, attached to the ceiling, looked romantic and out of place. Gloomy dead smoke sailed the air; and the car's heated closeness accentuated the stale odor of discarded sandwiches, apple cores, and orange hulls:

this garbage, including Lily cups, soda-pop bottles, and mangled newspapers, littered the long aisle. From a water cooler, embedded in the wall, a steady stream trickled to the floor. The passengers, who glanced up wearily when Kay entered, were not, it seemed, at all conscious of any discomfort.

Kay resisted a temptation to hold her nose and threaded her way carefully down the aisle, tripping once, without disaster, over a dozing fat man's protruding leg. Two nondescript men turned an interested eye as she passed; and a kid stood up in his seat squalling, "Hey, Mama, look at de banjo! Hey, lady, lemme play ya banjo!" till a slap from Mama quelled him.

There was only one empty place. She found it at the end of the car in an isolated alcove occupied already by a man and woman who were sitting with their feet settled lazily on the vacant seat opposite. Kay hesitated a second then said, "Would you mind if I sat here?"

The woman's head snapped up as if she had not been asked a simple question, but stabbed with a needle, too. Nevertheless, she managed a smile. "Can't say as I see what's to stop you, honey," she said, taking her feet down and also, with a curious impersonality, removing the feet of the man who was staring out the window, paying no attention whatsoever.

Thanking the woman, Kay took off her coat, sat down, and arranged herself with purse and guitar at her side, magazines in her lap: comfortable enough, though she wished she had a pillow for her back.

The train lurched; a ghost of steam hissed against the window; slowly the dingy lights of the lonesome depot faded past.

"Boy, what a jerkwater dump," said the woman. "No town, no nothin'."

Kay said, "The town's a few miles away."

"That so? Live there?"

No. Kay explained she had been at the funeral of an uncle. An uncle who, though she did not of course mention it, had left her nothing in his will but the green guitar. Where was she going? Oh, back to college.

After mulling this over, the woman concluded, "What'll you ever learn in a place like that? Let me tell you, honey, I'm plenty educated and I never saw the inside of no college."

"You didn't?" murmured Kay politely and dismissed the matter by opening one of her magazines. The light was dim for reading and none of the stories looked in the least compelling.

However, not wanting to become involved in a conversational marathon, she continued gazing at it stupidly till she felt a furtive tap on her knee.

"Don't read," said the woman. "I need somebody to talk to. Naturally, it's no fun talking to *him*." She jerked a thumb toward the silent man. "He's afflicted: deaf and dumb, know what I mean?"

Kay closed the magazine and looked at her more or less for the first time. She was short; her feet barely scraped the floor. And like many undersized people she had a freak of structure, in her case an enormous, really huge head. Rouge so brightened her sagging, flesh-featured face it was difficult even to guess at her age: perhaps fifty, fifty-five. Her big sheep eyes squinted, as if distrustful of what they saw. Her hair was an obviously dyed red, and twisted into parched, fat corkscrew curls. A once-elegant lavender hat of impressive size flopped crazily on the side of her head, and she was kept busy brushing back a drooping cluster of celluloid cherries sewed to the brim. She wore a plain, somewhat shabby blue dress. Her breath had a vividly sweetish gin smell.

"You do wanna talk to me, don't you honey?"

"Sure," said Kay, moderately amused.

"Course you do. You bet you do. That's what I like about a train. Bus people are a close-mouthed buncha dopes. But a train's the place for putting your cards on the table, that's what I always say." Her voice was cheerful and booming, husky as a man's. "But on accounta *him*, I always try to get us this here seat; it's more private, like a swell compartment, see?"

"It's very pleasant," Kay agreed. "Thanks for letting me join you."

"Only too glad to. We don't have much company; it makes some folks nervous to be around him."

As if to deny it, the man made a queer, furry sound deep in his throat and plucked the woman's sleeve. "Leave me alone, dear-heart," she said, as if she were talking to an inattentive child. "I'm O.K. We're just having us a nice little ol' talk. Now behave yourself or this pretty girl will go away. She's very rich; she goes to college." And winking, she added, "He thinks I'm drunk."

The man slumped in the seat, swung his head sideways, and studied Kay intently from the corners of his eyes. These eyes, like a pair of clouded milky-blue marbles, were thickly lashed and oddly beautiful. Now, except for a certain remote-

ness, his wide, hairless face had no real expression. It was as
if he were incapable of experiencing or reflecting the slightest
emotion. His gray hair was clipped close and combed forward
into uneven bangs. He looked like a child aged abruptly by
some uncanny method. He wore a frayed blue serge suit, and
he had anointed himself with a cheap, vile perfume. Around
his wrist was strapped a Mickey Mouse watch.

He thinks I'm drunk," the woman repeated. "And the real
funny part is, I am. Oh shoot—you gotta do something, ain't
that right?" She bent closer. "Say, ain't it?"

Kay was still gawking at the man; the way he was looking
at her made her squeamish, but she could not take her eyes off
him. "I guess so," she said.

"Then let's us have us a drink," suggested the woman. She
plunged her hand into an oilcloth satchel and pulled out a
partially filled gin bottle. She began to unscrew the cap, but,
seeming to think better of this, handed the bottle to Kay.
"Gee, I forgot about you being company," she said. "I'll got
get us some nice paper cups."

So, before Kay could protest that she did not want a drink,
the woman had risen and started none too steadily down the
aisle toward the water cooler.

Kay yawned and rested her forehead against the window-
pane, her fingers idly strumming the guitar: the strings sang a
hollow, lulling tune, as monotonously soothing as the Southern landscape, smudged in darkness, flowing past the window.
An icy winter moon rolled above the train across the night
sky like a thin white wheel.

And then, without warning, a strange thing happened: the
man reached out and gently stroked Kay's cheek. Despite the
breathtaking delicacy of this movement, it was such a bold
gesture Kay was at first too startled to know what to make of
it: her thoughts shot in three or four fantastic directions. He
leaned forward till his queer eyes were very near her own; the
reek of his perfume was sickening. The guitar was silent while
they exchanged a searching gaze. Suddenly, from some spring
of compassion, she felt for him a keen sense of pity; but also,
and this she could not suppress, an overpowering disgust, an
absolute loathing: something about him, an elusive quality she
could not quite put a finger on, reminded her of—of what?

After a little, he lowered his hand solemnly and sank back
in the seat, an asinine grin transfiguring his face, as if he had
performed a clever stunt for which he wished applause.

"Giddyup! Giddup! my little bucker-ROOS . . ." shouted the

woman. And she sat down, loudly proclaiming to be, "Dizzy
as a witch! Dog tired! Whew!" From a handful of Lily cups
she separated two and casually thrust the rest down her blouse.
"Keep 'em safe and dry, ha ha ha. . . ." A coughing spasm
seized her, but when it was over she appeared calmer. "Has my
boy friend been entertaining?" she asked, patting her bosom
reverently. "Ah, he's so sweet." She looked as if she might
pass out. Kay rather wished she would.

"I don't want a drink," Kay said, returning the bottle. "I
never drink: I hate the taste."

"Mustn't be a kill-joy," said the woman firmly. "Here now,
hold your cup like a good girl."

"No, please . . ."

"Formercysake, hold it still. Imagine, nerves at your age!
Me, I can shake like a leaf, I've got reasons. Oh, Lordy, have
I got 'em."

"But . . ."

A dangerous smile tipped the woman's face hideously awry.
"What's the matter? Don't you think I'm good enough to drink
with?"

"Please, don't misunderstand," said Kay, a tremor in her
voice. "It's just that I don't like being forced to do something
I don't want to. So look, couldn't I give this to the gentleman?"

"Him? No sirree: he needs what little sense he's got. Come
on, honey, down the hatch."

Kay, seeing it was useless, decided to succumb and avoid a
possible scene. She sipped and shuddered. It was terrible gin.
It burned her throat till her eyes watered. Quickly, when the
woman was not watching, she emptied the cup out into the
sound hole of the guitar. It happened, however, that the man
saw; and Kay, realizing it, recklessly signaled to him with her
eyes a plea not to give her away. But she could not tell from
his clear-blank expression how much he understood.

"Where you from, kid?" resumed the woman presently.

For a bewildered moment, Kay was unable to provide an an-
swer. The names of several cities came to her all at once.
Finally, from this confusion, she extracted: "New Orleans.
My home is in New Orleans."

The woman beamed. "N.O.'s where I wanna go when I
kick off. One time, oh, say 1923, I ran me a sweet little fortuneteller parlor there. Let's see, that was on St. Peter Street."
Pausing, she stooped and set the empty gin bottle on the floor.
It rolled into the aisle and rocked back and forth with a

drowsy sound. "I was raised in Texas—on a big ranch—my papa was rich. Us kids always had the best; even Paris, France, clothes. I'll bet you've got a big swell house, too. Do you have a garden? Do you grow flowers?"

"Just lilacs."

A conductor entered the coach, preceded by a cold gust of wind that rattled the trash in the aisle and briefly livened the dull air. He lumbered along, stopping now and then to punch a ticket or talk with a passenger. It was after midnight. Someone was expertly playing a harmonica. Someone else was arguing the merits of a certain politician. A child cried out in his sleep.

"Maybe you wouldn't be so snotty if you knew who we was," said the woman, bobbing her tremendous head. "We ain't nobodies, not by a long shot."

Embarrassed, Kay nervously opened a pack of cigarettes and lighted one. She wondered if there might not be a seat in a car up ahead. She could not bear the woman, or, for that matter, the man, another minute. But she had never before been in a remotely comparable situation. "If you'll excuse me now," she said, "I have to be leaving. It's been very pleasant, but I promised to meet a friend on the train. . . ."

With almost invisible swiftness the woman grasped the girl's wrist. "Didn't your mama ever tell you it was sinful to lie?" she stage-whispered. The lavender hat tumbled off her head but she made no effort to retrieve it. Her tongue flicked out and wetted her lips. And, as Kay stood up, she increased the pressure of her grip. "Sit down, dear . . . there ain't any friend . . . Why, we're your only friends and we wouldn't have you leave us for the world."

"Honestly, I wouldn't lie."

"Sit down, dear."

Kay dropped her cigarette and the man picked it up. He slouched in the corner and became absorbed in blowing a chain of lush smoke rings that mounted upward like hollow eyes and expanded into nothing.

"Why, you wouldn't want to hurt his feelings by leaving us, now, would you, dear?" crooned the woman softly. "Sit down—down—now, that's a good girl. My, what a pretty guitar. What a pretty, pretty guitar . . ." Her voice faded before the sudden whooshing, static noise of a second train. And for an instant the lights in the coach went off; in the darkness the passing train's golden windows winked black-yellow-black-yellow-black-yellow. The man's cigarette pulsed like the glow of a firefly, and his smoke rings continued rising tranquilly. Outside, a bell pealed wildly.

When the lights came on again, Kay was massaging her wrist where the woman's strong fingers had left a painful bracelet mark. She was more puzzled than angry. She determined to ask the conductor if he would find her a different seat. But when he arrived to take her ticket, the request stuttered on her lips incoherently.

"Yes, miss?"

"Nothing," she said.

And he was gone.

The trio in the alcove regarded one another in mysterious silence till the woman said, "I've got something here I wanna show you, honey." She rummaged once more in the oilcloth satchel. "You won't be so snotty after you get a gander at this."

What she passed to Kay was a handbill, published on such yellowed, antique paper it looked as if it must be centuries old. In fragile, overly fancy lettering, it read:

LAZARUS

The Man Who Is Buried Alive
A MIRACLE
SEE FOR YOURSELF

Adults, 25c—Children, 10c

"I always sing a hymn and read a sermon," said the woman. "It's awful sad: some folks cry, especially the old ones. And I've got me a perfectly elegant costume: a black veil and a black dress, oh, very becoming. *He* wears a gorgeous made-to-order bridegroom suit and a turban and lotsa talcum on his face. See, we try to make it as much like a bonafide funeral as we can. But shoot, nowadays you're likely to get just a buncha smart alecks come for laughs—so sometimes I'm real glad he's afflicted like he is on accounta otherwise his feelings would be hurt, maybe."

Kay said, "You mean you're with a circus or a side-show or something like that?"

"Nope, us alone," said the woman as she reclaimed the fallen hat. "We've been doing it for years and years— played every tank town in the South: Singasong, Mississippi—Spunky, Louisiana—Eureka, Alabama . . ." these and other names rolled off her tongue musically, running together like rain. "After the hymn, after the sermon, we bury him."

"In a coffin?"

"Sort of. It's gorgeous, it's got silver stars painted all over the lid."

"I should think he would suffocate," said Kay, amazed. "How long does he stay buried?"

"All told it takes maybe an hour—course that's not counting the lure."

"The lure?"

"Uh huh. It's what we do the night before the show. See, we hunt up a store, any ol' store with a big glass window'll do, and get the owner to let *him* sit inside this window, and, well, hypnotize himself. Stays there all night stiff as a poker and people come and look: scares the livin' hell out of 'em. . . ." While she talked she jiggled a finger in her ear, withdrawing it occasionally to examine her find. "And one time this ol' bindle-stiff Mississippi sheriff tried to . . ."

The tale that followed was baffling and pointless: Kay did not bother to listen. Nevertheless, what she had heard already inspired a reverie, a vague recapitulation of her uncle's funeral; an event which, to tell the truth, had not much affected her since she had scarcely known him. And so, while gazing abstractedly at the man, an image of her uncle's face, white next the pale silk casket pillow, appeared in her mind's eye. Observing their faces simultaneously, both the man's and uncle's, as it were, she thought she recognized an odd parallel: there was about the man's face the same kind of shocking, embalmed, secret stillness, as though, in a sense, he were truly an exhibit in a glass cage, complacent to be seen, uninterested in seeing.

"I'm sorry, what did you say?"

"I said: I sure wish they'd lend us the use of a regular cemetery. Like it is now we have to put on the show wherever we can . . . mostly in empty lots that are nine times outa ten smack up against some smelly fillin' station which, ain't exactly a big help. But like I say, we got us a swell act, the best. You oughta come see it if you get a chance."

"Oh, I should love to," Kay, said, absently.

"Oh, I should love to," mimicked the woman. "Well, who asked you? Anybody ask you?" She hoisted up her skirt and enthusiastically blew her nose on the ragged hem of a petticoat. "Bu-leeve me, it's a hard way to turn a dollar. Know what our take was last month? Fifty-three bucks! Honey, you try living

on that sometime." She sniffed and rearranged her skirt with
considerable primness. "Well, one of these days my sweet
boy's sure enough going to die down there; and even then
somebody'll say it was a gyp."

At this point the man took from his pocket what seemed to
be a finely shellacked peach seed and balanced it on the palm
of his hand. He looked across at Kay and, certain of her attention, opened his eyelids wide and began to squeeze and
caress the seed in an undefinably obscene manner.

Kay frowned. "What does he want?"

"He wants you to buy it."

"But what is it?"

"A charm," said the woman. "A love charm."

Whoever was playing the harmonica stopped. Other sounds,
less unique, became at once prominent: someone snoring, the
gin bottle seesaw rolling, voices in sleepy argument, the train
wheels' distant hum.

"Where could you get love cheaper, honey?"

"It's nice. I mean it's cute. . . ." Kay said, stalling for time.
The man rubbed and polished the seed on his trouser leg. His
head was lowered at a supplicating, mournful angle, and presently he stuck the seed between his teeth and bit it, as if it
were a suspicious piece of silver. "Charms always bring me
bad luck. And besides . . . please, can't you make him stop
acting that way?"

"Don't look so scared," said the woman, more flat-voiced
than ever. "He ain't gonna hurt you."

"Make him stop, damn it!"

"What can I do?" asked the woman, shrugging her shoulders.
"You're the one that's got money. You're rich. All he wants is
a dollar, one dollar."

Kay tucked her purse under her arm. "I have just enough
to get back to school," she lied, quickly rising and stepping
out into the aisle. She stood there a moment, expecting trouble.
But nothing happened.

The woman, with rather deliberate indifference, heaved a sigh
and closed her eyes; gradually the man subsided and stuck the
charm back in his pocket. Then his hand crawled across the
seat to join the woman's in a lax embrace.

Kay shut the door and moved to the front of the observa-
tion platform. It was bitterly cold in the open air, and she
had left her raincoat in the alcove. She loosened her scarf and
draped it over her head.

Although she had never made this trip before, the train was

traveling through an area strangely familiar: tall trees, misty, painted pale by malicious moonshine, towered steep on either side without a break or clearing. Above, the sky was a stark, unexplorable blue thronged with stars that faded here and there. She could see streamers of smoke trailing from the train's engine like long clouds of ectoplasm. In one corner of the platform a red kerosene lantern cast a colorful shadow.

She found a cigarette and tried to light it: the wind snuffed match after match till only one was left. She walked to the corner where the lantern burned and cupped her hands to protect the last match: the flame caught, sputtered, died. Angrily she tossed away the cigarette and empty folder; all the tension in her tightened to an exasperating pitch and she slammed the wall with her fist and began to whimper softly, like an irritable child.

The intense cold made her head ache, and she longed to go back inside the warm coach and fall asleep. But she couldn't, at least not yet; and there was no sense in wondering why, for she knew the answer very well. Aloud, partly to keep her teeth from chattering and partly because she needed the reassurance of her own voice, she said: "We're in Alabama now, I think, and tomorrow we'll be in Atlanta and I'm nineteen and I'll be twenty in August and I'm a sophomore. . . ." She glanced around at the darkness, hoping to see a sign of dawn, and finding the same endless wall of trees, the same frosty moon. "I hate him, he's horrible and I hate him. . . ." She stopped, ashamed of her foolishness and too tired to evade the truth: she was afraid.

Suddenly she felt an eerie compulsion to kneel down and touch the lantern. Its graceful glass funnel was warm, and the red glow seeped through her hands, making them luminous. The heat thawed her fingers and tingled along her arms.

She was so preoccupied she did not hear the door open. The train wheels roaring clickety-clack-clackety-click hushed the sound of the man's footsteps.

It was a subtle zero sensation that warned her finally; but some seconds passed before she dared look behind.

He was standing there with mute detachment, his head tilted, his arms dangling at his sides. Staring up into his harmless, vapid face, flushed brilliant by the lantern light, Kay knew of what she was afraid: it was a memory, a childish memory of terrors that once, long ago, had hovered above her like haunted limbs on a tree of night. Aunts, cooks, strangers— each eager to spin a tale or teach a rhyme of spooks and death, omens, spirits, demons. And always there had been the unfailing threat of the wizard man: stay close to the house, child, else a wizard man'll snatch you and eat you alive! He lived everywhere, the wizard man, and everywhere was danger. At night, in bed, hear him tapping at the window? Listen!

Holding onto the railing, she inched upward till she was standing erect. The man nodded and waved his hand toward the door. Kay took a deep breath and stepped forward. Together they went inside.

The air in the coach was numb with sleep: a solitary light now illuminated the car, creating a kind of artificial dusk. There was no motion but the train's sluggish sway, and the stealthy rattle of discarded newspapers.

The woman alone was wide awake. You could see she was greatly excited: she fidgeted with her curls and celluloid cherries, and her plump little legs, crossed at the ankles, swung agitatedly back and forth. She paid no attention when Kay sat down. The man settled in the seat with one leg tucked beneath him and his arms folded across his chest.

In an effort to be casual, Kay picked up a magazine. She realized the man was watching her, not removing his gaze an instant: she knew this though she was afraid to confirm it, and she wanted to cry out and waken everyone in the coach. But suppose they did not hear? What if they were not really *asleep?* Tears started in her eyes, magnifying and distorting the print on a page till it became a hazy blur. She shut the magazine with fierce abruptness and looked at the woman.

"I'll buy it," she said. "The charm, I mean. I'll buy it, if that's all—just all you want."

The woman made no response. She smiled apathetically as she turned toward the man.

As Kay watched, the man's face seemed to change form and recede before her like a moon-shaped rock sliding downward under a surface of water. A warm laziness relaxed her. She was dimly conscious of it when the woman took away her purse, and when she gently pulled the raincoat like a shroud above her head.